A PLUME BOOK

THE DEVIL'S PUZZLE

Margaret Smith

CLARE O'DONOHUE is a freelance television writer/producer. She has worked worldwide on a variety of shows for the Food Network, the History Channel, and Court TV, among others. An avid quilter, she was also a producer for HGTV's *Simply Quilts*.

ALSO BY CLARE O'DONOHUE

SOMEDAY QUILTS MYSTERIES

The Lover's Knot

A Drunkard's Path

The Double Cross

KATE CONWAY MYSTERIES

Missing Persons

The Devil's Puzzle

A SOMEDAY QUILTS MYSTERY

Clare O'Donohue

A PLUME BOOK

PLUME
Published by the Penguin Group
Penguin Group (USA) Inc., 375 Hudson Street, New York, New York 10014, U.S.A. •
Penguin Group (Canada), 90 Eglinton Avenue East, Suite 700, Toronto, Ontario, Canada
M4P 2Y3 (a division of Pearson Penguin Canada Inc.) • Penguin Books Ltd., 80 Strand,
London WC2R 0RL, England • Penguin Ireland, 25 St. Stephen's Green, Dublin 2, Ireland
(a division of Penguin Books Ltd.) • Penguin Group (Australia), 250 Camberwell Road,
Camberwell, Victoria 3124, Australia (a division of Pearson Australia Group Pty. Ltd.) •
Penguin Books India Pvt. Ltd., 11 Community Centre, Panchsheel Park, New Delhi – 110 017,
India • Penguin Group (NZ), 67 Apollo Drive, Rosedale, Auckland 0632, New Zealand
(a division of Pearson New Zealand Ltd.) • Penguin Books (South Africa) (Pty.) Ltd.,
24 Sturdee Avenue, Rosebank, Johannesburg 2196, South Africa

Penguin Books Ltd., Registered Offices: 80 Strand, London WC2R 0RL, England

First published by Plume, a member of Penguin Group (USA) Inc.

First Printing, October 2011
10 9 8 7 6 5 4 3 2 1

Ⓟ REGISTERED TRADEMARK—MARCA REGISTRADA

LIBRARY OF CONGRESS CATALOGING-IN-PUBLICATION DATA
O'Donohue, Clare.
    The devil's puzzle / Clare O'Donohue.
        p.   cm.—(A Someday Quilts mystery)
    ISBN 978-0-452-29737-1 (pbk.: alk. paper)   1. Quilters—Fiction.   2. Quilting—Fic-
tion.   3. Quilts—Fiction.   4. Murder—Investigation—Fiction.   I. Title.   II. Series.
    PS3615.D665D48 2011
    813'.6—dc22

                                                                              2011004474

Printed in the United States of America
Set in Granjon • Designed by Eve L.Kirch

*To my brother, Dennis, a man whose decency and kindness
I have always admired, and whose friendship
I will always treasure*

$\mathcal{A}$CKNOWLEDGMENTS

I only started writing this series in the fall of 2006 and now I'm publishing the fourth volume. Hard to believe. It's all thanks to many people who have helped make this possible: my agent, Sharon Bowers of The Miller Agency, who has taken every step with me; my editor, Becky Cole, who is my partner in getting each story exactly where it was meant to be; and publicity manager Mary Pomponio (my hero), who works incredibly hard getting the word out about each book. Also, to the men and women in sales and marketing, Nadia Kashper, and everyone at Plume who put this together, thanks, once again, for all the hard work. To those women who loaned their names to characters in *The Devil's Puzzle*: Molly O'Brien, Mary "Glee" Shipman, Dru Ann Love, Bunny Giordano, Kathryn Brigham, and Glad Warren, thank you. The characters are nothing like the people they are named after, but I do appreciate your letting me escape the hardest part of writing a novel: coming up with great names. To Dr. Brian Peterson, chief medical examiner for Milwaukee County, thank you, as always, for being a man with all the answers. To Julie Silber, who helped me with the sections on quilting history, thank you so much for your patience, expert knowledge, and quick responses. If there are errors in anything, don't blame Brian or Julie, blame me. I try, but don't always succeed, in getting things exactly right. Thanks to Margaret Smith, for all the photographs as well as the Sunday chats (you too, Brian). To my family, V, Kevin, and my many friends, your support has meant the world to me. And to the wonderful readers of both the Someday Quilts Mysteries and the Kate Conway Mysteries, thank you. Without you, I'd just be talking to myself (more than I already do).

The
Devil's Puzzle

CHAPTER 1

In any room full of people there are saints and sinners. There are those who would get out of bed at three in the morning to help a neighbor with a stalled car, and those who get out of bed at three in the morning, kiss a secret lover, and head home to their families with excuses about stalled cars. There are those who would die to save the life of a stranger, and those who would betray a loved one on a whim.

I looked around this room of esteemed citizens and wondered who fit into the first category and who fit into the second. They all seemed innocent enough, gathered together in the Archers Rest library, shifting on metal folding chairs, checking their watches and iPhones. Every one of them could easily be in the first group, the group of do-gooders. Perhaps they were here to help their neighbors, to help the town. But what if there was more to it? What if some people were harboring secret motivations for wanting to be in this room on this day? Maybe using this meeting as an alibi. Or a chance to spy on a neighbor.

Or maybe I was just bored.

✄

I glanced toward the door. If I planned it just right I might be able to make my escape without too much trouble. There were two dozen people in the library's reading room. They wouldn't be the problem. It was the woman sitting next to me. Every time I moved in my chair or even looked toward the door, she glared at me. But she didn't understand. I *had* to get out of there.

I checked my watch. 11:35 A.M. I was already late. I crouched a little and got ready to make my move. But just as I was about to bolt, her hand reached out and grabbed my arm.

"Nell Fitzgerald," my grandmother whispered at me, "if you don't sit still I'm going to nail you to that chair."

I settled back. This was ridiculous. I could have left anyway. I could have argued that as a grown woman I'm pretty much past the listening-to-my-grandmother stage. But there was no point. I'm stubborn; at least that's what everyone tells me. But my grandmother, Eleanor Cassidy, is immovable.

I rolled my eyes at her, but there was nothing to be done. Now seventy-four, with short gray hair framing her face, making her blue eyes all the more piercing, she was going to have her way. She was up to something; that much I could tell. But that was okay. So was I.

I turned my attention back to the front of the room where Gladys Warren, known to everyone as Glad, was going over the history of Archers Rest.

"As town historian," Glad said, "I've had the great privilege of spending hours digging into our town's past." At this she laughed slightly. I looked around. No one—including me—got the joke. "We have quite a history. As you all know I'm sure, we were founded by John Archer in 1661 or thereabouts. Unfortunately Mr. Archer died the first winter of our founding, along with most of the people who had ventured up the Hudson River with him. But despite this set-back, a town was born. And as others came after him, they recognized the sacrifices of John Archer and named this town for the place where Mr. Archer was laid to rest."

She paused and looked around. The audience nodded. We knew the story, knew the macabre reason for our town's name—it was named to commemorate a man's grave—and knew that Glad didn't care that we knew. She was going to tell us anyway.

As Glad launched into the story of John Archer's heroic deeds, his high moral character, and his ultimate sacrifice, she edited out what I considered the most interesting part about our founding father. He and his original group of followers were supposed to have come to Archers Rest seeking a quiet place to practice witchcraft. It was nothing more than legend, of course, as there were very few actual facts available about the man. Even most of Glad's version was fiction, or bits of truth heavily embellished by centuries of retelling. Either way, like everyone in the room, I'd heard it all before.

"I have to go," I whispered to my grandmother.

"Not yet."

I sighed heavily and dramatically. I couldn't tell her the reason I was needed at her house, but it was a good reason. I couldn't make up some story because she'd gotten very good at figuring out when I was up to something. And I couldn't just get up and leave because, well, because I'd never hear the end of it if I embarrassed her in front of what appeared to be the who's who of Archers Rest. Instead I sat back and waited for a good moment to break away.

From the podium Glad announced that the town would be hosting a special Fourth of July celebration to commemorate the 350th anniversary of the town's founding. If it had been 350 years. No one was quite sure. But that wasn't going to stop a celebration, especially one that might boost tourism.

There was a lot of talk in the town about that recently. The feeling was that we were being bypassed for other Hudson Valley towns that had more to offer the tourists. Local businesses apparently were missing out on cash-heavy New Yorkers coming up from the city and New Englanders coming south. A normal Fourth of July wouldn't cut it this year. We needed something that put Archers Rest in the newspapers.

Glad asked for volunteers to demonstrate, as she put it, "the kind of community spirit that would show nonlocals what a special place we live in, and give them a reason to return time and again." Several shop owners and restaurant owners offered to host parties or have special sales during the anniversary celebration. Carrie Brown, a fellow quilter and owner of Jitters, the local coffee shop, suggested a coupon booklet that would highlight town businesses and be handed out to visitors. That met with approval from everyone, and when she looked back to Eleanor and me, we clapped loudly as a show of support.

It was all going well, even if it was a little dull. I was just about to make a run for it when Glad announced that she wanted to introduce those who were chairing committees, and I could see Eleanor sit up straight. Mayor Larry Williams, who also ran half a dozen local businesses, told everyone he would handle the media and the fireworks display.

"I'll be posting updates of the anniversary celebration on my blog," the mayor said. "For anyone not familiar with it, it's a great way to keep up with all the exciting events in our little town. I'm not a writer, but I think I capture the flavor of life in Archers Rest." He then took out a half-dozen sheets of paper and read several recent postings. For nearly ten minutes.

After the mayor finally sat down, Ed Bryant, owner of the local movie theater, agreed to be in charge of the parade and carnival. And Maggie Sweeney, the town's former librarian and my grandmother's closest friend, took charge of the church bazaar.

Then Eleanor stood up.

"I thought it would be a lovely nod to our past to combine quilts, which as you all know is a tradition that predates the nation's founding, with the celebration of our town's history," she said. "I propose doing a quilt show."

Everyone applauded enthusiastically. If Eleanor was going to help, it wasn't entirely unexpected she'd help by offering quilts. She was, after all, the owner of Someday Quilts, which had been drawing folks to town for more than thirty years.

While the small crowd was applauding, Eleanor leaned down to me and whispered, "How badly do you want to get out of here?"

"Badly."

She nodded and stood up straight. "My granddaughter Nell is extremely busy with art school and working at Someday Quilts, so unfortunately she has to leave. But she has offered to take time from her schedule to organize the quilt show."

I stood up and was about to protest.

"You can go now if you need to." Eleanor took a deep and triumphant breath.

"This is why you dragged me here?" I asked her.

"I thought you might like to help your town."

As others applauded my willingness to help, I whispered to my grandmother, "This isn't over."

Eleanor smiled. It was over and she knew it.

CHAPTER 2

It was shaping up to be a quiet summer anyway, I reasoned, as I sprinted from the library, down Main Street, and toward home. It might be kind of fun to put on a quilt show. And it wouldn't be such a bad thing to help the town.

I'd lived in Archers Rest since September and it was now only mid-May, but I felt as though I'd been here forever. And that was a good thing. Mostly. But I realized since arriving in Archers Rest, I'd been stuck in a me-me-me kind of place. Worrying about boyfriends, jobs, art classes, a failure to get my borders to lay flat on the first bed-size quilt I'd made . . . and my grandmother had listened to all of it.

Now, with my twenty-seventh birthday in less than two months, I was starting to poke my head out of my world and focus on something really important. Not the quilt show. That wasn't exactly in my plans, but it was fine. I'd help the community, stay out of trouble, and get to be part of the town I'd grown to love. That was all wonderful, but it wasn't important. Not really important.

But what I was doing today was. What I was doing was going to pay Eleanor back for all the support, love, and friendship she'd given me these last few months. It would give me a chance to be a small part of what I knew would be one of the happiest days of my grandmother's life.

✂

As I raced into the driveway of the Victorian home I shared with Eleanor, I nearly ran into the landscaping trucks that were parked there. To someone else it might have looked like old pickups stuffed with lawn mowers, dirt piles, and shovels, but to me it was the most romantic gesture I'd ever been privy to.

Just a few months before, Eleanor had become involved with my art teacher, a well-known English artist named Oliver White. Oliver had spent most of his life accumulating honors, wealth, and girl-friends. Not exactly the kind of man I would expect the guarded and sensible Eleanor to fall for—but she had. In truth, I hadn't expected to watch my grandmother fall in love at all. Romantic love is so often, and so unfortunately, depicted as a privilege for only the young, and I guess I'd fallen into the trap of believing that at a certain age those feelings just evaporated.

But as I'd watched the relationship develop over the last few months, I'd seen how wrong that thinking was. Eleanor lit up whenever Oliver walked into a room. And Oliver never hid his admiration and attraction for my grandmother. They didn't play games or get into stupid arguments. They just accepted each other, adjusted to their differences, and fell in love.

Oliver and Eleanor had become serious pretty quickly, but because they were both senior citizens I'd had difficulty referring to him as her boyfriend. "Gentleman friend" sounded like something from a Tennessee Williams play, and "significant other" was a bit too modern for either of them. Usually I stumbled around when I introduced him, eventually referring to him as a family friend.

But Oliver was about to help me out with a better title. He was planning to propose to Eleanor in just a few hours.

As a gesture of new beginnings, he was planting a rose garden in the neglected backyard of my grandmother's Victorian home. Eleanor always grumbled about the mess her garden had become, but she never had the time or inclination to do anything about it. She told me once that her friend Grace Roemer, the former owner of the home, had a dozen different rose varieties planted there. But when she died, the garden died with her. It was a minor regret, but one Eleanor voiced every spring when the weeds took a stronger hold of what had once been a magnificent wash of color and fragrance.

Now, thanks to Oliver, it would be returned to its former glory.

I raced to the backyard to see how the work was coming, hoping I'd find rosebushes already planted. When Oliver and I first cooked up this plan we knew it would be nearly impossible to get the entire garden cleared and planted in one day, but we were confident we would make enough of a difference to give Eleanor a preview of things to come.

His plan was to show her the garden when she returned home in the late afternoon, then open a small box and reveal the diamond ring he'd bought. Ever the romantic, he'd found one that had been made the year she was born. Even though I wasn't actually going to be there for his proposal, I could picture the whole thing clearly and I was almost as anxious and excited as he was.

If the plan was going to work, then Oliver needed to get to his house, change his clothes, and pick up the champagne and cake he'd ordered. And I needed to supervise the workers and get dinner ready. But when I got to the back of the house, instead of seeing a rose garden in progress and a would-be fiancé ready to propose, I saw Oliver and several workmen standing over a hole, shaking their heads and speaking in low tones.

"Hi," I shouted, but no one made a move to look at me. I took a few steps forward. "Sorry I'm late, but don't worry, Oliver. Eleanor doesn't close the shop until four, so we still have plenty of time."

Oliver finally heard me and turned. He was tall, over six feet, with gray hair and a neatly trimmed beard. He was imposing, but in his soft blue-gray eyes, there was a sweetness I had come to adore.

"What's going on with the garden, Grandpa? Don't mind if I call you that, I hope." I smiled.

He didn't smile back. "We've run into trouble, Nell."

"Whatever it is, I'm sure the landscapers and I can work around it. You've got to get out of here so you can get ready for your big night."

Every time I had mentioned the proposal before, Oliver had shyly smiled. This time, though, a weary sadness crept across him.

"I don't think that I can go through with it tonight," he said.

"What? Of course you can, Oliver. Don't get cold feet now. Eleanor is madly in love with you. And you are madly in love with her.

We'll get this garden into shape. You'll get dressed. You'll say that beautiful speech you've been rehearsing. Eleanor will be thrilled. Everyone will be thrilled. And you and Eleanor and me, and the quilt group, can start planning a wedding, and more important, a wedding quilt." I smiled, looking for signs of optimism from Oliver, but there were none. I tried again. "Nothing, absolutely nothing is going to stop this proposal from happening tonight as planned."

Oliver nodded, but he didn't seem all that convinced.

He motioned for me to come toward the hole where he and the landscapers had all been looking. It wasn't deep, maybe two or three feet.

"I think this is going to stop it, Nell."

"No way," I said.

But as soon as I peered over, I realized he was right. We had run into the kind of problem that would likely change our plans for the garden, the proposal, and maybe much more. At the bottom of the hole, still half covered with dirt, was a body.

Or, more accurately, a skeleton.

CHAPTER 3

"I didn't put it there," Eleanor said forty minutes later, as she stood by the hole, shaking her head.

"No one thinks you did," I said.

When I'd called her at the shop and told her to close the store and come home, I'd only said there was a problem at the house. I hadn't said that the problem was a skeleton.

"I don't understand what you were doing digging up back here anyway," she said.

"Oliver and I just thought you would like it."

I wasn't about to tell her about the proposal, which hopefully was still on. No one wants to hear soft, romantic words in the vicinity of a dead body. At least I hope not.

"Is this why you insisted I take your shift at the shop?" Eleanor asked. "Why didn't you just tell me you were going to dig back here? Why do you keep me in the dark about everything?"

"I told you about this." I pointed toward the skeleton.

My grandmother just shook her head and stared at it. "Honestly, Nell, only you would dig up a rose garden and find a body."

She walked away from me, still mumbling about my knack for getting in the middle of things.

I didn't know if I had a knack, but I was a definitely in the middle of this. There were only twelve officers on the Archers Rest police department, and half of them were milling about around me, all over the backyard. Greg, one of the detectives, carefully photographed the skeleton and then stood back to stare at it.

"Crazy, isn't it," he said.

"It is."

"I sure wish Jesse were here."

"He'll be back tomorrow."

"You probably miss him, Nell. But right now I miss him more."

Jesse Dewalt, the town's chief of police and my significant other, had gone on a camping trip with his six-year-old daughter's Brownie troop. It was only one night. When he was debating whether he should be in the woods out of cell range, I laughed off his concerns.

"How much could happen in our sleepy little town in one night?" I'd said.

As it turned out, a lot.

"I don't know how comfortable I am removing the body, or whatever it is, without Jesse looking at it first," Greg said.

"Then don't. Just leave it here until tomorrow. It's obviously been here a long time, so one more day isn't going to hurt anything. I think we have a tarp in the garage you can use to cover the hole."

That seemed to relax Greg. He grabbed a couple of men and they went off looking for the tarp, something to hold it down, and crime scene tape to wrap around the trees and make the whole area off-limits. I moved closer to the edge of the hole and stared into the makeshift grave.

✂

It is an odd thing to look at what is left of a person after his skin has gone. The skeleton was a yellow white, with bits of what, I assumed, was tissue clinging to the bones and his empty eye sockets. The lower half of his jaw was detached from his skull and his ribs looked broken. Though he was nothing like the bleached white, almost cheerful depictions of skeletons I'd seen every Halloween, there was something haunted about him. He was a man robbed not just of his life but of the dignity of a real grave.

And, at least for the moment, of his identity. The skeleton seemed to be of a man. At least that was my guess by what was left of his clothing. Though they were heavily decayed, it looked as if he had on pants, a shirt, and a tweed jacket.

I crouched down at the edge of the hole and reached my hand toward the man's coat pocket. Nothing. I reached into the other. I came up empty again. I looked around. The officers, most of whom worked part-time for the force, were too busy trying to wrap trees with crime scene tape to pay any attention to me, so I stretched my arm out farther and dug my fingers into his pants pocket. There was something round and hard. Too big for a coin. I pinched it between my fingers and slid it out.

"A poker chip?" I said out loud without meaning to. I saw Eleanor turn to look at me, so I quickly stashed the chip back in the dead man's pocket and got up.

"What are you doing, Nell?"

"Nothing. Just looking."

"Well, stop right now. You're a grown woman, Nell Fitzgerald. I shouldn't have to tell you not to play in the dirt with skeletons."

I didn't bother to argue. I just walked over to the porch to join her and Oliver. "Grandma, do you have any idea who he is?"

"Of course not."

"He could have been there for years," Oliver pointed out.

"Maybe. How long has it been since you've done any work in the garden?" I asked Eleanor.

"I've never done any work in the garden, Nell. You've seen how it was. I've been terribly neglectful of it."

"So it's been undisturbed for how long?"

"I don't know. Years, decades, I guess."

"You've never had anyone work on the garden?"

Eleanor shrugged. "Yes, in the spring, to cut back the weeds and keep it from taking over the place. I had a gardener come for a while, but I've not planted anything there since my own children were small."

"Do you think it's been there since Eleanor moved into the house?" Oliver asked. "That was more than forty years ago."

"I don't know, but Jesse will want to look into it. A murder gets investigated no matter how long it's been."

My grandmother turned white. "You can't know it's a murder. That's just bones in that hole."

"Grandma, people don't just bury someone in the backyard if they die of natural causes."

CHAPTER 4

"Do you remember anyone going missing in town?" I asked Eleanor once we were alone in the kitchen making lemonade and sandwiches.

The officers were still in the yard covering the hole with a tarp, secured with a handful of bricks and some shovels we had in the garage. Oliver stood just outside the kitchen door, as if protecting us from any possible harm. The only male who had come inside was Barney, my grandmother's twelve-year-old golden retriever. He sat in his dog bed, half-asleep, half-annoyed at the commotion outside. He didn't seem a bit worried about our safety, and frankly, I trusted his instincts.

While I waited for my answer, Eleanor poured sugar into a bowl and searched for the right spoon.

"You didn't answer my question," I pointed out.

She looked at me, annoyed. "You're putting too little ham on those sandwiches. Those men are working hard out there, and they're hungry. Don't be stingy with the lunch meat."

"It's a police investigation, not high tea."

"I'm aware of what it is, Nell."

"What are you so nervous about? You said you didn't know anything."

"I don't."

"I'm sure Jesse will believe you. He's practically family."

She took a deep breath. "What did you mean by that? What do you know?"

"What do I know? I know you didn't bury a body in the backyard if that's what you're asking."

"No. About Jesse being practically family."

"I just meant that he's here a lot," I answered. "I know he really likes you. He's says one of the great benefits of dating me is that he gets to eat your cooking."

I noticed she was tapping her fingers on the kitchen counter. My grandmother doesn't rattle easily, but it seemed to me that she was rattled.

"Does it bother you that Jesse is here a lot?"

"No. It's just that . . ." She glanced out the kitchen window as if she were afraid of being overheard.

"It's just that what?" I was getting impatient.

"I think he's going to propose."

For a moment I felt the floor drop out from under me. I was almost afraid to ask what she knew that I didn't. It's not that I wouldn't have been happy. I think I would have been happy about a proposal from Jesse. It's just that we had never discussed anything even remotely like marriage.

Finally I found the words. "Why do you think that?"

"I shouldn't spoil the surprise, but I don't want you to get so caught up in what's happened in the backyard that you lose sight of what's important." She paused. "A few days ago Carrie saw Oliver and Jesse coming out of Fisher's jewelry store. She practically ran into them because she was on her way in to get an earring repaired. When she went inside Mr. Fisher was very happy. He told her he'd just sold a very expensive antique engagement ring."

I could barely keep myself from smiling. It had never occurred to her that Oliver had bought the ring. I hugged Eleanor.

"You didn't spoil the surprise."

"You knew?"

"I guess I knew that wedding bells were on the way."

I could see that she was fighting back a tear. "A good marriage is a wonderful thing. He's a lucky man."

"Yes, he is. I think proposing will be the smartest thing he ever does."

She rolled her eyes. "Don't get bigheaded about it. You're a lot of trouble. I hope he knows that. Now bring those sandwiches out to

the officers. And tell Oliver to get inside. He'll get heatstroke standing out there all day."

"You know he's practically family, too."

"What are you saying?"

Now that the door had been opened, I couldn't resist. "You just
said a good marriage is a wonderful thing."

"Oliver and I get married?"

"Why not?"

"That's the silliest thing I've ever heard you say."

"Why? You never thought about remarrying after Grandpa died?"

"Marriage is for young people with their lives in front of them.
Oliver and I . . . well, we're not young anymore."

"So just because you don't fit the fairy-tale image of a youthful
bride, you wouldn't want to get married? I've never known your age
to hold you back from anything before."

"That's not it," she said, an annoyance in her voice that was hard
to miss.

"Then why?"

She started to say something, then paused. After a long hesitation
she said, "I have my reasons."

"You love him, don't you?"

She softened for a moment. "I suppose."

"And he loves you. I know he does. If he proposed to you, you
would say yes."

"No, I wouldn't," she said. "Honestly, Nell, where do you come
up with these things? Get the sandwiches out there before those poor
officers die of starvation."

There was no sense pushing the point. I'd have to back off and
think of another way to bring up the subject. So I did what she
wanted for the moment. I took the plate of sandwiches and walked
out onto the back porch where Oliver was standing guard. He
seemed so nervous that I wanted to give him a hug. Instead I gave
him a ham sandwich.

"A bit of a hitch in our plan," he said.

I looked back through the window at Eleanor. "Something I
never would have anticipated."

CHAPTER 5

At 9:30 the next morning, I walked to the driveway, where Jesse's car was just pulling up. He jumped out, grabbed my arm, pulled me toward him, and kissed me before I'd even said hello.

"Aren't you afraid of what people will say?" I said when we came up for air.

"I know exactly what they'll say. They'll say Jesse Dewalt must have missed that crazy Nell Fitzgerald so much that he doesn't care he's breaking town ordinances against lewd public behavior."

"Kissing isn't lewd."

"The ordinance was put into effect in 1750 and it's never been updated, so technically . . ."

"And I'm not *crazy* Nell Fitzgerald."

"Really?" He was smiling, having fun. "I go out of town for one night and you get yourself in the middle of it again."

I made a face, which he ignored. Jesse seemed to think I took every opportunity to meddle in his police investigations, but this time the investigation had come to me.

"Don't you want to see the body?" I asked.

He nodded. The fun was over for the moment. Jesse was by nature a pretty serious person. Though only thirty-one, he was a widower with a six-year-old daughter to raise. He was careful, far more than I, but Eleanor seemed to think I brought out a playfulness in him. If only, my grandmother was fond of saying, he could bring out a bit of cautiousness in me.

"I guess we should see what we've got," he said.

We walked to the backyard, stopping at the spot that was supposed to be a beautiful rose garden.

He moved the bricks and shovel to one side and peeled back the tarp, revealing the skeleton, still half covered in dirt. Jesse crouched down, examining the remains from head to toe.

"Looks like he was hit with something on the back of the head." He pointed to a crack in the skull toward the back.

"Maybe that's how he was killed."

"Maybe." He moved lower, looking at the ribs, the arms. As I'd done the day before, he checked the pockets, coming up empty on three of them, but finding the same red plastic poker chip that I had found in the fourth pocket.

"No wallet. No ID. Just this." He held it up to me.

"A gambler?"

"He could have been." But Jesse wasn't interested in the chip anymore. His eyes had moved to the exposed shinbone on the skeleton's right leg.

"Anybody hurt themselves here yesterday? Maybe one of the men working on the garden."

"I don't think so."

"Anybody move anything after it was covered?" he asked.

"Meaning me?"

He nodded slightly.

"No, Jesse. I left the tarp exactly where your guys put it. And so did Eleanor. And so did Barney, for that matter."

"So it looks the same as it did when the guys covered it yesterday?"

"Exactly the same. Why?"

He pointed toward a reddish-brown spot on the skeleton's leg.

"What is that?"

"We'll have to check it in the lab, but I'd say that's blood, Nell."

I leaned over and examined the spot. "It wasn't there yesterday."

"Are you sure?"

"Yeah, I . . ." I hesitated more because of the teasing I'd face than any fear of Jesse getting mad. "I sort of examined him yesterday."

He didn't tease. "And there were no spots like this?" His eyes moved farther down the leg. "Or those?" He pointed to three more drops.

I shook my head. "Skeletons don't bleed." It was an obvious point, but under the circumstances I felt the need to say it.

"Something left blood." Jesse jumped from the hole. "I think while we're identifying the body, we'll also have to run labs on the blood, too."

><

After the coroner's office had taken the skeleton and agreed to call with results of the blood test as quickly as possible, Jesse and I went to his office at the police station. I looked through the photos Greg had taken of the skeleton shortly after it had been discovered and just as I'd remembered, there were no spots on the shinbone.

"Maybe an animal got in there," I suggested.

"But the tarp wasn't disturbed. You said it yourself."

Greg was at the door. "I'll bet it's some kind of ritual blood."

"What kind of ritual?" I asked.

"I don't know. Maybe John Archer's come back from the grave now that we're celebrating the anniversary. Plus, if those are his bones and we've disturbed them, maybe he would, you know, leave some blood as part of a ghostly spell or something."

"He's buried in the cemetery," Jesse pointed out. "And ghosts don't bleed any more than skeletons."

"Well, that's what the mayor thinks."

"You talked to the mayor about this?"

"No. It's on his blog," Greg said. "He asked me for a photo, so I e-mailed him the one that shows the whole body kind of reaching out from the dirt."

Jesse clicked the mouse of his computer and sighed. "Wonderful."

"What?" I leaned over to see his screen and had to stop myself from laughing. The mayor's blog featured a photo of the skeleton under the headline REVOLUTIONARY WAR HERO? PROHIBITION-ERA GANGSTER? SATANIC SACRIFICE? ARCHERS REST IS THE SITE OF MYSTERI-OUS SKELETON, UNCOVERED IN THE GARDEN OF HISTORIC HOME.

Jesse clicked off. "It's generally considered a bad idea to share evidence with the general public before we even know what we're dealing with."

Greg blushed. "The mayor asked for it, and you weren't here . . ."

I tapped Jesse's hand playfully. "Satanic sacrifice? Come on, Jesse. That's hysterical."

"I think the mayor's got a point," Greg said. "It could be anything. We could be onto a hidden part of the town's history."

"Or it could be a mundane crime scene," Jesse said.

Greg shrugged. "Well, the lab is on line two. Maybe they have an idea."

"You told me the John Archer theory first, before mentioning that actual scientific evidence is waiting for me on hold?" Jesse laughed and picked up the phone. "The whole town is nuts."

Greg left, but I waited to hear what the lab had to say. The call went on for a while, with Jesse mostly listening, adding in an occasional "okay," but otherwise giving me no clues as to the results. After several minutes and half a dozen okays, he finally hung up.

"Human blood. Less than twelve hours old."

"So sometime after midnight."

"Someone uncovered the tarp, probably looking for something. Whoever it was must have cut himself."

"Could be the killer."

"Or a treasure seeker. Or a curious teenager."

"Or John Archer's ghost." I smiled.

Jesse didn't. "Did you hear anything unusual last night?"

"Nothing, but my room faces the front of the house. Eleanor's faces the back. And knowing my grandmother, if she had heard noises in the backyard, she'd have gone outside to look."

"I have a feeling this is one of those cases that's going to take a lot of time and a lot of effort." He ran his fingers across my neck and smiled. "You must be excited; it's just the kind of thing you like."

I smiled back, but I didn't say anything. Jesse was half-right. I felt something, but it wasn't excitement.

CHAPTER 6

"He was going to *what?*" Carrie nearly dropped my espresso when I stopped in at Jitters, still feeling the same sense of dull panic I'd had at Jesse's office.

"Eleanor thinks Jesse is the one planning to propose," I told her. "Thanks to you."

She cringed. Carrie was a good friend and would never want to put me in a bad spot. We'd gotten to know each other through quilting, and quickly found it to be one of many common interests, including drinking coffee and meddling in other people's lives.

Carrie was older—and usually wiser—than me. A forty-something mother of two, married to a local pediatrician, she owned the coffee shop and was also a former New York stockbroker. On occasion, she unearthed financial information for my unofficial investigations. Not that we needed financial information at the moment. We already knew Oliver was a very successful painter. And since we had no idea who had been buried in my grandmother's backyard, background checks weren't going to help us there.

Which reminded me. "There was something else that happened yesterday," I said as I plopped down on the big purple couch that sat near the front of the shop.

Carrie sat next to me. "The skeleton. I read the mayor's blog this morning."

"You read that?"

"It's the best source of gossip in town, apart from the quilt group. How long do you think the skeleton's been there?"

"Jesse's looking into missing persons reports."

"But if someone was missing, we would know, wouldn't we?"

"Not if it was someone passing through town."

"Or a hundred years old."

"I don't think it's that old," I said. "There was rayon or some other man-made fabric in the shirt and pants. I think that's why the clothes are still partially preserved."

"How do you know it's man-made fabric?"

"I touched it." I could see her cringe. "It's just a skeleton, Carrie. It's not like he was going to reach his bony fingers out and grab me."

"You never know."

I rolled my eyes and turned my attention back to the investigation. "I do think it's been there for a while."

"Since before she moved in?"

"Maybe."

"And Eleanor bought the house from Grace," Carrie said.

None of us had ever met Grace Roemer, as she had died more than thirty years before. That didn't matter, though. She was a large presence in my grandmother's life, and through Eleanor's stories, Grace had taken on almost saintlike qualities for everyone in the quilt group. A wealthy widow with two grown children, ill, and in need of help, Grace had hired my grandmother as a live-in helper after my grandfather's death. The two became close friends, with Grace passing down her love of quilting to my grandmother. When she died, Eleanor bought the house from Grace's children and kept her memory alive by hanging several of her quilts in the shop and the house.

"Are you thinking Grace put the body there?" I asked. "From everything I've heard about her, she was always very frail."

Carrie was staring off into space. "When did Eleanor's husband die?"

I sat up. "What are you implying?"

Carrie laughed. "God, not that. I was thinking of the proposal."

I sat back again. "He died in 1965. And there was a funeral and a body." Then I added, "I assume."

"Can you imagine Eleanor killing some unsuspecting man and dumping him in the rose garden?" Carrie giggled.

"Well, if someone suggested Eleanor wasn't capable of raising her kids and running a business . . ."

"Or criticized her quilting."

Sitting with Carrie, the skeleton from yesterday was becoming abstract. I could almost hear the talk in town. "You'll never believe what Eleanor and that granddaughter of hers have gotten themselves into now." But when I flashed on the empty holes where eyes had once been, the unhinged jaw that had once been capable of smiling, I remembered that this was no game. There had been a real man lying in that ground.

Carrie, who had not seen what I had seen, was excited by the prospect of another puzzle to solve. We'd had several murders since I'd moved to Archers Rest, and while we certainly didn't enjoy having another murder victim in our midst, we both liked playing a part in solving the crime. "So what's the plan?" she asked.

I thought about it a minute, surprised by what I was thinking. "There isn't one. We're not going to get involved. We're going to leave the skeleton to Jesse."

✁

"We're not going to do anything? Not anything?" Natalie asked about ten minutes later.

Natalie was another member of the quilt group and worked part-time at Someday Quilts. A strikingly pretty blonde a year older than me, she was married to a local mechanic and had a two-year-old, Jeremy. In the short time Natalie had worked at the shop, Jeremy had become an unofficial employee, delighting customers and keeping Barney from sleeping the day away. When Jeremy had enough of being the shop's greeter, he rested in a crib set up in my grandmother's office, leaving Natalie free to gossip with me.

Natalie had opened the store and was already unpacking a new box of variegated threads when I came in. I'd brought her over some decaf tea and a muffin from Jitters, and some coffee and croissants for myself. All she wanted, though, was news about the skeleton.

I told her what I knew, what Carrie and I had just discussed, and then added that I was staying out of it. That got an exasperated reply. Natalie was seven months pregnant with her second child and was supposed to avoid stress. Obviously that wasn't happening.

"Jesse's the chief of police," I pointed out. "He doesn't need our help in solving a homicide." I could hardly believe the words were coming out of my mouth.

"But we always help," Natalie protested.

"I don't think Jesse always sees it as help."

"Is that why? Now that you and Jesse are a couple, you don't want to ruffle his feathers? I mean, that's fine for most people, but you, Nell. You always stick your nose in . . ." She stopped. "Well, you know what I mean."

"I do. But my nose has somewhere else to be right now."

I had just explained the whole situation to Carrie, about Oliver's planned proposal and Eleanor's lack of interest in remarrying, and now I explained it to Natalie.

"If Eleanor doesn't want to marry Oliver, or doesn't want to get married again, that's okay," I said. "But I think there's something else. Something she's not telling me. If she turns Oliver down, it will break his heart, and that will break her heart."

"And that will break all our hearts."

"Exactly," I said. "I know it's none of my business, but I just have to make sure she's not about to make a huge mistake. Plus, I have art school, the store, and now that stupid quilt show to plan. You're about to give birth. Carrie has her kids and Jitters. Maggie is working on the town's anniversary celebration. We can't do everything. Something has to give." As I said the words, the knot in my stomach started to relax and I knew I was making the right decision.

"So we leave the skeleton to Jesse and concentrate on Oliver and Eleanor," Natalie said, a note of concern in her voice. "Do you really think you can ignore a dead man in your own backyard?"

"Absolutely," I said, and I almost believed it.

CHAPTER 7

"Do you want popcorn?" Jesse asked me.

I raised an eyebrow.

"Dumb question." He laughed and turned to the kid behind the counter. "Two buttered popcorns, two Cokes."

"And Twizzlers."

"That's a lot of food, even for movie night," he said as we sat in our usual seats at Bryant's Cinema, the local classic movie theater— actually, the only movie theater in town.

"It's *Psycho*. Horror movies require a lot of snacking. Keeps me from screaming."

"You do make a lot of noise." He winked.

I tried not to smile. No sense in encouraging him.

Ed Bryant, the owner, was standing at the back of the theater, a look of exasperation on his face. "Sorry folks, I'm having a little trouble with the projector. It will be a few minutes before I can get the movie going."

"Don't worry about it, Ed," someone in the front row called back.

"Thanks." As he turned, Ed noticed Jesse. "Hey, Chief. Not on duty tonight?"

"Yeah," Jesse said, "I'm watching her. A one-woman crime spree."

"You're Eleanor's granddaughter," Ed said to me. He had a friendly face, making him seem younger than a man in his seventies. "Nice meeting you."

"You, too," I said. "I really like your theater."

"Thanks. We've been doing a lot of remodeling to it. I'm trying to keep the original spirit of the place, but just freshen it up a little."

"You're doing a terrific job."

His face lit up. "You should see the plans I have for this place. I could really make it something if I had the money."

Jesse coughed. "Ed, don't you have a projector to fix?"

Ed nodded. "Yeah, right. Sorry."

He ran out the door and presumably headed up to the projection room. I'd seen Ed at the library on the day of the big meeting, but we'd never actually met before. With just over five thousand residents, Archers Rest is a big enough town where you don't know everyone but small enough where no one is really a stranger.

While we waited for the movie to start, Jesse and I munched on our popcorn and he caught me up on the activities of his six-year-old daughter, Allie.

"So when are you going to ask me?" Jesse took one of the Twizzlers and tapped me on the head with it.

"Ask you what?"

"About the investigation," he said. "About the skeleton."

"I'm not interested."

He laughed so loud that another patron shushed him, even though we were staring at a blank screen.

"I'm serious," I said, and dug another handful of popcorn out of the bag. "I've given it a lot of thought and I really want to concentrate on Eleanor and Oliver."

"Maybe you would get into less trouble focusing on the skeleton than you will interfering in Eleanor's life."

"How many times have you told me to stay out of police work?" I asked. "And now you *want* me to get involved in an investigation? I'm getting mixed signals."

"I'm just looking at the lesser of two evils. This guy has been dead for a long time. Whoever killed him probably is in the cemetery himself, so I don't have to worry about you confronting a killer. If Eleanor thinks you're pushing her toward something she doesn't want, she'll never forgive you." He paused, seemed to think about what he wanted to say, and then turned to me. "Plus, you have a way of looking at things that can be very helpful sometimes."

The last remark took me by surprise. "You're complimenting me on my detective skills."

"Don't get carried away. I'm just saying you see things I don't sometimes. And that can be useful."

I chuckled. "I wish I were videotaping this. That way the next time you tell me to butt out, I would have evidence that you actually like working with me on your cases."

Jesse shifted in his seat. "I knew I shouldn't have said anything."

"No. I'm glad you did. I'm not going to get involved in your investigation." I could see the skepticism in his face. "But if you want to bounce ideas off me, maybe I'll think of something you wouldn't have. And maybe if you have ideas about Eleanor and Oliver . . ."

"Deal. Just know that you and Eleanor are a lot alike, and if you push her toward Oliver, she'll go the opposite way just to be stubborn."

"I'm not trying to push her anywhere. I just want to make sure she's turning Oliver down for a good reason. I don't want her to make the wrong choice because she's scared or something."

"She's not scared. She's just independent." Jesse kissed me lightly. "And she's lucky to have you."

"With my keen investigative skills, apparently so are you," I teased. "So what have you found out?"

"Nothing, really. I checked the missing persons reports for the county going back to 1960. There's no one matching his description that's been reported missing in over fifty years."

"What description? He's all bones."

"A forensic anthropologist from Albany came down to examine the remains. He was able to determine that it's a white male, thirty to forty-five years old, roughly six feet, one broken leg, but it happened years before his death."

"Can he figure out how long the body has been in the ground?"

"There are tests for that kind of thing, but it takes time and it's expensive. Archers Rest doesn't really have the budget. We may have no choice if I can't figure out any other way to identify this guy, but I'm hoping there's another way."

"What about his clothes?"

"As you suspected, there was rayon in his pants and shirt. You quilters really know your fabric," he said. "The jacket was tweed, not that there was much left of it. But there was a label from a shop on Savile Row, in London."

"Expensive."

"Very. Assuming the jacket was his."

"Maybe the shop has records of its purchases. Particularly if the jacket was tailored for him."

"Already checking."

"Okay." Since he had already thought of every one of my ideas, I was wondering if he really did need my help, but I kept going. "The doctors in town would have records of past injuries. Maybe someone set a broken leg?" I suggested.

"I'm checking on that but nothing so far. We've got three doctors in town that have been practicing for more than thirty years and what records they have don't show anyone with those injuries."

"No one?"

"No one who's unaccounted for, I should say. But we're still looking into it. I've got two officers checking on stored files from retired doctors, and if we have no luck there, we'll spread out countywide, then statewide if we have to."

"What about dental records?"

"Nothing that matches in Archers Rest. Though the coroner did say the man's teeth were well cared for," he said. "That's the confusing part. His teeth were in great shape, but his leg wasn't set properly, as if he hadn't gotten good medical care. If he had the money to look after his teeth, why didn't he have the money to get his leg set?"

I didn't have an answer for that, only another question. "What about DNA? Can you identify him that way?"

"I'd need DNA to compare it to," Jesse said. "I'd need a relative."

"What about the blood spots you found?"

"No match in the national criminal database."

"I'm sure people in town would volunteer to give samples of their DNA. All you need is to swab their cheek, right?"

"Yeah, but to do the whole town would take a lot of money and a lot of time. I'd rather start with asking around. Maybe someone remembers a man who passed through Archers Rest, or has a relative that's been unaccounted for all these years. We . . ." He smiled. "Sorry, *I* just have to start asking everyone if they know anything."

Just when I was about to ask if the coroner had been able to provide a cause of death, Ed announced that he'd fixed the projector. Despite reminding myself that I wasn't going to get involved in this investigation, I was puzzled about how a well-dressed man that no one in town had reported missing had ended up in Eleanor's garden. It was all I could think about until Janet Leigh stepped into the shower, and then I grabbed Jesse's arm and got lost in the movie.

CHAPTER 8

"Hi, Nell."

The next morning I sat at the front counter of the shop, paging through the latest issue of my favorite art quilt magazine and trying to stay awake when Glad Warren snapped me to attention.

"Just popping my head in to see how things are going."

'They're going well, Mrs. Warren.'

"Glad. Call me Glad. Anyone who would give so much of herself to help this town is a friend, and my friends call me Glad."

"Okay. Well, I'm working on some plans for the quilt show and hoping to get some other regulars at the shop involved."

Glad took a step into the store. It may have been her first time. She had a fussy, won't-break-a-nail quality about her. Correcting other people's manners and checking for dust seemed more likely to be Glad Warren's hobbies than anything as useful as quilting.

She sniffed at the general warmth of the place and then turned on a concerned—aka annoyed—expression when she looked at me. "This is a big responsibility, Nell. A well-designed quilt show can be a huge draw for us, or it could be a disaster if it's just thrown together. I hope you're taking it seriously."

"I've got a terrific plan for the show," I assured her. "I just want to go over it with the other members of the quilt group and then I'll clear it with you."

She eyed me suspiciously. "Is Eleanor helping you, dear?"

"She'll contribute a quilt or two, I'm sure, but she's leaving the show to me."

"Well, I suppose she knows what she's doing. Your grandmother sometimes can exhibit an inexplicable faith in people."

"I don't think she's ever been wrong."

She raised an eyebrow. "It's good that you have such confidence in your grandmother's judgment. Just let me know what you need before you get in over your head."

"Will do."

I watched her glance around the store before leaving. While I did sense that Glad approved of handmade things and the continuing of tradition, I also felt that she would never bother with the actual effort involved in making anything from scratch, and was wary of anyone who would. For Glad, the only duty of a prominent citizen was to form a committee and find some poor idiot to do all the work.

"Who's that?" Kathryn Brigham, a regular customer of Someday Quilts, had been pulling bolts of bright neon pink fabrics.

"One of our town big shots. I somehow got myself put in charge of a quilt show this summer."

"It sounds like you have some great ideas for it," she said.

"It does sound that way," I admitted.

Truth was, between the skeleton and helping Oliver, I hadn't really thought much about it. Now, with the Fourth of July weekend less than two months away and Glad looking over my shoulder, I had to start thinking. And fast.

Kathryn had gone back to the bolts, choosing, rejecting, then re-choosing fabric after fabric until she'd accumulated a pile. She ran her hand along Alex Anderson's newest collection, a colorful medley of polka dots and stripes. I could see she was debating, the way quilters do, whether she should indulge in them.

"Are these new?" she asked.

"Just came yesterday."

"I don't know what I'm going to do with them."

"When has that ever stopped a quilter?"

She laughed. "I'll take a yard each. I'm trying to get my daughter interested in quilting, and I think she would love these. I think it's wonderful the way quilting has been passed down from one generation to the next."

"It is. You could trace the entire history of the country just by looking at antique quilts," I said. "I've always thought of it as a really subversive way that women have expressed themselves. Over the centuries we've used quilts to make political statements or religious statements, show off our wealth with expensive fabrics, show off our talents with amazing stitch work . . ." I stopped myself from rambling. It was a subject I could talk about all day. "I'm always so humbled when I think about all the amazing quilters there have been."

"It's a good thing we have shops like this one, to keep the tradition alive," she said, looking around. "Maybe I should pick up a couple of reproduction prints while I'm here."

"We've got a great selection," I told her. "They're getting so popular we can hardly keep them in the store."

Kathryn grabbed a few bolts of Civil War reproductions, then went back for some 1970s psychedelics. Like so many of our regular customers, she'd come from quite a distance to check out the newest fabrics we had in stock and didn't want to miss something special. Someday Quilts was the only quilt shop for about thirty miles. Quilt shops, just like any other specialty business, suffer from dips in the economy, competition from the Internet, and the changing interests of their customers.

Somehow, though, my grandmother's shop was doing better than ever. She'd doubled the square footage over a year ago and because of it had been able to hold more classes and bring in more specialty fabrics. And now the shop was offering quilting services. Or, rather, Natalie and I were, as we'd become quite good at the longarm machine we'd convinced Eleanor to buy.

It was turning out to be the shop's best year. As Jesse had said, she was an independent woman used to running her business—and her life—without interference. It was something to be proud of, and as her granddaughter, something to aspire to. But I didn't think the shop was the reason—at least not the entire reason—why Eleanor was shying away from a marriage to Oliver.

I could see Eleanor at her desk in the tiny office at the back of the shop. Barney, as usual, was curled up at her feet and there were piles of newly arrived books sitting on the edge of her desk.

After I finished waiting on Kathryn, I walked back to Eleanor, looking for an excuse to talk.

"Do you want coffee?" I asked.

Eleanor looked up at me, startled, as if I'd woken her from a dream. "I don't know what to do," she said, more to herself than to me.

CHAPTER 9

"About what?"

She blinked at me a moment, then seemed to wake up. "About all this work I have." She took a breath. "Did you want something?"

"I asked if you wanted coffee."

"Desperately," she said. "And I'm guessing you could do with a cup yourself. You didn't get home until early this morning."

"Four," I admitted.

I yawned. I hadn't slept well the night before, as I rarely did on nights I was with Jesse. After the movie, we'd gone back to his place so he could be home in time to put Allie to bed. Jesse and I would take turns telling her stories and then, when we were sure she was asleep, we'd retire to his bedroom. Problem was, neither Jesse nor I were sure how Allie would feel if she found me there in the morning, and we weren't ready to find out. So it had become my routine to spend the first part of the night at his house, then drive back to mine and catch the last few hours of sleep in my own bed.

"Maybe you can make an early night of it," Eleanor suggested as she saw me yawn a second time. "I'm sure the girls won't mind if you miss the meeting."

It was Friday, which meant our weekly quilt meeting. And while I loved hanging out with the members of the group, I wanted nothing more than to crawl into bed and close my eyes. But I knew that on this particular Friday, I couldn't.

"The quilt show," I reminded Eleanor. "If I'm going to get it together I'll need everyone to start helping tonight. Even with help I have no idea how I'm going to manage."

"Well, you shouldn't volunteer for things if you don't have the time."
I could see the corners of her lips turn up as she tried not to laugh.

I threw a skein of decorative yarn at her, which she caught and
dropped on the desk.

"Wasn't someone going to get coffee?" she reminded me.

I sat on the chair opposite her. "That would be great, Grandma.
I'll take mine black."

She met my smile with one of her own. "I guess I deserved that."

"That's almost an apology. What's your angle?"

"No angle. I just realized that I should enjoy you while I can.
Once you're a bride-to-be, you'll be too busy for your old grandma."

"It does take a lot of time, planning a wedding."

"It can. You and Jesse will try to keep it simple, I imagine, but
these things have a way of becoming big and complicated."

"Was your wedding big and complicated?"

"No. It was your grandfather, a minister, my sister and parents,
and his brother. We got married in the church at ten in the morning
and then we all went to lunch."

"Where did you go on your honeymoon?"

"Niagara Falls."

"Was it nice?"

"It was a honeymoon. It would be a crying shame if it wasn't nice.
And yours will be nice, too."

"So you and Joe were in love?"

"Yes. We were very young. I was eighteen. He was twenty. We didn't
know a thing about what marriage really was, but we were in love."

"What was he like?"

She leaned back in her chair. "He was a football player in high
school, so he had a strong build. He was very athletic. He played
baseball and tennis, and really any sport he was interested in. And he
was good at all of it. He liked to watch them, too. He used to take me
to New York to see Yankees games and tell me how his dad had seen
Babe Ruth and Lou Gehrig play. He knew all the statistics. We used
to have so much fun."

"That's where you got your love of baseball," I said. The only time

I'd ever heard my grandmother swear was when the Yankees lost to the Red Sox in extra innings. "What else did he like?"

"Lots of things. He was smart. Not an intellectual, but he had a curious mind. He was good at reading people. He could tell if someone was ready to buy insurance or wasn't."

"That's right, he sold insurance. I'd forgotten that."

"And he was popular. He knew everyone. We'd walk into a store and he'd know the owner, the owner's wife, the owner's dog." She laughed. "It was strange when I first moved to Archers Rest because nobody knew him. That's when I realized he was really gone."

Joe, my grandfather, had been dead since my mother was six and my uncle Henry was five. There were photos of him in my grandmother's bedroom, but she rarely spoke about him, and growing up, I never heard my mother mention his name. He was a ghost in our family. A man who had big plans, big ambitions, but ended up with his car wrapped around a tree after a night out with friends. He left my grandmother a widow at twenty-six, with two small children and a pile of debt.

"Did he make you happy?"

"We were kids, with kids. We didn't think about being happy." She paused. "But I guess we were."

"Was he the love of your life?"

"When did you become a romantic?"

"I've always been one."

"I would have thought you had more sense."

"I have enough sense to believe in love," I said.

"I'm sure Jesse will be happy to hear that."

I sighed. "I just don't know if I'm ready for all of that. I feel like I'm just beginning to grow into myself. But I do love Jesse," I said, "and I know you love Oliver. I'll bet he's the love of your life."

"Not everyone has that kind of happiness, Nell. Or deserves it."

"What does that mean?"

"I'm going to get that coffee before you fall asleep." She got up and walked to the door of her office. "Jesse is a good man. He'll be good to you, and you'll have a nice life together—you, Jesse, Allie, and whatever children you bring into the world. If you want to be happy, you will be. It's more of a choice than you think."

I nodded. So why wasn't she choosing to be happy, I wondered as I waited for her to return. Was the specter of my grandfather, or the long-ago pain of losing him, keeping her from marrying Oliver? Or was it as simple as feeling too old and too settled to become a wife again? Or was it something else? Whatever the answer, I was pretty sure I wouldn't hear it from Eleanor.

CHAPTER 10

"Okay, no time for gossip," I said once all the members of our quilt club had arrived. "We have serious quilting business to discuss."

Carrie and Natalie were both at the counter eating oatmeal raisin cookies, but stopped when I spoke. Natalie sat next to her mother, Susanne, the award-winning art quilter in our group, and Carrie sat next to Maggie, my grandmother's best friend and the only person I knew who could win an argument with Eleanor.

"I thought we were going to talk about the skeleton," Bernie said. Bernie was our local pharmacist, an ex-hippie, sometime psychic, and my go-to person whenever I needed cheering up.

"We're not talking about the skeleton," I said. "We're talking about the quilt show that I somehow got roped into organizing."

I looked over at Eleanor, who shrugged.

These Friday night get-togethers had been going on long before I moved to Archers Rest, but I was welcomed as a member before I even knew how to quilt. Theoretically we gathered to share quilt ideas, show off new projects, and spend some uninterrupted time engaged in our favorite hobby. But soon after I joined the group I came to realize that the quilts everyone brought to a meeting served mainly as an alibi for outsiders. We did talk about quilting once in a while. But what made our meetings a not-to-be-missed occasion was the opportunity for seven women to share the events of their week, and whatever gossip happened to be floating around town.

"I heard he was a gambler," Susanne said, ignoring my plea to talk about the quilt show.

"They found a poker chip in his pocket," I told her, "but I don't know if that makes him a gambler."

"There's a casino not far from here," Carrie said.

Bernie shook her head. "Oh, that was built less than ten years ago, and he's been in the ground for at least forty."

"Why do you think that?" Maggie asked.

"Well, he had to be buried there when Eleanor moved into the house or else she would have noticed someone digging in her garden."

Carrie turned to my grandmother. "When did you move in, Eleanor?"

"Nineteen sixty-five," Eleanor said. "And the garden was in good shape for several years."

"You don't remember anyone digging in it?" Carrie asked.

"No one but the gardeners, Larry Williams, and his father."

"The mayor?"

"He was a teenager then. His father was a gardener. These days I suppose you would say he had a landscaping business, but back then he was just handy with a garden hoe. Larry would tag along with his father and help as he could. When he got to be a teenager he took over tending to the place. He kept that rose garden in beautiful condition." Eleanor smiled at the memory of it. "It's a shame I didn't keep it up, but after Grace died and I bought the place, there were so many other priorities . . ."

"You did the best you could," Maggie jumped in.

"She did," I agreed. "And she did a wonderful job. But that isn't why we are here. I'm in serious trouble unless we figure out what we're doing about the show and start dividing up the work. So we have no time for investigating mysterious deaths."

Bernie laughed.

"I'm serious."

Carrie nodded. "She is. She says she's staying out of this one."

"Jesse can handle it," I said.

"What else is there for him to do?" Bernie jumped in. "Aside from keeping Nell happy, which I'm led to believe is a full-time job . . ."

"It is." Eleanor laughed.

"But what about the break-in at the high school?" Susanne said. "There were a couple of windows smashed early this morning. Nothing was taken, but I think Jesse was there most of the day."

"One small break-in," Bernie said. "That's probably the most excitement we'll have in town all year."

"We've had lots of excitement," I reminded her. "Even in the shop." I nodded toward the door, where we had once found a local man dead. "Frankly, I would think you would all be frightened to hear about another odd death in our little town."

"This is different," Maggie said. "This is a skeleton. There's no killer walking around."

"Exactly," Susanne spoke up. "It's more like town history than murder."

There was a general chattering of agreement on that point—chattering that would get out of hand unless I put a stop to it.

"If we're done with the town news, we have a quilt show to put on," I reminded the group, feeling like a broken record. "I'm a little freaked out by how much work this is, but I may have an idea, and I need your help. I had a conversation this afternoon with one of the shop regulars about how much the history of this country is reflected in the history of quilting. And it got me thinking. I want to do something that's tied in with the history of Archers Rest," I said. "I think that would work well with the idea of it being the 350th anniversary."

"Maybe we can do a quilt that celebrates different events of the town," Susanne suggested. "We could do appliquéd blocks. Each block would represent people or events. Sort of a Baltimore Album. I've always wanted to do one of those."

"I have to admit I'm not sure what that looks like," I said.

"It's a style of quilt made of ornately appliquéd blocks, with floral themes, ships, animals, things like that. It was done in Baltimore in the 1840s, for just a short time," Susanne explained.

Eleanor leaned forward. "You've seen them, Nell, it's just that you've seen ones with holiday subjects and contemporary fabrics. Beautiful quilts, really. It would be nice to make one."

"It will take too long. It can take months, even years, to do one of those," Bernie said. "We've got how long?"

"Seven weeks," I told her. "What if we do quilt patterns that were popular in the past, maybe tied to a particular decade? We could use reproduction fabrics to make quilts to represent the Civil War, the Depression . . ."

I could see everyone getting excited.

"I have a crazy quilt I made," Susanne said. "It's really beautiful silks and satins and hand embroidery. They were popular in the 1870s to the end of the century."

"And I could do a broderie perse to represent the early years of our nation," Maggie offered.

That one I knew. Broderie perse quilts were made from cutting flowers and other images from a fabric and appliquéing them onto a different fabric. It was a way to use up the scraps of beautiful printed fabrics at a time when imported prints were expensive and hard to get. Now it's a great shortcut to appliquéd quilts.

"I'd like to do a Hawaiian quilt with pineapples and flowers. It could represent the late 1950s when Hawaii became a state," Bernie jumped in.

"Aren't they complicated to make?" Natalie asked.

"Simple, really," Bernie assured her. "You just fold a piece of fabric into eighths, cut out an image, and unfold the fabric. Presto, you have a circle of repeating images, kind of like making a paper snowflake or string of paper dolls. It's fun."

"We would need something contemporary," Eleanor said. "I'd like to put my name on something modern, something that speaks to the future of quilting. It's important people realize that this isn't just a piece of history, but a part of our present lives and our futures."

"And not just bed quilts, but pieces of art," Maggie agreed. "It's a pity so many wonderful quilt artists are unknown to us because they didn't think to sign and date their quilts. We're left guessing who they could have been. I suppose they didn't understand how valuable those quilts would be to future generations."

Bernie leaned forward. "I'll tell you why they didn't value it: because it was a woman's art. If the majority of quilters were men, quilting would be taken more seriously as the art form it is, instead of treated as a quaint old custom."

"It's not just that it's mostly women," Carrie argued. "It's also that it's utilitarian. It's something you sleep under, so people forget it's also art. That's why it's not as valued an art form as, say, a painting."

"A vase is utilitarian, but no one says ceramicists aren't artists," Bernie shot back.

"Okay," I stepped in. "Bernie, we're not turning this quilt meeting into a protest march. We all agree that people don't fully realize the work and talent of the millions of women through the centuries who have designed and made quilts, or for that matter of all the men who've also quilted. But we're going to teach them. Our show will make it clear that quilters from the past influence current quilting, but there is also room for growth and change." I was getting interested in organizing the show for the first time. "Anybody else want to volunteer to make something?"

"I could do a whole cloth. That could represent the quilts brought over from Europe," Natalie offered. "That way I wouldn't have to piece or appliqué, and I could get started right away quilting on the longarm. I'm due July 26th, but just in case I'm early . . ." She patted her growing belly.

"Great," I said. "And I can do something from the thirties. I've always wanted to make a grandmother's flower garden."

Natalie laughed. We all looked at her, puzzled. "Nell, considering the circumstances, it might not be the best choice," she said.

A grandmother's flower garden uses only one shape—a hexagon—to create the impression of brightly colored flowers. It's a beautiful quilt pattern and one I'd been dying to try, but Natalie was right. I'd have to think of something else.

"It's a shame that a skeleton is dictating our quilt patterns," Bernie said. "But it is fascinating how things work. Some gambler comes to town and then, twenty, thirty, even forty years later, he eliminates a perfectly beautiful quilt from our show. It's that butterfly effect the scientists talk about. One small action has repercussions you would never expect."

Maggie pointed a finger at Bernie. "Don't be too sure he was a gambler. I was thinking how they used to give poker chips out at the movie theater. You remember, Eleanor?"

Eleanor nodded. "It was some promotion. You collected them and you got a free movie pass or something. But that was years and years ago."

"When years ago?" I asked.

"Your mother and uncle collected them. They had jars of them. I would say your uncle Henry was about fourteen or fifteen."

"That would put it in the early seventies," I said.

Maggie pointed toward me. "I'll bet that we could ask Jesse if it was just a regular poker chip or a special one, something that was given out at the movies. I'll bet there's a way to tell. We should look into it."

"We could," I said reluctantly, "but we're kind of getting off track. We're supposed to be planning a quilt show."

"Oh, we'll get to that," Bernie scolded me, "but don't you think we need to discuss the skeleton first?"

Eleanor laughed. "Well, you tried to get them to talk about quilting, Nell. You should give yourself a little credit for effort."

"I don't think Glad will see it that way when I have nothing to display at the quilt show."

Maggie shook her head. "Don't overdo it, Nell. You don't make a quilt in one go. You make it piece by piece, choice by choice. Tonight you decided on the theme. That was enough. Now let's just enjoy ourselves, and talk about the body in Eleanor's garden."

CHAPTER 11

After the meeting, and another hour of conjecture about the skeleton and the break-in at the high school, I stayed at the shop and pored over pattern books. There were dozens of possibilities, from elaborate appliquéd pieces to simple nine patches. And the names were all evocative of the experiences of past quilters, dealing with whatever life brought them, from broken dishes to bear's paws, shoofly to double wedding ring. Since quilting was—and is—an informal art form, many quilt patterns go by several names. One person might call a quarter-circle block surrounded by small triangles a crown of thorns, another might call it a New York beauty, but the pattern is the same. As I went through the pattern books, the problem I was facing was not a lack of options, but too many. I'd been through three books on quilt history and I still hadn't found what I wanted to make.

Finally, after a desperate search through Internet sites, something jumped out at me. A devil's puzzle, a pattern first made popular in the late 1800s. The name referred to several different patterns, but the one I chose was an easy block of rectangles and triangles that when put together create a kind of lattice effect. It seemed like something I could make quickly but would appear to have been the result of a lot of effort—sort of how I wanted the quilt show to turn out. And it had a cool name that fit my mood. Everything these days felt like a puzzle—the quilt show, Eleanor's love life, and especially the skeleton—and I knew that somehow quilting was going to help me through it all.

When I'd first come to Archers Rest, I was a bit of a mess. I was confused about who to love, where to live, and what kind of work I wanted to do. Quilting, with its dual need for logic and creative thinking, had helped me find my way. But so had looking into the few odd deaths that had occurred in town. Solving homicides, it turned out, required the same balance of logic and creative thinking. Maybe figuring out why Eleanor was so against remarriage would also make use of those skills.

But there was something about this particular mystery that bothered me more than any other I'd been involved with: It wasn't any of my business. Not that this had ever stopped me before. As Jesse and Eleanor were fond of reminding me, I'd jumped into murder investigations as if they were nothing more than a logic puzzle with a body. I was getting something of a reputation for it, which I wasn't entirely thrilled about. For me uncovering the truth had always been the motivation, and for the most part I hadn't worried about where that led. This time, though, I was worried about Eleanor.

There was no one in the world I loved more than my grandmother. She had taken me into her home, her shop, and her circle of friends. I didn't want my attempt to repay her to turn into an unintended betrayal of our friendship. I thought about just staying out of it, but what she had said earlier—"Not everyone deserves that kind of love"—nagged at me.

I decided I would call Maggie in the morning and ask for her opinion. Maggie had known my grandmother since they were both in their twenties. And like Eleanor, she wasn't shy about telling me to mind my own business.

✄

I locked up the shop and headed for home. Eleanor had taken Barney with her at about ten o'clock, when the meeting had broken up, and she'd also taken the car. As sleepy as I was, I was glad about that. It was a beautifully warm May evening, and walking the mile back to the house would be the perfect way to get me ready for sleep.

Downtown Archers Rest, if you can call it that, is only a few blocks long, with a cemetery on one end and on the other, a winding road that leads to—among other places—my grandmother's old Victorian. Bordering it to the west is the Hudson River, and to the east, farmland and several old homes that date back to the colonial days. The homes are all museums now, available for tours led by people in Revolutionary War costumes—a kind of poor man's Williamsburg. Beyond the homes is a highway that, if you went south on it for three hours, would take you to New York City.

Archers Rest isn't particularly unique or filled with interesting sights, but its citizens are proud of it. George Washington had been up and down the Hudson River Valley, but as far as I knew had never so much as hoisted a tankard in Archers Rest. There were skirmishes during the Revolutionary War, but anything of even the smallest historical significance had taken place elsewhere. The town's main claim to American history was that in 1777 the British had briefly considered Archers Rest as a place to wage a battle before deciding to go farther south.

I knew the point of the Fourth of July celebration was to get tourists to visit Archers Rest, and maybe it would, but I liked the quiet. It was a shame that tourists coming up for a parade and a fireworks display would miss out on all this quiet. At least they would get a good quilt show. Hopefully.

Walking home, I got to enjoy the quiet. I looked at the darkened shops and empty streets, and listened to the only sound there was: crickets calling out to each other. Tonight, though, I didn't feel alone on the streets. It was as though someone was walking with me. I looked around repeatedly as I moved toward home. Despite the hair standing up on the back of my neck, as far as I could tell, I was all by myself.

"Maybe it's the ghost of John Archer," I said, trying to laugh off my fears. I knew, as Jesse had said, that Archer was safely buried in the cemetery. It wasn't *his* grave we'd uncovered. It wasn't *his* ghost we'd upset. "Go haunt someone else, will ya? I'm tired," I called out to the night air.

As the words came out of my mouth, I heard a loud bang behind me. I turned but there was nothing, just a sudden cold breeze that I told myself was only the wind coming off the river.

I kept walking and got to the house just after midnight. I thought I heard noises coming from the backyard, so I walked through the kitchen and opened the back door. I was tired and should have gone up to bed, but something in the yard caught my eye. I went over to the hole in my grandmother's overgrown rose garden. There was nothing different about it. The skeleton had been removed and it was now just a hole, dark earth, and small stones. I decided I must have been seeing things. But as I turned back toward the house I heard the noise again, this time from the trees.

I took a deep breath and walked toward the trees, looking for any sign of an intruder. I told myself it probably was a squirrel or a deer. But it didn't seem like animal noises. It seemed like someone's heavy breath. I could feel my heart beating just a little faster. I moved my foot forward, but I couldn't make myself take a step. Instead I stood as still as I could, and listened.

My grandmother's house is on several acres, and toward the back of her land the trees are densely planted. Little light can penetrate, especially on a night like this, with a new moon in the sky. And beyond the trees is the river, a sheet of black on even the brightest night. I could hear what sounded like rustling, maybe an animal, but heavier than a squirrel. And larger. Whatever—whoever—had left blood on the skeleton might be back, looking for something else.

I thought about walking into the woods to find the source of the noise, but my feet were only interested in moving toward the house. As my pace quickened, getting me closer to safety with each step, I told myself that my curiosity wasn't worth coming face-to-face with whatever had retreated there.

"Maybe I'm maturing," I said once I was on the porch. "I just have to make sure Eleanor doesn't find out or she'll take all the credit."

When I walked into the kitchen I bumped into Oliver, putting two cups of tea on a tray.

"Did you hear anything in the back?" I asked him.

"No. I just came down to make your grandmother some tea. I think a cup of tea is a perfect way to end the day," he said. "What did you hear in the backyard?"

"Nothing. Just animals," I said, deciding that was, in fact, what I'd heard. "I'm going to sleep, but I may be the only one in the whole town. I keep seeing, or think I'm seeing, something out there in the dark."

"There are more secrets per capita in a small town than in a big city," Oliver said. "In a big city you don't have to keep your life secret because no one cares. But in Archers Rest . . ."

"Everyone knows everything. Or tries to."

"Which brings up an interesting point: How long do you think I can keep Eleanor from finding out about the engagement?"

I could feel myself blush. "A little while longer," I said. "I think you can wait until things are cleared up with . . ." I motioned toward the hole in the backyard.

"That ring is burning a hole in my pocket." He seemed excited, and I couldn't tell him that he might be—we both might have been—wrong about Eleanor's reaction. "You were the one who thought this was a good idea, Nell. You're not changing your mind?"

"Not a bit. I just think you should wait a little longer."

Maybe with time I could turn Eleanor's answer to a yes. Or at least find a reason that would soften the blow Oliver would feel if Eleanor turned him down.

Oliver assembled his tea tray. "She's going to make a lovely bride, isn't she?"

"She will," I said. In my heart, I added, "I hope."

CHAPTER 12

"You're up early." Maggie greeted me at the door a little after seven, a cat tangling itself in her legs.

"He must be new."

"Showed up a few days ago. Must have heard I was a soft touch. Come into the kitchen. I've got some rhubarb muffins I just baked."

We sat in the kitchen enjoying muffins and coffee, and talked about the quilt show and quilting in general. I was halfway through a sentence about some new batiks that had arrived in the shop when Maggie leaned back in her chair.

"Okay, enough small talk. What's this about?"

"I just wanted to visit."

"You saw me yesterday. Nothing much has happened between ten o'clock last night and seven this morning," she said. "Is this about the skeleton? Do you know something you didn't want to say in front of Eleanor?"

I put down my coffee cup and nodded. "It's not about the skeleton, but there was something I didn't want to say in front of my grandmother."

"Jesse," Maggie said.

"What?"

"You know Jesse is going to propose."

"Eleanor told you that, I assume."

Maggie smiled. "He's a wonderful man. Just perfect for you."

"He's not going to propose."

"Well, he's not nearly good enough for you anyway."

I laughed. There might be nearly fifty years between us, but Maggie was a true girlfriend, willing to spin 180 degrees at a moment's notice just to back me up.

"Oliver. He's the one planning to propose," I said.

Maggie stared off into the distance, the shock evident on her face. Then she smiled slightly and nodded to herself before turning back to me. "How much time do we have to make them a wedding quilt? They probably won't have a long engagement at their age, so it will need to be a simple pattern, but very, very special."

"There may not be an engagement. Eleanor thinks getting married again is ridiculous. She doesn't know Oliver is planning anything. She's just against the idea in theory. But if he asks, I think she'll say no and . . ."

"The poor man." Maggie shook her head. "Did she give you a reason why she wouldn't marry him?"

"No. That's why I'm here. I don't want to interfere in her life, but I don't want her to make a mistake she'll regret."

"You want my permission?"

"Maybe 'advice' is a better word."

"Well, if the situation were reversed, and you were against marrying Jesse but wouldn't give a reason, what would she do?"

I laughed. "She'd lecture me and nag me and bug me until I either married him or gave her a good reason why I wouldn't."

"Then that's your answer."

I felt a weight lift off me. "Okay, then, Maggie, you've known Eleanor longer than anyone . . ."

"Since she was your age," Maggie agreed.

"So I thought you might know about her marriage to Joe."

"I didn't meet Eleanor until after Joe died. She came to Archers Rest with her two little ones and got a job as Grace Roemer's live-in assistant, I guess you would say."

"I know that part of the story. But how did she get that job? She never told me."

"I don't actually know. Grace's own children were grown and living far away, so she needed Eleanor as a companion and a kind of nursemaid, and Eleanor needed a home for her children. However Eleanor got it, it was just what she needed."

"Did Eleanor ever say anything about Joe?"

"Of course. The memories were fresh then. The pain was front and center. But she had your mother and uncle to raise. She put aside her pain and got on with her life."

"Would there have been something in her marriage that would stop her now, after all these years, from getting married again?"

"Meaning?"

"I don't know. Maybe they were really happy and she felt he was her one true love."

"I can't picture Eleanor uttering the words 'one true love.'"

"She thought I was nuts when I suggested it," I admitted. "Was the marriage really unhappy and she doesn't want to repeat a nightmare?"

"I don't think so. Eleanor loved your grandfather and she spoke of him fondly, as she still does. From what I learned about him, he was a well-liked man, but maybe he wanted more than he could afford. In those days folks like us didn't have credit cards, but we could still get things on credit at stores. I gather he did that. Their car wasn't paid for. Their house was behind on the mortgage. There were debts and nothing in the bank to pay them."

"Was he a gambler?" Suddenly the poker chip popped into my mind, and I tried to push away what I was thinking.

Maggie shook her head. "I don't think so. I think he was just a dreamer. He might have been able to achieve his dreams if, well," she paused. "I understand the weather was very bad that night."

"It must have been heartbreaking," I said.

"It was, of course, but she got on with life and did whatever she had to for the sake of her children."

"Any romances after Joe?"

Maggie lowered her eyes for a moment. "Your grandmother's past is hers to tell."

"Which means yes."

Maggie poured me another cup of coffee. "Did I show you the picture my kids gave me for Mother's Day? They had a professional portrait done. All the kids and grandkids." She got up from the table and left the room, coming back with a large framed photo. "I don't think you've met all of my kids."

"Only one or two of them."

I took the photo and looked at the dozens of smiling faces. Maggie had eleven children, thirty grandchildren, and one great-grandchild. As Maggie pointed to each of her children, I couldn't help noticing that the people Maggie identified looked nothing alike, with a mix of races and ethnicities that would make the UN proud.

"You never told me you adopted," I said.

She shrugged. "My kids are my kids, no matter where they come from. Hank and I took in Emilio when his parents died," she said, pointing to a man of about fifty in the center of the photo. "He was our first child. Then, I gave birth to three kids: Thomas, Sheila, and my youngest, Brian. In between, we took in the others as they needed us."

"It looks like a nice family."

She nodded. "They're good people. That's what matters. They're close to each other, and they help each other, and they help others. Two of the kids are teachers, one is a nurse, Emilio is a lawyer, working for Legal Aid, and Brian . . ."

"He's planning on running for Congress," I said. "Eleanor told me."

"He'll do good things for people. He'll contribute. That's all I ask of my kids and grandkids. And myself. We all make mistakes, have regrets, but we can't be judged by our mistakes. If you look closely at a quilt, it's full of mistakes, but if you step back and look . . ."

"You only see the beauty of the entire quilt. Eleanor is fond of saying that." I took a deep breath. "We sort of got off the subject, though, Maggie. I was asking about Eleanor's life after Joe died."

"I don't know that there's anything your grandmother hasn't already told you."

"Humor me."

She sighed. "Your grandmother and I became friends because our children played together. When Grace taught Eleanor how to quilt, I sat in on some of the lessons and picked it up myself. So we had that in common as well. No one quilted in the sixties," she said with a laugh, "and the fabric was awful. We didn't have the beautiful cottons we have today. We used bedsheets for the backs. We made templates for our quilt patterns using the cardboard from empty cereal boxes. It's amazing we stuck with it."

"But you did."

"We did. And a few months after Grace died in '75, I think it was, Eleanor opened the quilt shop. Perfect timing, too. That was right before the bicentennial. All the colonial-era crafts were making a comeback: quilting, candle making, iron work. Ironic really, because quilting wasn't that popular during the colonial years. It's one of the myths about quilting . . ." She smiled. "I'm getting off track again. The point is that Eleanor just hit at the right time. And of course, Eleanor has a knack for people, for helping them find their own creative voice."

"That shop has been her life," I said.

"And it's been a good life."

"But you didn't answer my question."

"I've answered several of your questions."

"About Eleanor's love life after Joe."

"I actually did, Nell. You just didn't like the answer. If you want to know about that, you can ask Eleanor."

"But she won't tell me."

Maggie considered it for a moment, then sighed. "Then perhaps there isn't anything you need to know."

CHAPTER 13

After I left Maggie's, I walked toward town trying to figure out what she had meant. She wasn't saying there was nothing in Eleanor's past, just that I didn't need to know it. But at the same time she'd encouraged me to keep pursuing the matter, as Eleanor would have done if the situation were reversed. I would have stayed and pushed Maggie to explain the contradiction, but Maggie, like my grandmother, wasn't easily pushed.

Instead I headed toward Someday Quilts. I wasn't on the schedule to work, but I hoped to pick out some fabrics for my devil's puzzle quilt and make phone calls to some shop regulars to see if they would have quilts to contribute to the show. But when I passed the movie theater, I changed my mind and made a phone call.

"Can you meet me at Bryant's with the red poker chip?" I asked.

I could hear Jesse laugh on the other end of the phone. "Is that code for something?"

"No." I knew what was coming next.

"But the poker chip is tied to the skeleton we found," he said, "and since you're staying out of that investigation, you can't possibly be asking me about that."

"If you want to mock me, you'll never know what I was going to tell you."

"Five minutes."

True to his word, Jesse met me in front of the theater just a few minutes later. I told him what Maggie had said about Eleanor.

Rather than the expected reminder that Eleanor's love life was none of my business, Jesse asked, "What does that have to do with a poker chip?"

"Maggie has a habit of casually slipping important information into a conversation. I felt like she told me something important about Eleanor this morning. I just have to figure out what it was."

I held up my hand to stop Jesse from asking the question about the poker chip a second time.

"As I was thinking about it, I remembered how Maggie had mentioned that the theater used to give out poker chips as part of some promotion they had in the seventies. I thought maybe Ed would know something about it."

"That's a great idea." He smiled. "Nice to have you back on the case."

"I'm not on the case. I'm just passing along information."

"So you're not going to stay while I talk to Ed?"

I considered walking away, heading to the shop and working on my plans for the quilt show, but I just couldn't do it. "I'll just wait for you. Maybe we can get some coffee afterward and hang out."

He laughed. "I knew you wouldn't be able to keep out of this."

I didn't bother to protest, but I did promise myself I would just listen and not ask any questions. It had become a matter of honor. Everyone assumed I would butt into the investigation, that I didn't have the willpower to leave it alone—and the one quality that usually trumped my curiosity was my stubbornness. If everyone was betting I would jump in, I was determined to stay out. Mostly.

Ed met us at the front door with apologies. "We're closed until this evening," he said. "I had to have the plumber in to work on some leaks in the soda machines. I really should replace them, but I don't have the funds right now."

"We're not here for a movie, Ed," Jesse told him. "We're actually looking into an incident over at Eleanor Cassidy's house."

"The skeleton?"

Jesse smiled. "I guess you heard about it. We found something with the body that you may recognize." He held up the poker chip, encased in a sealed plastic evidence bag. "Does this look familiar?"

"Should it?"

"I understand your father had a promotion at the theater in the early seventies. Something that involved poker chips?"

Ed nodded. "Oh, I do know what you're talking about. I didn't own the theater then, my dad did. I was still teaching at the high school."

"When did you take it over?" I asked.

"Only about ten years ago, after my father passed away. I couldn't let the old girl be turned into a fast-food place or some such nonsense, so I took over. I was retiring from the school anyway. I needed something to keep me busy."

"The poker chip," Jesse said, nudging us back to the topic.

"Right. My dad used to have silly promotions all the time. He had as much trouble keeping the bills paid as I seem to. I guess I'm as crazy as he was, wanting to own a movie theater, but I love it, and he loved it."

"And the poker chips?" Jesse asked again.

"It must have been in '74 or '75, he had these coded poker chips he handed out to patrons. You got one when you saw a movie and one if you bought a combo of popcorn and a soda. If you collected ten, you got into a movie for free."

"What stopped people from just buying a box of poker chips and handing those in?" I asked.

"Dad had the chips specially made. There's a code on the back of each one of them." Ed pointed to the poker chip in the evidence bag. Engraved into the chip and painted a faded gold were two small letters: "'B.C.' It stands for 'Bryant's Cinema,'" Ed continued. "Each movie was a different color chip. *Young Frankenstein* was yellow; *The Sting* was green . . ."

"What movie was red?" Jesse asked.

"*Towering Inferno*." Ed smiled. "I loved that movie. I must have watched it at least a dozen times."

"That would mean the chip is from 1974," I said. "Do you know what month it played here?"

"Not off the top of my head. I know it wouldn't have played right when it was released. We got movies after they had played at the bigger theaters." He thought for a moment. "It was the summer. I remember that because I was off school. If you give me a minute, I can look at the records. I have all my dad's files in my office," Ed said, and then frowned. "I'd offer you a Coke while you wait, but . . ." He pointed toward the broken soda machines.

Jesse shook his head. "If you can tell me when that poker chip was handed out, it will be a big help."

"Anything for you, Chief."

Ed seemed like a nice man. He was almost completely bald and kept what hair he did have almost military short. He had a bit of weight around the middle, but he was quite tall so he carried it well. Most of all he was friendly, and Jesse seemed to like him, so that counted for a lot.

Once Ed went to his office, Jesse turned to me. I could see he was about to speak, so I spoke first.

"I know what you're going to say," I said, assuming he would kid me about asking Ed questions when I'd promised not to.

"I was going to ask how you knew *Towering Inferno* came out in 1974."

"I like disasters."

"I know that," he said. "And I know you. Which one did you have a crush on—Paul Newman or Steve McQueen?"

"So I only could have liked the movie if I liked one of the actors?"

"Enough to know when it was released? Yes."

I shrugged. No sense in pretending he was wrong. "Robert Wagner."

Jesse looked at me for a minute. "No kidding?"

"No kidding. He's very suave."

"Like me." A wide grin spread across his face.

I laughed. "Exactly like you."

A few minutes later, Ed returned. "We had the movie for two weeks in the summer of 1975. It opened here on the Fourth of July."

"And that's the only time your dad would have given out this particular poker chip?"

"I think so. He had lots of colors, maybe thirty different chips. He figured it would encourage people to buy popcorn and stuff, to get a free movie faster."

"Did it work?" I asked.

"It did. In fact, that promotion did well enough to keep the doors open that summer. Dad was going to have to shut down if he didn't fix some things in the building and get it up to code, but he did well enough that year to fix everything and take home a salary. But then things slid downhill and he was barely hanging on after that. He was like me. He even looked like me." Ed ran his hand across his balding head. "Big guys with big hearts and no brains." He laughed. "At least that's what my mother used to say."

"Do you know how many of these chips he would have given out?" Jesse asked.

"No idea. Maybe a hundred or so."

"It's a long shot, but he wouldn't have kept a record of who got them?"

"Heavens no," Ed told him. "We just handed them out to whoever came through the door for a movie. I worked the ticket booth in the summers. I probably was the one who gave out that very poker chip."

I perked up at that. "Do you remember giving a chip out to a stranger?" I asked. "A tall man?"

"Not that I recall, Nell. But if you find my fingerprints on the chip, I just want you to know how they got there." He slapped Jesse on the back and laughed a loud, friendly laugh.

CHAPTER 14

"So, assuming that our friend went to the movies and collected a chip, he was in Archers Rest sometime between July 4th and July 18th of 1975," Jesse said as we walked into Jitters for our usual cappuccinos and chocolate-dipped biscotti.

He settled into the corner of the purple couch and I sat close enough for him to put his arm around me, while I rested my hand on his thigh.

I sipped my coffee. "But you've already checked missing persons in the seventies, haven't you?"

"Yes. And got nothing. The thing to do now is ask about those years . . . you know, to find out what she remembers."

"You mean Eleanor?"

"She was living there in 1975. She has to know something." My head did an involuntary jerk as I pulled back from Jesse. He grabbed my arm to keep me from moving farther away. "I'm not saying Eleanor did it. Obviously she didn't kill him. Eleanor wouldn't harm anyone," he said. "But even if I didn't know Eleanor I'd still say it was pretty unlikely she killed a man in his prime, someone over six feet tall, all by herself. She wouldn't have had the strength."

I relaxed back into his arms. "Just to play devil's advocate, couldn't she have shot him?"

"Yes, but if she had, there would be bullet wounds. There aren't. From what the medical examiner has been able to tell, he was hit over the head with something. Repeatedly. It would take someone pretty strong to do that."

"And you figure Eleanor wasn't strong enough?"

"You and she are about the same size. You're only a few years younger than she would have been then. I'm about the same height and probably the same weight as the victim. Maybe a few years younger than he would have been. How many times could you hit me with something without my stopping you?"

"If you were asleep, I could get in enough blows to kill you."

"I'll sleep with one eye open from now on."

"But assuming the victim was asleep when he was killed," I said, "then someone would have had to drag him out to the backyard, dig a hole, and dump him in."

"So asleep or awake, the killer would have to be pretty strong . . ."

"And probably male." It was hard to argue with his logic. "Unless the killer had help."

"Or a wheelbarrow," Jesse admitted. "Then maybe she could have moved the body on her own. Or he could have. And if the victim were drunk, or drugged, his reflexes would be slower, making it easier to get a blow in." He sighed. "With just a skeleton to work with, there's no way of telling whether there were drugs in his system. So I guess we haven't eliminated someone Eleanor's size."

"Not yet. What's the next step? We talk to Eleanor?"

"Which she won't like."

I sat up. "What if you came over for dinner? You, me, Oliver, and Eleanor. You could slip it into the conversation somehow." I hesitated before adding, "But just so you know, she's going to hint around about a wedding because she thinks you're about to propose."

"She thinks what?"

"She knows you and Oliver went to the jewelry store together and figured it was you buying the ring."

"Amateur sleuthing runs in the family."

"The point is, just go along with it because we don't want her suspecting that it might be Oliver. Not until we're sure why she's against remarrying."

"Until *you're* sure. I'm staying out of that. Even if you are helping with the murder investigation."

"I'm helping you talk to Eleanor in a way that will be open and relaxed, so she won't think you're accusing her of something."

"Oliver and I are lucky men to love such interesting women."

I grazed his lips with mine. "It's amazing how often we agree these days, isn't it?"

I had just settled back into his arms when I heard a booming voice from above. "Hello, lovebirds."

I looked up at our mayor, smiling at us, his favorite green tea in one hand and a double-chocolate brownie in the other.

"I like to balance my bad habits with good ones," Larry said when he saw me looking at his food.

"Smart man." I smiled.

With him was a young woman in her late teens or early twenties with an intense, almost angry look. She had long black hair—so dark that it could only be from a bottle—long black fingernails, and a large Celtic cross hanging from her neck. But she was wearing a soft pink lipstick that matched her outfit, a light T-shirt, and khaki pants. She looked as though she were trying to be Goth enough for her friends and country club enough for her parents, though neither look was a perfect fit.

"This is Molly O'Brien. Summer intern down from Newton. She's helping with the anniversary celebration. She'll coordinate with the committee chairs," the mayor nodded toward me, "on anything they may need."

Molly smiled vaguely at us but seemed bored.

"And Molly," he turned to her, "this is our chief of police, and this is Nell Fitzgerald. It was in her grandmother's garden that we found our skeleton."

Now Molly was interested. "I saw the mayor's blog," she said, her voice more animated with each word. "It's so cool. A dead body just buried in your backyard all these years. Any idea who he is?"

"Not yet," Jesse said.

The mayor sat on the arm of the couch and leaned in. Larry Williams owned the local travel agency, sold insurance, and from January to April did the taxes of nearly half the town. He'd even set his sons up in a hardware store that served as one of his many unofficial campaign offices. And when Larry wasn't working, he was helping.

He had a jovial, laid-back way about him, but he was absolutely passionate about Archers Rest.

"We have to talk about this skeleton situation, Chief," he said.

"We're doing everything we can to identify the victim," Jesse said.

"Oh, I'm sure you are. It's just I'm thinking of the big celebration this Fourth of July."

Jesse nodded. "And you don't want this becoming bad publicity for the town. Which is why posting pictures on your blog is a bad idea . . ."

The mayor waved him off. "On the contrary. I want this to be huge publicity for the town. A skeleton in a backyard in a small town like Archers Rest? If we can get you a few interviews with some of the New York papers, talking about how the town is full of secrets, maybe even ghosts . . ."

"Ghosts!" I nearly spit out my coffee.

"City folks love staying in haunted bed-and-breakfasts, visiting old houses where spirits still roam," he said, with a confidence that suggested he'd done a study of it.

"Mayor," Jesse interrupted, "there aren't any ghosts in this investigation."

"You don't know that," Molly jumped in. "The house with the skeleton has to be full of ghosts. I'd love to see it sometime. Poke around for spirits. It's at least a hundred years old, isn't it, Nell?"

"A hundred and thirty," I told her. "But no ghosts."

"But those New Yorkers don't have to know that." Larry looked around as if he were afraid of being overheard, which was likely considering how loudly he spoke. "We have a picturesque little town here, right on the banks of the beautiful Hudson River. We have the nicest people in the world, the best shops, great little coffee places like this one. What we don't have is tourism."

"We don't really have anything that sets us apart from all the other picturesque towns on the Hudson," Jesse said. "Sleepy Hollow has the Washington Irving story, Hyde Park has Roosevelt's home, and West Point has—"

Larry practically jumped up. "That's my point. We're losing out to those flashier places. We need something unique, something that gets people interested in Archers Rest."

I didn't want to burst his bubble, but I didn't see it. "Why would a decades-old murder investigation get people interested in coming here for the anniversary celebration?"

"We have to dress it up a bit. Make it more exciting. And that's where Jesse comes in. We don't have to run around solving this thing right away. We could maybe suggest that it might be a Revolutionary War hero. Or something else, I don't know—maybe a pirate, or a duel gone bad. There are lots of scenarios."

"A pirate?" I looked over at Molly, who was listening intently. "Would pirates be interesting enough for you to come to a town like Archers Rest?"

She glanced at the mayor, seemed to consider her words, and said, "I think murders are always interesting. Even—maybe especially—old ones."

"Exactly," the mayor said. "This is an old town. That body could be hundreds of years old. No sense in solving it tomorrow and making it another mundane homicide when it could be the jumping-off point for a story that would get us on the map."

I could feel Jesse tensing up. "Mayor," he said, "I'm interested in identifying this man, and if possible, solving his murder. That's my job. I'm not interested in parading the body of a dead man around so some bored New Yorkers can have a bit of weekend fun."

Larry stood up and sighed. "Well, you'd better be, Jesse Dewalt, or this town will be looking for a chief of police who cares about the welfare of its living residents."

CHAPTER 15

To his credit, Jesse didn't seem too worried about the mayor's threat.

"He's a little manic about this place," Jesse reassured me once we'd left Jitters and walked across the street to Someday Quilts. "Sometimes he forgets he's the mayor and imagines he's the king."

"When are you going to tell him that his pirate was wearing synthetic fabrics and had a poker chip in his pocket?"

"Not today, that's for sure."

"He'd be an idiot to lose you," I said. "And if he doesn't know that, then the rest of the town does."

Jesse looked at me for a long time before gently kissing me. "I'll see you at this dinner party tomorrow," he said. "And I have a favor to ask. I need to send Allie over to the shop, just for a couple of hours this afternoon. My mom is doing some errands."

"That's not a favor. I love having Allie at the shop."

"She loves being there. She told me she wants to be a quilter when she grows up."

"She's already a quilter. Eleanor has been teaching her. Allie will be at the Friday meetings before you know it."

He laughed. "I'd say that was harmless fun, but I have a feeling a lot of dangerous talk goes on at those meetings."

"You don't want to know."

We kissed again and I watched as he walked toward the police station.

Inside the shop a couple of women were wandering through the aisles of fabric. Eleanor was at the front counter ringing up a sale and

Natalie was in back, working on the longarm machine, trying to finish a growing pile of quilts.

The quilting world used to be divided into two camps: the hand quilters and the machine quilters. Now there's a third category, those who quilt by checkbook—people who make quilt tops and send them out to be quilted by someone like Natalie or me. The advantage of sending out a quilt top is, of course, that it will actually get quilted. For the folks who do it all themselves, making the entire quilt is a way to stretch their skills and create something completely their own. For those who send them out, it seems like the perfect way to make more quilts in less time. Personally, I thought they were both right.

I made ten phone calls to ten regular customers of the shop, explained about the quilt show, and got ten promises to make reproduction-style quilts to fit the theme of the show. As I picked out some fabrics for my devil's puzzle quilt, I congratulated myself on how smoothly things were going. I even left a message for Glad telling her the theme, and how, not surprisingly, quilters from all over town were contributing their work to what I knew would be a great show. At least something was going right.

"Nell Fitzgerald, I want to speak to you."

I was hoping I hadn't spoken too soon. Just as I was feeling relaxed, Glad entered the shop. Even though she was dressed in a soft green skirt and matching jacket, as if she were stopping in on the way to tea, her whole demeanor was that of a woman ready to do battle.

"Hi Glad. What can I do for you?"

"It's about this skeleton," she started, "over at your grandmother's."

"What about it?"

"We cannot have that kind of scandal in our town with the anniversary celebration coming up. How would it look?"

"I don't think it's a scandal, exactly."

I looked toward Eleanor, who was quietly moving toward her office. I was a little annoyed that she would leave me to deal with Glad alone, but I had to admire her ability to make a quick getaway. Barney, on the other hand, stayed by my side in a show of loyalty. Or maybe it was that he'd found a fabric cat one of the customers had made for him and he was having fun chewing on it. Glad looked down at him and scowled.

"Isn't it against some health code to have a dog in a shop?"

"It's a fabric shop, Glad. We don't serve food here."

"Still, an animal wandering around . . ."

"You wanted to talk to me about the skeleton."

"Yes," she sniffed, as if she'd suddenly developed an allergy. Barney, now walking around her feet, didn't appear to take offense. But then, he never did. As I watched him, I noticed a mark on Glad's leg. It looked like several long, narrow cuts on the side of her calf.

"What happened there?" I said, pointing to her leg.

Glad reached down and patted her leg through her nylons. "One of my sister's many cats," she said. Then she stood up straight and stared into me. "Nell, this skeleton is exactly the kind of bad publicity that we don't need. We are a safe, quiet town with good people. People with values. People with manners." Her voice, which had been getting progressively louder, suddenly turned into a whisper. "If people hear about this after everything that's happened this year, they'll think the whole town is full of killers."

"The mayor . . ."

"The mayor is shortsighted."

"So you know about his idea?"

"There is very little that goes on in this town that I don't know about."

I had no doubt about that. "Well, then you know there really isn't anything I can do about it."

"You can tell Jesse Dewalt to identify this . . . person as quickly as possible."

"That's what he's trying to do," I said.

"It should be his only priority to put this matter to rest as quickly as possible. Solved or unsolved. In fact, it might be the best thing for everyone if he just buried the bones of that poor person and let that be the end of it."

"That poor person had a name, Glad, and Jesse plans to find it.

And solve his murder. I know he's putting every available officer on the case."

"Tell him that it must be dealt with quietly, and with respect for the reputation of this town."

"I'll tell him what you said, but, for future reference, you don't need to go through me to give Jesse a message. The police station is one street over to the left."

She blinked her eyes slowly. "I realize the reason Eleanor foisted this assignment on you is that she didn't want to spend time with Ed Bryant . . ."

"The theater owner?" I'd never heard my grandmother even mention his name, let alone suggest she disliked him.

"Obviously." Glad was losing whatever patience she had with me. "And since you are in charge of the quilt show, I'm hoping that you care about this town as much as I do, Nell. I'm hoping you want this celebration to be a success."

"I actually left you a message with an update on the show and . . ."

"That's fine. Thank you." She smiled at me, though it was clear that she wasn't happy. "You can tell me all about it at the organizers' meeting tomorrow. You do remember we're getting together promptly at four p.m. to discuss our progress, don't you?"

"I didn't know . . ."

"Well, you do now. You'll be there?"

"Absolutely," I said—to no one, because Glad had walked out of the store, slamming the door behind her.

I walked into Eleanor's office, where she was ordering fabric, and Barney followed, bringing his fabric cat with him. I shook my finger at Eleanor. "Chicken."

She looked up. "That woman scares me."

"Nobody scares you."

"Glad does." Eleanor looked through the door of her office, as if she were making sure Glad was gone. "When I met her, she was a child, and she was just as forceful then. Her father was the town banker. And I think the mayor for a time. She thought she owned the place then. She thinks she owns it now."

"She'll have to fight it out with the current mayor. He's gotten awfully possessive of it."

"Larry's just a nice man who wants to make his mark," Eleanor said. "He worked for his success. Glad thinks she got hers by divine right."

I looked back at the door that Glad had slammed just moments before. "How old would she have been in 1975?"

"Why?"

"Just curious."

"I don't know. Maybe seventeen or eighteen."

"Was she athletic as a teenager?"

"I don't remember. I don't recall her being on any sports teams. She seemed more interested in shopping. When Grace and I would go into the bank to check on Grace's investments, Gladys and her sister, Glee, would often be there, getting money from their dad." Eleanor shook her head. "He was a soft touch. 'Anything for my girls,' he'd say. I don't think he ever said no to them."

"Glad has a sister named Glee?"

"Mrs. Shipman, Mary Shipman. The woman who lives in that big house near the highway. I don't think you've ever met her."

I shook my head.

"She keeps to herself these days," Eleanor continued. "Funny you should ask about Glad being athletic. Mary was the athlete in that family. I remember she played softball and girls' field hockey, I think. She was quite good, too. She even held a protest march, one woman strong, if I recall, about getting on the wrestling team. To prove she was up to it, she pinned one of the local boys to the ground. Not that he minded." She laughed to herself. "It didn't get her on the team, but you had to admire her spunk."

"Is that why everyone called her Glee?"

"Everyone didn't. Her mother called her Glee for some reason. Strange mother, if I recall. Very theatrical."

"She named her daughters Glad and Glee. Maybe she was just happy."

"Well, if she was," Eleanor said, "she didn't pass it on to her children."

CHAPTER 16

Jesse's daughter, Allie, dipped her hands into the pile of bolt ends and other fabric scraps we kept in a large box labeled DISCARD PILE. We said it was there for anyone to take needed fabrics, but the truth was, we didn't have a discard pile. We just told Jesse that. He insisted on paying for any fabric Allie used from bolts on the sales floor, so Eleanor, Natalie, and I had started cutting small scraps of brightly colored fabric and putting them into a special "Allie pile," so she would be free to play without Jesse feeling obligated to pay for anything.

Allie loved going through that pile and getting her first taste of what addicted most quilters: the endless choice of fabrics. When she found a piece she liked, she would place it on Barney's back, using him as a kind of display wall. She would stand back and stare at the fabric as he stood perfectly still, letting her decide if it was worth keeping. For Allie, a pretty piece of fabric was always worth keeping, so she would add piece after piece to Barney's back. After a few minutes he ended up looking like a circus clown. Not that he minded. He followed Allie around as if she were his secret crush.

"Can I put purple polka dots with green stripes?" Allie asked me.

"You can if you want to," I told her. "There aren't any rules about what goes with what when you make a quilt."

"Are you sure?" She scrunched up her face worriedly. Even at six, she had reason to doubt that a place without rules existed.

"It's your quilt. You can do what you like."

She looked up at me with the same serious expression that Jesse had whenever he didn't quite believe what I was saying. "I'm not making the quilt for me, Nell," she said. "It's kind of for Daddy, so it has to be colors he would like."

"He'll love whatever fabrics you choose." Eleanor came into the room and grabbed Allie, sending the little girl into a fit of giggles.

"What do you mean it's 'kind of' for Daddy?" I asked.

"It's for you and Daddy when you get married."

Eleanor and I exchanged surprised glances. I was glad to see from the look on her face that it wasn't my grandmother who had put the idea into Allie's head.

"Well, then you have plenty of time to choose colors," I said, without any idea of what else to say.

"But I want to make you a wedding quilt," she said. "That's what you do when people get married."

I could feel my face turn red. "It is," I agreed. "But . . ." I looked toward Eleanor for help.

"If I help her, maybe we can figure out what to make," Eleanor volunteered. That wasn't exactly the help I was looking for, but for Allie's sake, I just smiled.

Natalie, who had been working quietly in the back of the room the whole day, stopped quilting at the longarm machine and came over to us, stretching her arms tiredly. "I think that's all I have in me for the day," she said. "The baby is kicking up a storm and it's wearing me out. Nell, do you want to grab a quick cup of tea at Jitters before I head home?"

"I'd love the break," I said. "Is it okay to leave Allie?" I asked Eleanor.

"Okay? Allie and I have a quilt to plan."

"Don't get too carried away," I said, but she wasn't listening. She and Allie were walking through the aisles of the shop adding fabric to the polka dots and stripes.

"This is getting out of hand," I said to Natalie when we entered Jitters.

Carrie looked up and smiled. "This is your fourth time today, Nell. Even for you, that's a lot of coffee."

"I'm not here for the coffee," I said. "I'm here for help."

The shop was enjoying a rare quiet moment, so Carrie left the counter and joined Natalie and me at a table. I told her and Natalie about my conversation with Maggie, and Glad's strange comment that Eleanor was avoiding Ed Bryant.

"He's a nice man, isn't he?" Carrie asked. "He comes in here every morning for coffee and a muffin. Always apple spice." She smiled. "Then in the afternoon, he comes back for another one. He's so gentlemanly. Why would Eleanor dislike him?"

Natalie shrugged. "Maybe that's just Glad trying to be mean. You know, saying something provocative to show you how much she knows about this town. That would be just like her."

"Maybe," I said. "But there is something. I think Maggie knows what it is, but she's too loyal to Eleanor to tell me."

Natalie nodded. "And if you asked Eleanor, she would just stonewall you, or start talking about your engagement."

"Poor Jesse," I said. "You should have seen the look of terror on his face when I told him that Eleanor thinks he's the one ready to pop the question."

"It wouldn't be such a bad idea, though," Carrie said. "Maybe it could be a double wedding."

"Maybe in the fall," Natalie agreed. "How sweet would that be? You and Jesse, Eleanor and Oliver. It would be such a testament to the enduring power of love."

"That's enough of that," I said. "Let's just focus on Eleanor and why she apparently dislikes Ed Bryant."

"Aside from his order, all he talks about is the movie theater. Poor guy, he doesn't seem to be making much money at it," Carrie said. "He just gets his coffee and muffin and sits at the corner table reading the paper. Every day."

"Does he ever talk to anyone?"

Carrie shook her head. "Not that I've noticed, but it gets very busy here in the mornings."

"Does he live alone?" I asked.

"As far as I know," Natalie said.

"What about a wife, kids?" Carrie asked.

Like me, Carrie was a transplant, having arrived in Archers Rest just a few years ago. Natalie had grown up in the town, so we depended on her for any gossip that dated back more than five years. And she was happy to oblige.

"I don't think he ever married," Natalie told us. "I don't think he even has relatives in town. He was a teacher at the high school, but he retired when I was a freshman, so I never had him. My mother said he's friendly when you talk to him, but mostly he keeps to himself. Just him and his movies. Like a hermit, really, locked away in his projection booth most evenings. I do know that he hasn't really been involved in town activities before, at least since I was a kid."

"But he volunteered to be in charge of the parade and carnival," I said.

"And he can't be too much of a hermit if he comes to Jitters every morning," Carrie added.

"Don't you think that's strange?" I said. "He's lived here for years, never gets involved in anything outside the theater, and now he's suddenly joining up to help the town."

"Maybe he just got lonely," Carrie said.

"So why would Eleanor dislike him?" I asked. "Assuming Glad isn't just playing games with me, what could be the reason?"

"Maybe they dated and he left her, broke her heart," Natalie suggested.

"Eleanor's not the type to hold onto hurt feelings," Carrie said. "And we're talking about something so big that she would pass a quilt show on to Nell so she wouldn't have to be in the same room with him."

"Don't say it that way," Natalie scolded her. "You make it sound like Nell can't handle the quilt show."

"I barely can," I admitted.

Natalie thought for a moment. "I could ask around and see what kind of reputation he had as a teacher. Maybe he had a run-in with Eleanor about her kids."

"And I can mention Eleanor's name to him tomorrow when he comes in," Carrie said. "Just something casual. See if there's a reaction."

"And I'll ask Jesse what he thinks of Ed," I volunteered. "Maybe see if there's an old arrest on the records, something that would be bad enough that Eleanor wouldn't forgive it." I tapped the table impatiently. "And I'll see him at that silly committee meeting tomorrow. That should be fun."

Just when I was feeling charged about making headway on Eleanor's secret, I looked up and saw Oliver walk into the shop. He looked tired, but he winked when he saw us. "May I join you ladies?"

"Always," I said, and matched his smile with one of my own. "Everything okay?"

"Working on a new painting, for the anniversary celebration. A new project always invigorates me. It gives me something to think about besides myself and, well, anything that might be troubling me." He smiled at Natalie and Carrie, who met his expression with worried faces. "Everything okay, ladies?"

"They're fine. We're fine," I said. "We were just talking about Ed Bryant, the man who owns the movie theater. Have you been there?"

"No. I tried to get Eleanor to go to see *His Girl Friday* when it was playing there a few weeks back, but she wouldn't hear of it. She can't stand Cary Grant—can you imagine?" He laughed. "Who doesn't like Cary Grant?"

Natalie looked at me, and I knew she was thinking what I was thinking. Maybe it wasn't Cary Grant that my grandmother didn't like.

"She prefers the theater by my house," he said. "She said the one in town is kind of broken-down. Unlike her not to support an Archers Rest business, but I guess we all have our quirks." He looked toward me.

"I don't have quirks," I said, a touch too defensively.

Carrie, Natalie, and Oliver all laughed. Carrie patted my hand. "Of course you don't, Nell. Being curious isn't a quirk, it's a lifestyle."

I knew it was all in good fun, but the label was beginning to annoy me. I sat back and smiled, half of me wanting to tell them I was perfectly capable of minding my own business, while the other half wondered what Ed had done to make Eleanor dislike him.

CHAPTER 17

A t four the next day, I walked into the committee meeting and realized I was the first to arrive. After waiting a few minutes in the library's conference room, I walked into the main area and looked around for any of the other committee members. Finding none, I headed toward Dru Ann Love, the head librarian, who was sitting at her desk, deeply engrossed in *War and Peace*.

"I'm supposed to meet Glad Warren for the anniversary committee meeting," I told her.

"At 4:30."

"She told me four o'clock."

Dru smiled. "You must have done something to annoy her, and this is payback."

I sighed. "That's a little petty, wasting a half hour of my time."

"That's Glad. You might as well just wait in the conference room. There's some coffee in there that's pretty fresh. Glad will be here at 4:30, all smiles, insisting you misheard her. I'm actually surprised she hasn't been in, what with the problems we've had today."

"What problems?"

"Didn't you hear? Someone got into the library last night and tipped over carts, threw books on the floor, just made a real mess of the place."

"Was anything stolen?"

"Not that I can tell. The computers are all accounted for, our videos and CDs. Even the money from the late fees was still here. It's only about thirty dollars, but if someone were going to steal, you would think they'd take the cash." She shook her head. "I think they were looking for something."

"Like what?"

"Don't know. But when I told Jesse that the books that had been displaced were in our New York history section, he seemed very interested. We keep some of the rarer ones in a glass case over by the window." She pointed toward a wooden and glass case with cardboard taped to it and caution tape wrapped around the cardboard. "Someone broke into the case, left glass shattered all over the floor. We've been cleaning up all morning."

"I wonder what they wanted."

"Well," she leaned toward me and whispered, "one of the books was a short history of the town written by Glad's father. Years and years ago, of course. There were pages ripped out."

"Which pages?" I whispered back.

"I don't know. Jesse took the book as evidence." Dru looked around and lowered her voice even more, so it was barely audible. "It's the sort of thing *she* would do."

"She who?"

"The witch on the hill."

The mayor had talked of ghosts and pirates. Now Dru was adding a witch. Archers Rest was turning into quite the colorful community. "What witch?" I asked.

"Glad's sister. She's done a lot of crazy things in this town. Years of it. She once threatened to blow up city hall. Now Glad keeps her locked up in that house so she won't cause any more trouble."

"That can't be true." I didn't like Glad, but I doubted she would keep anyone, least of all her sister, a prisoner. "How did she—how would anyone—get into the library?"

She pointed the tip of her pencil toward the far corner. "Whoever it was broke a window in the office around back. Perfect spot for it, too. It's surrounded by bushes, so she—I mean, whoever broke in—was completely hidden."

"What about a surveillance camera?"

Dru laughed. "I talked to Glad about getting one over a month ago, or at least an alarm system, but she said we don't have the money. Maybe she was afraid of what her sister might do and she didn't want it caught on tape." She paused, looking slightly horrified. "When Glad does show up for the meeting, do me a favor and don't mention anything I said about Mary Shipman."

I headed back to the conference room after glancing into the office and seeing the boarded-up broken window. Kids, I guessed, just trying to have some fun. Far more likely than a crazy relative of Glad's.

As I waited, I paced the floor of the conference room, my mind going back and forth between the skeleton, the situation with Eleanor, and the growing impatience I felt for Glad's childish way of asserting her authority. I was building up to a confrontation that would make the break-in—and for that matter, the skeleton—seem dull by comparison.

"I thought I was early." Ed walked into the room.

"She told me four," I told him.

"She told me 4:15."

"Apparently she told everyone else 4:30."

He laughed. "Everyone has a fiefdom. For people like Glad and the mayor, Archers Rest is their little piece of the world and they are going to control everything in it for as long as they can. I guess we're on the receiving end of that lesson today."

"Except they might be at odds over the latest town event." I told him about the opposite reactions that Glad and Larry had to the discovery of the skeleton.

"Well, you can't blame them. In a way, they're both right, aren't they? It is publicity for the town, maybe it will get some people interested in coming up here, but it's not exactly the kind of thing you want to be famous for—a dead body in someone's garden," he said. "Any progress yet on who he is?"

Glad walked into the room. "Haven't we had enough unpleasantness? Can't we put that sad business at Eleanor's behind us?"

"Not yet," I said. "But we have found out that the person likely went missing in 1975. It's just that there are no missing persons reports filed on anyone in '75 that match the description: male, about six feet tall, maybe mid-thirties to forties. It could have been someone maybe passing through town . . ."

"In 1975?" Glad asked.

"We think so. That is, Jesse thinks so. I'm just an interested observer."

"You aren't able to identify him?"

"Not yet. There really isn't anything remarkable about the body," I said. "Except he was wearing a suit coat from Savile Row in London and his teeth were well cared for, but he had a broken leg that hadn't been properly set."

I could see that Glad wasn't really listening. She lowered herself into a seat and rifled through some papers. She was trying to appear disinterested, but her face was pale and her breathing seemed erratic.

"Are you okay?" Ed asked.

"Winston," she muttered.

"You know who it is?" I crouched down so I could look at her face. She wouldn't meet my eyes. "You said 'Winston.' Is that his first name or his last?"

"Winston Roemer," she whispered.

"Roemer," I repeated. "Like Grace Roemer? The woman who owned my grandmother's house?"

She nodded.

"And Winston was related to her?"

"Her son."

I wanted to ask her why she was so sure, but Glad's breathing had begun to alarm me, and I could see Ed felt the same way. He grabbed a bottle of water that had been left on the table and poured Glad a glass. She sipped it and seemed to relax, though she was lost in her own thoughts.

"I can't believe it," she said, shaking her head.

"Do you really think it's him?" Ed was saying, more to himself than to either Glad or me.

Maggie walked into the room and smiled at first, but then looked at our faces, filled with shock and confusion. "What's wrong?"

I looked at her. "Did you know someone named Winston Roemer?"

She didn't move, didn't even blink, but it seemed to me that she looked frightened.

CHAPTER 18

"Four thirty, exactly on time," Glad looked at her watch. After excusing herself for about five minutes, she'd returned with a fresh coat of lipstick and a peaceful expression. She had, apparently, recovered from the fright of identifying the body and now wanted to pretend it hadn't happened.

"So glad everyone is here." Glad counted heads. "Except the mayor. Well, I suppose he has pressing business, so we can't fault him. I suggest everyone take a seat and we'll go around the room and share our progress."

Maggie slid into a seat near Glad, keeping her back to me. She'd turned a shade of white when Winston Roemer's name was mentioned, but she'd been saved from answering any questions by Glad's decision to "end the discussion on such a disagreeable topic and begin the meeting."

I didn't care about any discussion, disagreeable or not. I was desperate to get out of there and head to Jesse. "Glad," I said, "I've been waiting since four o'clock, and now I have somewhere to go . . ."

"Yes, I'm sorry about the mix-up, Nell. I meant to call you at the shop and forgot." It was an unusual admission of failure and it left me unsure of what to say. "Just give me a few minutes," she continued. "I have some very important news to tell all of you as soon as the mayor arrives."

I reached for my phone and texted Jesse. "Skeleton may be Winston Roemer. Glad ID'd." Then I sent the same text to Carrie and Natalie, with an additional line: "Maggie shook up at mention of his name."

I could have—and maybe should have—given Jesse that last line of information, but I didn't want him thinking I considered Maggie a suspect. It was suspicious, though. Why would the mere mention of Grace's son have gotten such a strange reaction from her? Even now, as we waited for the mayor to arrive, I could see Maggie sitting tense and angry. And why was Glad so shook up? I knew almost nothing about Grace's children except that they would have been much older than Glad. I shifted in my seat and tried to focus on the meeting, not my growing desire to ask questions of everyone present.

"Sorry. Sorry, everyone," Larry announced as he walked in the room with doughnuts. He was followed closely by Molly, loaded down with a cardboard tray filled with cups of to-go coffee. "We stopped at Jitters to pick these up and got talking. Everyone wants something from me. They think their public officials should be able to solve any problem." He laughed and gestured for Molly to sit, while the rest of us went after the coffee and doughnuts.

Except for Glad. She was sizing up Molly, and Molly was doing the same in return. Neither woman seemed very impressed with the other.

"You've obviously met Glad," I said to Molly.

"What makes you say that?"

"She's chairing this committee to create the anniversary celebration. You're the intern who is helping with it. Or did I misunderstand the mayor?"

"You didn't misunderstand, Nell," the mayor answered for Molly. "You just jumped the gun. I haven't had a chance to share our good news about having an intern. It's going to take a load of work off everyone's shoulders to have someone full-time to help coordinate our little shindig."

"Always glad of the help." Glad glanced toward Molly but didn't smile. If Molly was insulted or intimidated, though, she didn't show it. Glad turned to the rest of us. "Now that we're all here, I suggest we each report on the progress of our events. How about you first, Maggie?"

Maggie cleared her throat. "I'm handling the church bazaar. I've decided to focus on selling handmade things, such as knitted scarves, artwork, pottery, and the like. The high school art classes are all working on small pieces that can be sold, and I'm putting in several of my quilts. And of course if anyone has pieces they would like to donate for sale, the money raised will be used to make some much-needed repairs of the oldest headstones in the cemetery."

"I'm sure everyone at the shop will want to donate something," I said to Maggie. "And I have some paintings I've done. Nothing amazing, but you're welcome to them."

Maggie gave me a tense smile. "That would be wonderful, Nell. Thank you. And the big news is that Oliver White has agreed to donate a small painting of the town square he's working on. If we sell raffle tickets . . ."

Glad jumped in. "We could make thousands on that alone. That is amazing! We must make sure the New York and Boston media know that Oliver White is a resident of Archers Rest."

"He isn't actually a resident," I told her, leaving out the word "yet."

"He's practically one," Glad said. "He's here all the time. Some sort of acquaintance of your grandmother, isn't he?"

"He's her . . ." I stumbled, hating the endless search for a simple answer when I so desperately wanted to say "fiancé." "He's her boyfriend."

Glad rolled her eyes, then, obviously unwilling to discuss the matter further, turned to Ed. "And Ed, how is the parade coming?"

He nodded slightly. "The school marching band, the cheerleaders, and the fire department are all ready to go. I need to order flags and secure the permits from the police chief, but I'm not expecting a problem."

"And yet problems occur, don't they? Are you able to handle the carnival as well?" Glad asked. "I'm so worried that could turn out to be a distraction from the important events that day."

He turned a little red. "I think it will be fun," he said. "I've booked a very reliable vendor for rides, and several prize booths. I'd love to have a dunking booth with some of our more esteemed citizens as the draw. If anyone would like to be dunked . . ."

"I'm in." The mayor grabbed his second doughnut and laughed.

Ed turned to me. "Do you think Jesse would do it?"

"I can ask him," I said. "He might be busy with work."

"He'll have sorted out the skeleton thing by then," Ed said confidently. "He's a smart guy."

"Hopefully," I said. "I know he's trying, but there have been a few things happening around town that have taken his attention."

"There are a lot of people with parking tickets who might want to see Jesse get all wet, so he'll just have to make sure he's available," the mayor said. "That's the sort of thing that shows what a nice town we are. What good people we are. I like it, Ed."

Glad sighed loudly. "I suppose," she said. "And Mayor, are you ready with the press releases?"

"Ready to be printed whenever we have all the details worked out. I've contacted papers in a fifty-mile radius to let them know about the celebration," he said. "I've also booked the fireworks display for nine p.m. on the Fourth. Right over the Hudson River, same as last year, but bigger. Much bigger."

"But tasteful," Glad said. "I hope."

The mayor gave Glad a small, almost unnoticeable look of disdain, then quickly smiled. "I've been taking care of the fireworks for years, Gladys. Nothing to worry about. I've also had these made."

He dropped a half-dozen campaign-style buttons on the table. Each was a photo of the gazebo in the town park and read: ARCHERS REST: 350 YEARS OF AMERICAN LIFE.

"They're nice," I said.

"Do we need these?" Ed asked. "It's another expense. Shouldn't we have voted on it?"

Larry chuckled. "Honestly, Ed, you can't nickel-and-dime everything in life. You have to spend money to make money." I could see Ed grit his teeth. "Besides," Larry continued, "I only had these few made, at my own personal expense. I'm bringing them here to see if we want to get them made for the celebration. Everyone take one and look at it up close. It's a really nice little piece. Same guy who does my reelection buttons."

We each took one and examined it. They were nice. I didn't know what it cost to make them, nor did I really care. I had a skeleton with a possible ID and I needed to talk to Jesse. As we started to hand them back, Larry put up his hand.

"Keep 'em. If we decide to get these made, we'll have plenty more."

"They're lovely," Glad said as she pinned one to her blouse. "I vote yes. Let's move on." Without waiting for the rest of us to vote, Glad turned to me and said, "Nell and I spoke yesterday. She has assured me the quilt show is coming along quite nicely."

"Except for a location," I admitted, as I dropped the button into my purse. "The parade is using the high school to set up and the church is having the bazaar, so I'm going to chat with Dru about using the library . . ."

"That's fine," Glad cut me off. "And I have some news."

She sat back in her chair as we all waited, but Glad just sat there, relishing the anticipation.

"Well, what is it, Glad?" the mayor finally asked.

She smiled. "I've convinced my husband that we should donate a statue of John Archer to be placed in the park near the gazebo. It will be unveiled after the parade."

"Does anyone know what he looked like?" Ed asked.

"He was obviously a strong-looking man." Glad's jaw clenched as she spoke. "Tall, a full head of gray hair, strong jaw. Masculine. Dutch extract. I think we can assume these things."

"Why can we assume that?" I asked.

She looked through me. "Because we know what he did. The sacrifices he made. Only a certain kind of man would do what he did."

"A man with a full head of gray hair?" I could see it was annoying Glad, but I couldn't help myself.

"Maybe we could draw a pentagram on the ground around the statue and give him a broom and a big pointy hat," Larry said. "Salem has made quite the tourist trade out of that kind of thing."

"He was not a Satan-worshipping witch," Glad spat out.

"I don't think witches are Satan worshippers," Ed said, chuckling. "I think that's something different altogether, though I can see how people mix them up, since they both wear black a lot and do things in the forest." He turned to the mayor. "We really need to find out exactly what John Archer was up to so we can be historically accurate. Maybe he left a spell book . . ."

"This is absurd." Glad's face was getting redder.

"That's enough." Larry glanced at Glad and blushed. "John Archer, whatever his personal views, was the founding father of our town. As mayor, I will not have him mocked." Given that he had just been doing some of the mocking, his sudden sternness was more comic than serious. At least to everyone but Glad.

"Thank you, Larry." Glad put her hand over her heart. "It's so important to preserve the image of this good man."

"But," Larry continued, "if you don't mind my saying so, Glad, the man you're describing sounds a lot like your late father."

She snorted. "Well, if none of you think it's a good idea, far be it from me to overrule the committee. But I do want to point out that I was planning to pay for the statue with my own personal funds and the donations of some leading citizens." Glad stood up. "But obviously a tasteful statue that honors our founding father doesn't fit into the mayor's plan, which is to turn the town into an amusement park."

At that she grabbed her Louis Vuitton handbag and left the room.

"So what do we do now?" Molly asked the mayor.

Larry frowned. "We keep doing what we're doing. The thing that's going to get people up here is the events—the carnival, the parade, the quilt show. People are going to want to shop, eat lunch, and see a nice fireworks display. That's how we hook 'em. Not a single person will drive three hours from New York to see a statue."

"Maybe I should talk to her," I suggested. "I was a little rude with the comment about the hair."

"I'll talk to her," Larry said. "My fault, actually, with the crack about her father. But I swear she was describing him perfectly."

Maggie smiled. "She really was. I remember him. Bit of a spineless fellow, I thought, despite the strong jaw. Though with Glad, her mother, and her sister always picking at him, it's a wonder he functioned at all."

Larry grabbed the last doughnut. "Well, since Glad isn't here to do it, I officially adjourn this meeting. Great job, everybody."

We exited the conference room as a group. I wanted to talk to Maggie and Ed, but now was not the time. Instead I went looking for Dru to ask about using the library for the quilt show. But I was too late. Dru was deeply engrossed in a conversation with Molly, and they both were looking in the direction of the broken glass case. Molly handed Dru the anniversary button the mayor had given us and Dru pinned it to her sweater. They looked very chummy. They, like everyone else in the library, were gossiping about the break-in. Even Maggie and Ed were looking over the damage. Only Glad left the building without even glancing at the mess.

CHAPTER 19

"Wash the lettuce, will you, Nell?" Eleanor directed me around the kitchen as we prepared for Oliver and Jesse to arrive.

"How's the salmon looking?" I asked.

"Wonderful. And the rice is coming along nicely," she answered. "When you finish with the salad, check the asparagus."

"No problem."

It had been like this all afternoon. We talked constantly but said nothing of substance to each other. I was dying to speak to Jesse about Winston Roemer but had only gotten a short text in reply to mine: "Thanks. Checking into it. Love you." Carrie had sent her own text: "Natalie and I are on it. Good luck with dinner." But that was all I'd heard since leaving the library.

The dinner had been planned as a gentle push to get information from Eleanor about the summer of 1975, when the body had likely been placed in the garden. But now that we might be able to put a name to the skeleton, it was all I could do not to mention it while Eleanor and I were alone in the kitchen. The only reason I didn't was because there was a chance—maybe a good chance—that Glad had been wrong.

Whatever thought I had to bring it up ended when Oliver arrived. He brought a large bouquet of flowers for Eleanor and—smart man that he was—a brand-new bone for Barney. Jesse was only a few minutes behind him, with a bottle of wine and an excited look on his face.

"I was thinking we could take a walk before dinner," he said.

"No way," Eleanor called out. "Dinner will be ready in less than ten minutes. Open the wine and put the plates on the dining room table. That will keep you occupied until I'm ready."

With Oliver and Eleanor wandering in and out of the room, Jesse and I were forced to keep our conversation to non-skeleton-related topics, such as my meeting at the library and Glad's strange offer to build a statue that would, apparently, be more a tribute to her father than to the town's founder.

"He was an awfully nice man," Eleanor said once we'd sat down to eat.

"I thought you said he was a soft touch who spoiled his daughters," I told her.

"He did. But he was also a nice man," Eleanor said. "He gave me a loan to open the shop, and I'll always be grateful to him for that."

Jesse speared an asparagus with his fork and lifted it but put it down again. He'd been doing that since he'd arrived, making one choice and then backing away from it. The result was that he'd been unusually quiet most of the evening and his dinner was still on his plate. Finally he looked up.

"When did you open the shop, Eleanor?" he asked.

"April 23rd, 1976." She smiled. "It was a beautiful spring day. Not that I noticed it much. I was so scared. I thought that I was going to sit with all that fabric and no one to buy it. But Maggie came. She was my first customer. And then, of course, other women came. Nearly all the quilters in those days were women. It was tough going at first, but little by little the quality of fabric got better and we went from cutting our own templates to plastic rulers and rotary cutters. The books and patterns came out, and before you knew it there were quilt shows and magazines and, well, here we are."

Oliver took her hand. "It's given you many wonderful years."

"I'm not retiring, if that's what this is about. I have no intention of giving up that shop."

"No one is asking you to," Oliver said. "Though you might want to take a week off now and then."

She looked at him for a moment, then laughed under her breath.

"I knew there was some hidden agenda to this dinner." Eleanor raised an eyebrow at me. "Nell's been fidgeting all afternoon."

"Actually, I was fidgeting because I've been wondering..." I started, but when I looked at Jesse I could see he was subtly shaking his head. I took a deep breath and started again. "I've been wondering if you would take a vacation, Grandma. Seeing as you trusted me enough to run the quilt show, I figured you might trust me enough to run the shop for a week or so."

Eleanor looked at me suspiciously, then at Oliver and Jesse the same way. "I feel outnumbered. I don't need a vacation. I enjoy going into the shop every day." She paused. "But if it will make you all happy for me to take a week off, I'll be happy to. Maybe in July. The shop tends to slow to a dead stop in the summer anyway. Some people have a hard time making a quilt when it's ninety degrees outside."

I looked over at Jesse and he nodded slightly. What was he waiting for? If he had some grand plan, he wasn't letting me in on it. He just speared another asparagus, let it sit on his fork for a moment, then dropped it on his plate.

"Why did you open the shop?" he asked Eleanor.

She looked at him. "Why all the curiosity about Someday Quilts?"

"I've always wondered. I just never asked."

"Well, I guess since you are practically family, you have a right to know a little more about us."

Jesse nodded as if his being family were already decided. I just sat quietly and bit my lip.

"I needed to make a living," Eleanor said. "Grace had passed away in early August, so that job was over. It was harder than I thought to lose Grace. I'd been her aide, and her friend, for nearly ten years by that point. She had been so kind to me. And to the children. I felt like she'd given me a chance to reimagine my life and I didn't want to waste it. Plus, I had the kids to support and this big house to run. I know I could have gotten a job somewhere, but I..." She paused. "Well, I guess Grace talked me into opening the store."

"I thought you said she was dead?"

"She was. But in the months before she died, she and I talked about our lives. What we had done, what we'd failed to do. She taught me to quilt and I'd come to love it, and I said to her that someday I'd like to open a shop that had all the supplies in it a quilter would need," she said. "In those days, quilt shops were a rare thing."

Oliver nodded. "You were seeing the future, Eleanor."

"I suppose I was." She smiled at the compliment. "Anyway, Grace said that when you say, 'Someday, I'd like to,' you're making a promise to yourself. She told me it's just as important to keep the promises you make to yourself as it is to keep the ones you make to other people. So when she died, I decided that the best way to honor her was to keep that promise and open the shop."

"Is that why you named it Someday Quilts?" I asked.

She laughed. "I thought I'd told you that."

"No," I said. "I always thought it was a reference to how all the fabric would someday be a quilt."

"I suppose it does mean that now," she said. "Or at least someday all this fabric will end up in a quilter's stash, to be lovingly cared for and dreamed over but never actually used."

Both Eleanor and I laughed. We knew that quilters fall in love with fabric, love having it, folding it, and looking at it. It's calming just to be around fabric, strange as it might sound. While the goal is to turn all the fabric you own into quilts, a beautiful piece of fabric, even if it's never used, is still worth having.

"I'm surprised Glad's father gave you a loan with no business experience, no money, and no idea that quilting would grow the way it has," Jesse said.

"He wasn't that much of a pushover. I had to put the house up for collateral," she said. "Now, who would like a piece of chocolate cream pie?"

CHAPTER 20

The air was still warm from the day as Jesse and I took Barney toward the river for his nightly walk. I took in a long, deep breath. I loved the coming of summer. The days were long, the wind soft, and there was color everywhere.

"Have you been digging around the hole since we found the skeleton?" Jesse asked.

"Digging?"

"Or maybe Barney?"

"Why?"

"I stopped by here earlier and I happened to notice a few odd things in the dirt," he said. "An old key chain and a few coins. They weren't there when we recovered the body, so I was wondering if you found them when you were searching the hole for evidence."

I smiled. "I haven't been. Hadn't thought about it, which in retrospect is a missed opportunity. I guess Barney could have been digging in there, but these days he mostly sits. Do you think they were from the skeleton?"

"Maybe. The weird thing is the coins are Civil War era and the key chain is from a drugstore that went out of business in 1948."

"So the skeleton is a Civil War soldier who owned a drugstore in the forties?"

"Who knows? I'm chasing my tail with this case. I feel like as soon as I sit down to really think it through, something pulls me away from it."

"I heard about the library and the book with the torn pages."

"*The History of Archers Rest*," Jesse's voice boomed in a mock-serious tone.

"Do you know what was torn out?"

"Sort of. I spoke with Glad about it. First she spent twenty minutes telling me that her father was an amateur historian, just like she is. Then she told me she remembered what the pages said."

"She remembered? She doesn't have any copies of the book?"

"Not a one. But she did say the missing pages were about John Archer's days before coming up here. According to Glad's father, Archer was plagued by rumors of various kinds . . ."

"Witchcraft."

"That, and apparently he killed a neighbor and buried him in the yard."

I slapped Jesse's arm. "You're kidding me? Just like our skeleton."

"Do you think you've solved the case?" He laughed. "I should go down to the graveyard and arrest John Archer. He does seem like quite a character."

"I think he was just the victim of a lot of stupid rumors," I said. "If you ask me, that's why he came up here. To get away from gossips and create a town where he was free to be himself. Too bad he died the first winter."

"Which is really the only fact we have about him," he said. "And the funny thing is, Archer died in about 1661 and we know only a little less about him than we know about what happened in this garden in 1975."

I leaned into Jesse's shoulder and kissed his neck. "So why didn't you just ask Eleanor directly about Winston instead of all those questions about the quilt shop?" I asked.

"I was wondering, I guess," he said. "Don't you think it's odd that your grandmother came to live with Grace in 1965 with no money, debts from her late husband, and two children to raise, and ten years later she had enough money to buy a four-bedroom house on five acres of land?"

"She probably saved money from her salary."

"How much could she have earned? She was living here—probably her food was paid for. When you have live-in help, usually the salary is really small, just spending money."

"You have a lot of experience with live-in help, do you?" I smiled playfully, but I wasn't really feeling playful. I was getting the distinct impression that Jesse was suggesting Eleanor had done something wrong. As we passed the hole still left in the rose garden, I started to worry about what *exactly* he might be thinking she had done.

I stopped him, grabbed his waist, and pulled him toward me. "You're just wondering about Eleanor because the skeleton is Grace's son."

"We don't know that for sure."

"Are you looking into it?"

He smiled at me. It was a warm, romantic, maybe slightly amused smile. "Yes, Nell, I am looking into it."

"What have you found out?"

"Not that you're interested in the case, right?"

"If it has to do with Eleanor, I'm interested."

He nodded. "Winston Roemer was alive and well early in 1975, and nothing since. No use of his Social Security number. No loans. No bank accounts. No credit cards. No property bought or sold. No crimes committed by or against him. And there's no death certificate that I can find. At this early stage of the investigation, it looks like a strong possibility that Winston may be our man."

"And what does that have to do with Eleanor having enough money to buy this house?"

"I don't know. Maybe nothing."

I hugged him closer and whispered in his ear. "She didn't kill him."

He leaned his face against mine. "Of course she didn't."

"So why don't you go in and ask her about him right now?"

"Because I need to know more about the case before I question any . . ." He stopped.

"Suspects." I finished the sentence.

"Witnesses."

"That's not what you were going to say."

"Nell, you said you were staying out of this. I can't tell you that you have to." He smiled. "I guess I could, but you wouldn't listen anyway, Nancy Drew."

"Enough with the jokes—what are you leading up to?"

"I'm just asking that you not talk to Eleanor about Winston being our victim just yet."

"Why not?"

His jaw clenched. "Because I'm a good cop and you trust me to find the truth and you know I will include you in anything pertinent to the case."

"I like how you made that something I would not be able to argue with," I said.

"Good."

"So when can I talk to her about Winston being buried in her backyard?"

"When we know it's him—how about that?"

I could tell that was all he was going to say on the matter. Jesse had a soft, kind voice when he and I were alone, but when he was on duty or when he was shutting me off from an investigation, as he was doing now, his voice was authoritative and deep. There was no room for disagreement at those times, unless I wanted to turn the discussion into an argument.

"You know who you should be looking into?" I said. "That new intern, Molly O'Brien."

"She wasn't even born when Winston disappeared. And she's not from town. What reason would I have, exactly, for checking her background?"

"I don't know, but it's just . . ." I hated when I couldn't explain my hunches. "Glad doesn't like her."

Jesse laughed. "Glad doesn't like you. Or me. Or anyone as far as I can tell."

"Maybe. But there's something."

"Okay, Nell." Jesse leaned in. "But I still have to look into people who were actually alive at the time of Winston's disappearance."

Just as he was about to kiss me, Barney came toward us, tired and wanting to go inside. Jesse gave me a peck on the cheek and said, "We're on the same side."

I wanted to be reassured, but somehow I wasn't.

CHAPTER 21

"It was a nice dinner," Eleanor said once the men had left. Oliver usually would have spent the night at the house, but he was making sketches for the painting that would be auctioned at the anniversary celebration, and he was aching to get to his studio to work on them. Jesse wanted to check in at the station before heading to his mother's to pick up Allie. And I wanted to talk to Eleanor alone.

"I always think of you as so strong and independent," I said.

"I would say thank you, but I have a feeling you don't mean it as a compliment."

"I do, actually. I just forget that you must feel overwhelmed sometimes, the way I do."

"You never feel overwhelmed, Nell. You barge into every situation with all the optimism and curiosity of a puppy."

"Now *that* doesn't sound like a compliment," I said. "And I do feel overwhelmed sometimes, and scared."

"What's this about?"

"When you were talking at dinner about opening the shop, it got me to thinking. It must have been so hard for you, moving into a stranger's house after having a house of your own."

She cocked an eyebrow. "I suppose."

"Did you know anyone in Archers Rest at the time?"

"No. Your grandfather and I both grew up about an hour's drive from here. But you know that, Nell." She handed me a dirty plate. "Load the dishwasher, will you? I'm tired."

"Keep me company," I said. "I'll make you a cup of tea."

She sat at the kitchen table, and Barney immediately rested his head on her lap. "Did you and Jesse have a nice walk?" she asked.

"We did."

"Did he ask you anything? Is that why you're suddenly feeling so overwhelmed?"

"We talked, but not about the future," I said. "We talked about the past."

"No word at all on an engagement?"

I thought about the plans Oliver and I had made for her garden and their lives. "I think that's on hold for the moment," I said.

"Maybe on your birthday. That's coming up July 3rd."

"Don't get your hopes up, Grandma."

"I suppose he has a lot going on," she said. "Still, he can't wait his whole life for the right moment to propose. Someone once said to me that a woman can live her whole life without a man and be complete, but a man needs a woman. We women have our friends to share our feelings with, you see. But for many men, they only really open up in the company of the woman they love."

I put a mug in front of her and poured her tea. "Was the someone who told you that Grace?"

"Not all my pearls of wisdom come from Grace, though that one happened to."

"And the house did, too," I said. "Did you inherit it?"

"No. I bought it."

"From her children?"

"Yes."

"And neither one of them wanted to keep it?"

"Why? Her son was in South America and her daughter was in California. I think they were pleased it was going to someone who was as close as family," she said. "By then, I guess they thought of me that way. I certainly thought of Grace that way."

"And you were close to them? Her children, I mean?"

She sighed. "I was close to the daughter. Winston, Grace's son, was a difficult man to be close to."

"Have you kept in touch with them?"

"Letters at Christmas." She pointed to a drawer in the kitchen where she kept cards and letters too precious to throw out.

"Both of them?"

"What's the sudden interest?"

"Curious, I guess."

I knew I was getting very close to breaking my promise to Jesse, but I comforted myself with the fact that I'd actually only promised not to talk about Winston being the skeleton—I hadn't said I wouldn't talk about Winston at all.

"Did they pay you well?" I asked. "Grace and her children?"

"Why?"

"You bought the house. It must have been pricey."

"Your grandfather sold life insurance, Nell. He would have been a poor salesman if he didn't own some of it himself." She was tired and growing impatient with me. "What's the sudden interest in this house? Are you and Jesse hoping to move in here once you're married?"

"How did we get back to that?" I laughed. "He has his own house, Grandma."

"It's a tiny little place. Not enough for three, or eventually maybe four or five of you." She sat back in her chair and looked around the kitchen. "It wouldn't be such a bad idea, really. I could clear out the sewing room. That's really the master bedroom anyway. You and Jesse could take that, and Allie could take your room, and that still leaves another bedroom for a nursery down the line. And then when I go, you could take over the house."

"You're not going anytime soon," I said. "Unless you moved in with Oliver."

"I'm a little old for living in sin, Nell."

"You could marry him. Make an honest man out him."

She swallowed the last of her tea and got up from the chair. "And you accuse me of bringing up the same conversation again and again." She turned to the dog. "Come on, Barney, we'll go to sleep and let Nell clean up the kitchen."

✂

Once I was alone, I grabbed the cards and letters from the kitchen drawer and began sorting through them. Most were from the past year. A few birthday cards, postcards from my parents who were still traveling the globe, a letter from Eleanor's sister who lived in Phila-delphia, and more than a dozen thank-you cards.

Eleanor's generosity and kindness, I was glad to see, had not been forgotten by the people of Archers Rest. She was thanked for the donations of money, time, and quilts to everything from an AIDS fundraiser to a children's choir. Whatever may have happened years ago, however she got this house, it was obvious Eleanor had led a good life. Not that I was, even for a moment, suggesting, even to myself, that Eleanor had done anything wrong. I knew her too well to think something like that.

At the bottom of the pile there were a few Christmas cards. Most were from friends in town, but one was from California. The return address said it was from Elizabeth Sullivan. The card was simple, just an illustration of a Christmas tree, and inside there was only a short message:

> Eleanor,
>
> Another year gone by. I miss them so much. And miss you, too. I'm glad to hear your children and grandchildren are well. My youngest grandchild is in college in Boston now. Time has flown, hasn't it? Seems like yesterday we were all together with the future ahead of us. Have a won-derful Christmas in the old house.
>
> Love,
> Elizabeth

There was no mention of Grace. No last name of Roemer. But it had to be Grace's daughter. She'd moved to California. Eleanor had said they kept in touch through Christmas cards and this was the only one from someone I didn't know. Maybe that was little to go on, but it was all I had. If it was Winston buried in the yard, then Eliza-beth would be our best chance at a DNA match, and maybe an answer to why he had ended up there.

CHAPTER 22

"I need to do a search on a woman named Elizabeth Sullivan," I told Natalie the next morning as we opened the shop. "I have her address, so it shouldn't be hard to find her phone number."

"First I have to tell you about Winston," she said. "I did a little digging after I got your text. Is he the skeleton?"

"We're not sure yet. What did you find out?"

"He was the oldest child of Grace and William Roemer," she said. "Born in New York. He went to Harvard for undergrad. Graduated in 1953. He studied ancient tribes there, and eventually got a doctorate in anthropology from Columbia University in 1958. He wrote three books, all out of print, having to do with ancient tribes in South America."

"Eleanor said something about his being in South America," I told her. "That's why he didn't want the house."

"But maybe he did," she said, smiling. "He had accepted a job teaching at Avalon University, to begin in the fall of 1975. They were just starting an anthropology department and he was going to chair it."

"That's less than an hour from here," I said. "Maybe we should go there and see if he's still teaching there."

She shook her head. "Already called. I talked to the current chair of anthropology and he referred me to a retired professor who had started with the department in '75. So I called him, and he said that Winston never started the job. According to this professor, Winston came in, made a big impression on everyone, donated some huge sum of money to the school, and practically insisted on chairing the department. Then, after the school set up the department, Winston decided to go back to South America instead."

"That's a lot of information for one day. You're getting good at this."

Her son, Jeremy, pulled at her jeans and Natalie struggled to lean down to pick him up, so I did it for her.

"I'm too pregnant for bending," she said, "but at least I can use the computer. And it's amazing how much I could find out just looking at the newspaper archives from the Hudson Valley. I had no idea how prominent Grace's family was in the area at the time. Everything they did was in an article somewhere."

Natalie touched her computer screen and brought up several newspaper articles with fuzzy black-and-white photos. The first one had a caption that identified Grace and her adult children, along with several other people, standing in front of the library.

"That's Winston?" I asked, pointing to the tall, stern-looking man with glasses who stood to Grace's right. "He'd be good-looking if he smiled."

"Doesn't seem the type to smile," Natalie said. She pointed to the woman at the edge of the picture. "Guess who that is?"

I looked closely. "Maggie. I guess that makes sense. She was the town librarian." I looked closer. "Wow, she looks so pretty. Not that she isn't pretty now."

"I agree on both counts. And notice, she's looking right at Winston."

She was. But I couldn't tell from the grainy image if she was smiling or scowling.

Natalie pressed another key on her computer. "There's even a photograph of Grace with Glad's father and one in front of the movie theater."

"Any news on Winston after South America?" I asked, as Jeremy tugged at my hair.

"Not a thing. He must never have come back to the area."

"Or he never left."

Natalie sighed. "Do you really think it's him?"

"It makes sense, doesn't it? It was his house, after all."

"How did someone with his background end up buried in the backyard?"

"Someone put him there."

"It's weird," Natalie said, "considering we never met her, but it just breaks my heart for Grace that her son could have been murdered."

"I feel the same way."

We were both silent for a moment before Natalie finally spoke. But she'd moved on to another mystery we were trying to unravel.

"By the way, I made a couple of calls about Ed Bryant. No one had anything bad to say about him, at least as a teacher. He was friendly but not too friendly. He was fair in his grades. He wasn't big on school activities, but he did what was required of him," she told me. "The only interesting piece of gossip was that he had an affair, or that's what people thought, with someone named Glee."

"Glad's sister?"

"You're kidding! The only sister I've ever heard of is Mrs. Shipman, that recluse of a woman who lives in the ugly brown house."

"That's the one. Apparently her nickname was Glee."

"We have to find out more," she said excitedly.

"Why, Natalie? What does that have to do with Eleanor not wanting to get married or a skeleton in the backyard?"

"I don't know. It's just interesting." Natalie curled her lips into a frown. "What's happening to you, anyway? You used to be the town—"

"Busybody, snoop, nosy neighbor . . ." I finished her sentence for her.

"I was going to say 'the town's most curious citizen.'"

"Any way you say it, it's not exactly the reputation I want to have for myself. Besides, we can't just run around looking into the secrets of everyone in town." I could see Natalie's disappointment. "If it has something to do with the rest of it . . ." I started.

"We won't know unless we look, right?"

"I guess."

I was worried about more than my reputation. We were pulling a thread from a sweater, unraveling an entire town's secrets, for no good reason. It was the sort of thing that probably had driven poor John Archer to come to this area in the first place. Digging up the past, literally and figuratively, was turning out to be a complicated proposition.

"Can you watch the shop by yourself for a while?" I asked Natalie. "Eleanor will be in at noon. I just need to run a few errands."

"Sure. It's not exactly busy this morning and I'm just working on my quilt for the show." She headed toward the back of the shop and the longarm machine.

I put Jeremy into his playpen and stared for a moment at the young boy as he picked up and dropped a stuffed toy. He picked up the toy a third time and handed it to me, laughing, and then lay down and wrapped himself in the blue and white log cabin quilt that lined the bottom of his playpen.

"It's hard to believe that we all start off as innocent as Jeremy, and somewhere along the way, some people become killers—and others their victims," I said, more to myself than anyone. Then I called back to Natalie, "I'll be back in a couple of hours." I left with the hope I'd have some answers to something before I returned.

✂

As I walked out to my car I saw Carrie across the street, waving to me.

"Everything okay?" I called over to her.

She ran across the street and met me at my car. "The shop got broken into this morning."

"What? Are you okay?"

"Fine. Nothing was stolen. Someone broke the lock on the back door and dumped the trash all over my office. Luckily, nothing was done in the rest of the coffee shop, but I've been cleaning up all morning," she said. "Can you imagine someone doing that? I called Jesse and he filled out a report, but he didn't think there was any chance we'd figure out who it was. It made it completely impossible for me to look into the Winston thing."

"It seems like a pretty pointless thing to do," I said. "Someone breaks in and just messes up the place? Why?"

"I'm just grateful it wasn't worse. I'd already made the deposit at the bank, so I guess whoever it was didn't find anything to steal."

"I suppose you're right. Listen, don't worry about researching Winston Roemer. You have enough going on, and I think it's under control. Natalie found out a lot."

"Thanks," Carrie said, "but I do have some information for you. When Ed came in this morning for his usual coffee and muffin, I mentioned the anniversary celebration this summer. Just casual, you understand." She stopped—waiting, I guess, for a reaction.

"Yes," I prompted. "What did he say?"

"Nothing interesting about that. He just said he was doing his part to help the community, and I told him that it looked to be a wonderful celebration."

"I'm interested, Carrie, but you have a shop full of hungry customers." As she talked, I watched four people walk into Jitters.

"Yeah, you're right." She looked back toward her store and then began talking faster. "Anyway, we started chatting, and I told him that I was making a quilt for the show that would be part of the celebration. I said something about how much I've loved quilting and how I learned everything from Eleanor." She took a breath. "And his whole expression changed."

"Angry?"

"No. The opposite. His face just lit up. He went on and on about what a good woman Eleanor Cassidy is, how much she has helped the community and been an example of the sacrifices of motherhood. He said I'm lucky to count Eleanor as a friend."

"So why would Glad say Eleanor doesn't want to be in the same room with him?" I asked.

"Maybe she's lying."

"Maybe. But why?"

"I don't know." Carrie shrugged and glanced toward my windshield. "I need to get back. And you need to figure out why Jesse gave you a parking ticket."

As she ran back to Jitters, I saw a piece of paper stuck underneath my driver's-side wiper blade. It didn't look like a ticket. As I unfolded the paper, I saw that it was a handwritten note with very careful printing in large block letters that read: MIND YOUR OWN BUSINESS, NELL FITZGERALD. OR YOU'LL REGRET IT.

I steadied myself against the hood of the car. It was a threat. And it had to be tied to the skeleton—to a murder that had taken place long before I was born that I wasn't even, technically, investigating.

"Unless someone really doesn't want me to run the quilt show," I said, hoping to lighten my mood. It didn't work. I could feel my shoulders tense up and that knot in my stomach begin to tighten again.

I drove the block to the police station. Jesse wasn't in, and I didn't feel like sharing the note with any of the other officers, so I left the name and address of Elizabeth Sullivan, the woman I assumed to be Grace's daughter, with one of his detectives. Knowing Jesse, it was likely he had the information by now, but if he didn't there was no use in him wasting time looking for something that had already been found.

I stuffed the note in my pocket and tried to ignore the strange reality that someone was trying to intimidate me. I drove over to see Maggie, the one person who actually might have answers to all the questions that were crowding my brain—about Eleanor, the house, Ed, and Winston. Assuming, of course, she was willing to tell me.

CHAPTER 23

"Two visits in one week. Either you're lonely or I am," Maggie said as she motioned for me to sit in the same kitchen chair I'd been in days before. "I have some oatmeal cookies if you're hungry."

"I'd never turn down a cookie," I said.

She handed me a plateful and poured me a coffee. It was my third and it was barely ten o'clock, but I drank it.

"It's just as well you're here," she said. "I've gone through some of my quilts, and I have several reproductions that would look lovely in the show. Where is it going to be?"

"I don't know," I told her. "I tried to get the library, but Glad already has it booked for a special reception. I may end up showing quilts in the alley or out of the back of my car."

"That's not a bad idea," Maggie said.

"Are you serious?"

"Outside. We could hang them outside in store windows and in the park and all around town. There are several places, like Sisters, Oregon, that have outdoor quilt shows. People wouldn't have to come to the quilt show. We would bring it to them."

"That's a great idea." I took a deep breath. All it would take would be permits from the police chief—Jesse would give me those—and the permission of a few shop owners. Somehow, amazingly, this show was coming together. "I appreciate the idea, Maggie, but I'm not really here to talk about the quilt show."

"You're here about Winston," she said. "I'm surprised you didn't run after me yesterday."

"Eleanor and I had the guys over for dinner last night. I needed to go home and cook."

"So this is your first chance?"

"Yes," I said. "I can tell you what I know so far. Winston was Grace's son. He worked in South America a lot. He got his doctorate in 1957, so that probably would put him in his forties in 1975."

"I think so."

"So you can fill in the rest."

"Like what?"

She was being deliberately coy, which was very unlike the forthright, opinionated Maggie Sweeney I'd come to know.

She sighed. "This is just a lot of old memories, and it's making me feel sad, I suppose. I don't like to talk about the old days. I prefer to live in the here and now. Keeps me young."

"Well, here and now, there is a lot going on in Eleanor's life, and I'd like to help, if I can."

She looked away for a moment but then met my eyes. "What about Winston would you like to know?"

"I don't know. For starters, was he in Archers Rest in 1975?"

"I wasn't his travel secretary, Nell. He was Grace's son. He came and went. He was always on some archeological dig or something."

"He was an anthropologist."

"Okay, he was always on some anthropological something or other. I had kids to raise. I didn't pay that much attention to Winston."

"His sister's name was Elizabeth, though, right?"

"Yes. Lovely woman. She was married and living out west when I met her. She would come back to visit her mother from time to time."

"When's the last time you saw her?"

"Grace's funeral, I suppose."

"And that was in August of 1975?"

She shrugged. "I guess. Your grandmother would know better than I would. I remember it was summer. It was a very hot day. I was pregnant with Brian. Very pregnant. I didn't stay long at the funeral."

"What about Winston? Was he at the funeral?"

She thought about it for a moment. "I don't remember."

"If he was, then that's fine. But if he wasn't, there might have been a very good reason."

"Such as?"

"If he didn't show up for his own mother's funeral, it may have been because he was buried in Eleanor's yard."

"What? You think he's the . . . does Eleanor know?"

I shook my head. "Jesse wanted to find out what we could about him before we said anything. Besides, I know how close she was to Grace's family. If I said anything and I was wrong, it would just upset her."

"So you don't know for sure?"

"No. But he seems to have disappeared after 1975."

"Good heavens. All this time . . . in the backyard of his own house?"

"Maybe," I cautioned. "Anything you can tell me would really help."

She poured me another cup of coffee, and I drank it. Her hands were shaking slightly, but so were mine. It may have been the caffeine, but I sensed it was something else.

"I didn't like him much," Maggie admitted after she'd poured the last of the coffee for herself. "He was smart and he cared for his mother, but he had the arrogance of a man who thought inherited wealth made him better than the rest of us, instead of just luckier."

"Did Eleanor like him?"

"More than I did. But your grandmother had such affection for Grace, it spilled over to her children."

"Was she in love with him?"

"No."

"And you're sure about that?"

Maggie cocked her head. "If you're imagining that Winston was the love of your grandmother's life, and a broken heart is what's keeping her from marrying Oliver, you're wrong."

One theory shot down. "Was he in town a lot?" I asked.

"I don't know. I only met him a few times. He came in '65 or '66, when Eleanor was new at the house. I think he was checking to make sure his mother was well cared for. Then he went on one of his trips and didn't come back for years. He stayed a little longer that time. It was maybe in '73 or '74, but he left again. And then he came back one last time, shortly before Grace died. And that was the last time I saw him, as far as I remember."

"Did he make enemies?"

She laughed. "What a thing to say. He wasn't the type of man who made enemies. He was a snob, maybe. Archers Rest had been the family's summer home, so he'd never bothered to get to know any of the locals well. I think he regarded all of us as inferior. But did anyone dislike him enough to kill him? I doubt that."

"Someone must have," I pointed out.

She looked at me, taking it in. "I suppose so," she muttered. Then she sat back and for a long while seemed lost in her own thoughts.

CHAPTER 24

As I drove back toward the shop, I noticed Molly O'Brien walking out of city hall gripping a legal-size file folder. I parked in front of the police station.

"Just the person I was looking for," I lied.

Molly looked like a deer in headlights. "Me?"

"Yeah. You are supposed to help the committee members with the celebration, right?"

"What do you need?" As she spoke she tightened her hold on the folder.

"I need to get a permit to have the quilt show outdoors."

"Who do I get that from?"

"The police chief." I said it with a straight face, hoping she'd forgotten who I was with the day we met.

She hadn't. "Isn't he your boyfriend?"

"Yes, but . . ." I hadn't thought this through. All I wanted was a peek at that file folder and now I sounded like an idiot. "We're kind of fighting, so . . ."

She nodded. "That's too bad. But he does seem a little more, I don't know, straightlaced than you. And the mayor said you were always getting in the middle of his cases."

I bit my lip. "What have you got there?" I pointed toward the file folder. "You've got quite a death grip on it."

She looked down at the folder as if she were just noticing it was there. "Just something the mayor asked me to look at."

She tried to hold the folder more casually, which was just the opportunity I needed.

Before she could object, I grabbed it and flipped it open. Right on top was the deed to my grandmother's house.

"What do you need with this?" I asked.

"That's where the body was found."

"Which has nothing to do with the anniversary of the town."

Molly grabbed the folder back. "Well, I got the folder for the mayor, so I guess you'll have to ask him."

I smiled just a little, in my best Clint Eastwood imitation. "I will, Molly. I'll ask him right now."

✂

"So what did the mayor say?" Natalie asked when I got back to the shop. Eleanor was sitting in the office going over the receipts. Barney and Jeremy were rolling a plastic ball back and forth, to their mutual amusement. There were no customers, so Natalie and I had the front of the shop to ourselves. But even though there was no danger of being overheard, we whispered as I told her about running into Molly.

"He wasn't in his office at city hall," I told her. "I checked the travel agency, too, and it was closed. Weird that he'd close it in the middle of a workday, don't you think?"

Natalie shrugged. "So what did Molly do?"

"Nothing. She just walked away with the folder and a copy of the deed to my grandmother's house."

"What would she need that for?"

"Confirm ownership," I guessed.

"Or to find out when she bought the place," Natalie suggested. "Maybe to find out if Eleanor was living there when the skeleton was buried. Maybe the mayor wants to know."

"He worked at the house," I pointed out. "He doesn't need to confirm when Eleanor took over. He was there. Molly took those documents for herself or for someone who might not have been as personally involved in Eleanor's life at the time."

Natalie's eyes got wide. "Like who?"

"I don't know. At the meeting yesterday there was something

weird going on between Glad and Molly. They said they'd never met, but they both seemed uncomfortable."

"I saw Glad about twenty minutes ago. She was heading to the library. She stopped in to see if you'd found a location for the show. She's very worried you're going to mess it up."

I let that pass without comment. I didn't have time to be insulted. "I guess I'll have to reassure her," I said, and headed out the door to look for her.

✂

As I walked past the movie theater toward the library, I had the same feeling I'd had days earlier, that I was being watched. I caught a glimpse of something in the ticket booth, but when I moved closer, there was nothing there. I really wanted to talk with Glad about Molly, but if someone was watching me, I wanted to know who, so I reached for the door to the theater. Just as I was about to pull on the handle, the door flew open.

I waited. Nothing. I peeked inside. No one was there. All I could see in the darkened theater was a poster for *Friday the 13th*, the movie playing that day. I took a step inside.

From behind me I heard a man call out. "Anything I can do for you, Nell?"

I jumped. When I turned I saw Ed walking up the street, a large to-go coffee in each hand.

"The door opened as I was walking by," I told him.

He laughed. "Spooky, isn't it? Unless I lock the door, it does that when the air-conditioning comes on."

I felt a little foolish. I stepped back onto the street. "No one's in there?"

He laughed. "It's just me today. And I went out for a little coffee." He held up one of the cups.

"It looks like you went out for a lot of coffee."

"One for now. One for later." He paused. "I microwave it. Saves me walking up and down the street." He walked past me and stepped inside the theater. "The movie starts at eight if you want to come back." Then he put one of the cups on the other and with his free hand pulled the door shut behind him.

✂

Dru Love, the librarian, was deep in a Stephen King novel when I arrived. I was more shaken up by my conversation with Ed than I was by the door opening for no reason. He'd lied to me about what caused it, I knew that much. It was a heavy metal door with a pull-down bar that often took two hands just to open it. Even unlocked, a mere blast of air-conditioning would not have been enough to cause the door to swing open. But unless I could prove it had something to do with the skeleton, Eleanor, or the quilt show, I reminded myself, I had to let it go.

"Dru," I said once I got her attention. "Have you seen Glad?"

She nodded toward the library conference room. "Private meeting with someone."

"Who?"

"I didn't see anyone come in. Must have come in the back way."

"Do you know what it's about?"

"All I know is that it's private. Glad said that no one could disturb them under any circumstances. And you know how Glad is about getting her way." She pulled her sweater tightly around herself and I could see she was still wearing the anniversary button.

"Molly gave you that," I said.

"She didn't want it. Not too fond of this town, I think."

"But you two seemed to be getting along pretty well the other day. What were you talking about?"

"You, actually. She wanted to know all about you."

"And what did you say?"

"That if anyone could figure out about that skeleton, and about everything else that's been going on in town, it would be you and Jesse."

"Thanks, Dru. And if I were stumped on a literary reference, I'd know just who to ask."

She blushed. Anyone working closely with Glad probably would go a long time between compliments.

"I wish I knew who Glad was meeting with," I said.

Dru looked around. "When they built that conference room where the employee lunch area used to be, they only put a thin wall between it and the office. Money saver, that's what Glad said. If someone were sitting in the library office, right next to the conference room, they probably could hear every word that was being said."

I smiled. "Enjoy your book, Dru."

I walked to the office, closing the door behind me, and leaned against the wall it shared with the conference room. It was, as Dru had promised, paper thin. I could hear two very distinct voices: one was Glad and the other was a deep male voice. It took a minute of listening, but I was sure it was the mayor's voice.

"I don't know how much more I can do," the mayor was saying.

"You don't have any choice," Glad said. "There is too much at stake here. My reputation. Your reputation. We can't let that ridiculous woman ruin everything."

The mayor answered her, but it was muffled, as if he were moving. I took a few steps backward and banged into the desk.

I froze, but I knew I'd been overheard. I could hear the door to the conference room open, and within seconds Glad and Larry were standing in the office, staring at me.

"What in heaven's name?" Glad said.

"I was waiting to talk to you," I said. "I had a question about the quilt show."

"What about it?"

"Is there," I stammered, "a limit on the number of quilts I can have in the show? I'm getting quite a lot of interest."

"Isn't that more or less up to you, as the chairperson of the quilt show?" the mayor asked.

I smiled nervously and moved toward the door. "Well, that answers that."

"That's why you were sitting in the office?" Glad clearly wasn't buying it.

"Not entirely," I admitted. "I also wanted to ask you about Molly. How do you know her? And don't say you met at the meeting, because that's obviously not true. Neither of you liked each other, before you'd even been introduced."

"If you must know, Nell, and obviously you must, Molly came to me and asked for a job with the historical society, and I turned her down," Glad said. "Too inexperienced. The next thing I heard she was interning for the mayor."

"You had a problem with that?"

"No. But I did have a problem with the fact that she was snooping around in the office of the historical society, much as you're doing now at the library."

"I was waiting for you."

"And she said she was lost. But you were both snooping. I don't know why Jesse finds that an attractive quality, Nell, but he may tire of it. I would watch all your interfering, or you'll lose him to someone better suited to a man in his official position."

CHAPTER 25

"Tonight, my house?" Jesse called my cell as I was leaving the library, my thigh bruised from the desk and my ego from Glad's scolding. "I got the note you left. I think I may have a surprise for you."

"You've ID'd the skeleton as Winston?"

"Not exactly. Come to the station around four."

"Any hints?"

"You're going to laugh."

✂

Four o'clock was a long way away, so I headed back to the shop. Natalie was there, but she was busy with customers, so I couldn't fill her in on what I'd been up to. As much as I tried, I could not figure out what Jesse had in his office that would make me laugh, so I decided not to focus on it. Instead, I started work on my devil's puzzle quilt.

Like so many quilt blocks, it looks complicated—intersecting rows form secondary patterns and it's hard to see where one block starts and another ends. But it's actually quite a simple quilt. I used just three fabrics: a bubblegum pink, a dark brown, and an olive green. An odd color combination for today's quilter but quite in keeping with the period I was representing. I reminded myself that having an odd-looking quilt was not my biggest problem and set to work cutting the rectangles and triangles that would make up the quilt.

By midafternoon I'd sewn my blocks—brown rectangles with a pink triangle sewn to each long side and pink rectangles with a green triangle sewn to either long side. Using the felt design wall we had in the shop's classroom, I positioned my blocks, alternating colors, and stepped back to admire my work. I still had to sew the blocks together, add borders, and quilt it, but for a day's work it wasn't bad.

It was almost three o'clock and I'd forgotten to eat, so I was about to run across the street to Jitters for a sandwich when I saw Oliver pacing outside.

"What are you doing?" I opened the door to the shop and invited him in. Well, forced him in would be more accurate, as he seemed unusually reluctant to cross the threshold.

"Just came to see Eleanor."

"You're not going to . . ." I whispered. "I don't think you should right now."

"No. I thought about what you said, about it not being the right time. It's just . . . I have to talk to her about something else."

He looked past my shoulder to Eleanor's office and saw what I saw—Barney's paw. And where Barney was, Eleanor was. He took a deep breath and stepped toward the office before I could stop him. If he proposed now, it would likely be a disaster.

I started to follow him, hoping that somehow I could delay his mission, but before I could reach the office, Oliver closed the door.

✂

At four o'clock Eleanor's door was still closed. I couldn't hear anything coming from inside, which probably was a good sign. As much as I wanted to stay and make sure everything was okay, I had to get to the police station. I hurried over there and saw Jesse standing outside the door to his office.

"So what will make me laugh?" I asked.

"Nell Fitzgerald, meet Molly O'Brien."

"We've already met," I pointed out.

"Not officially." Jesse smiled broadly. "Molly is . . ."

I remembered Elizabeth's Christmas card, and the mention of a grandchild in college in Boston. The mayor said Molly was going to college in Newton. I hadn't put it together before, but Newton is a town just outside the city and home of Boston College. Suddenly it all made sense—why someone like Molly would practically insist on an internship at city hall, even after Glad turned her down. "You're Grace's—"

"Great-granddaughter," she finished my sentence. "I'm here about my great-uncle Winston."

"Is she providing DNA?" I asked Jesse.

"No. Winston's sister, Elizabeth, gave a swab to a facility in California. We're waiting on the results."

"But it has to be Winston," Molly said, with a touch too much enthusiasm in her voice. "We assumed he was dead," she told me. "He just disappeared and my grandmother said that if he were alive, he would have gotten in touch at some point. He and Elizabeth were very close, but even if they weren't, there was an inheritance he would have claimed."

"Will you excuse me for a moment?" I grabbed Jesse and pulled him several feet away. "Why would this make me laugh?"

He smiled. "You'll see." He moved me back toward Molly. "It's okay to tell Nell what you told me."

"I'm studying criminology in Boston, so when I saw the mayor's blog about the skeleton, I figured I should come down and see if I could help with the investigation."

"You thought you would what?" I asked.

"You know, help, in whatever way I can. As long as I don't get in the way."

"Archers Rest has a very capable police force," I told her. "Jesse was a detective in New York."

She looked embarrassed. "I'm sure everyone's great. It's just that I have a great mind for puzzles and I'm good at reading people. I'm only a freshman, but I've taken two criminology classes and got an A in both of them."

"So you thought you would just come up and see if you could solve Winston's murder?"

She nodded.

"So why didn't you just say all of this the other day, instead of pretending to be an intern helping with the anniversary celebration?"

"I'm not pretending. I took the internship." She sat up straight, trying to look more imposing. "I didn't know anything about this town, so I wanted to find out what I could and see if any of the suspects were still around. If I said who I was, people might not be willing to talk to me."

"So why say anything now?"

"You said you were going to talk to the mayor about the file. I knew he'd tell you he hadn't asked for it, and you'd probably bring it to the chief."

"What was in that file, aside from a copy of my grandmother's deed?"

"Just old papers about the history of the house. I thought I might find something that explained how your grandmother got the house, but there really wasn't anything that helped."

"You took them from the historical society," I said.

She blushed. "Glad caught me. But I made up an excuse about being lost, and I think she bought it."

I turned to Jesse. "And this was supposed to make me laugh?"

"It made *me* laugh."

CHAPTER 26

Jesse and I had settled back in his office. He was behind his desk, I was leaning against the window, and Molly was in a chair facing us. The police department in Archers Rest didn't have an interrogation room. Usually there was no need for one. But today I felt like it would have been nice to have a long metal table and a two-way mirror, just like they do in the movies. Obviously Molly wasn't a suspect in her great-uncle's murder—she'd been born almost twenty years after his death—it was just that she was . . . I don't know. I just didn't like her, and that was reason enough for me to want to sit in while she and Jesse talked.

"What do you know about Winston Roemer?" I asked.

Molly smiled at me but directed her answer to Jesse. "From what I understand he was very smart, well respected. He was close to his sister and mother."

"Didn't anyone in your family wonder where he'd been all these years?" Jesse asked.

"No. He spent years in South America in the 1950s and 60s, going to some places that were unstable. It was understood in our family that he must have been killed on one of those trips."

"Did he have any financial issues?"

"No. He was quite well-off, actually. He had an inheritance from his father, as well as money he'd made on his own. And of course, he was set to inherit an even larger estate from his own mother when she passed away."

"What about romantic issues?"

She shrugged. "As far as I know, he didn't have a wife, or kids, or anything like that. I can't say whether he might have been involved with someone."

"Your grandmother never mentioned a woman to you? Or a man, for that matter?"

"No." She smiled. "But she was his sister. Do you talk about your love life with your sister?"

Jesse smiled back. "I don't have a sister, but I take your point. I couldn't find any legal problems, and if he had no financial or romantic ones, then it's unlikely he just took off to start a new life."

"Very. As I said, he was close to his sister and his mother."

"When's the last time anyone had contact with him?"

"My grandmother says that they spoke last in the summer of 1975, shortly before Grace died. Winston had visited Grace and was concerned," Molly said.

"Concerned in what way?"

"I'm not sure. But he was quite worked up about something. That's the impression I got. He felt she was being taken advantage of."

I stood up. "Who did he think was taking advantage of her?"

"I don't know. I don't think he told Elizabeth. She was his younger sister and she was three thousand miles away in California. I think he wanted to protect her. Until he was sure."

"Sure about what?" I asked.

"If it was true. Grace was a trusting person, and apparently Winston believed that someone was abusing that trust," Molly said. "I don't know all the details. It wasn't really talked about much because it was so long ago, and Grace was dead, and we assumed that Winston had died on one of his trips. But I always thought that it was possible that Winston knew something, and that's why he disappeared." She sat back. "And, well, it looks like that's turned out to be the case."

"So you're suggesting someone killed Winston to stop him from exposing a mistreatment of Grace?" I said my words carefully, as calmly as I could. "Is that why you stole a copy of my grandmother's deed?"

"I just wanted to see when she took over the place." Molly was getting defensive. "It was my family's property."

"Until they sold it," I pointed out.

Jesse looked back at me and quietly shook his head. "Let me ask, Nell."

I leaned back against the window and crossed my arms. I finally knew why I didn't like her. She was here to accuse Eleanor of manipulating Grace and possibly killing Winston, a charge that was not only untrue, it was outrageous.

Even from my vantage point I could see Jesse smile at Molly, but it was a cop smile, not a friendly one. "Assuming this is your great-uncle, did anyone in your family have medical records or dental records on him? It might help us make a preliminary ID as we wait for the DNA results."

"I don't think so," she said. "Not after all these years. But I do know he broke his leg when he was in his twenties. He was on a ship somewhere, going on one of his trips. Apparently he limped slightly."

"That fits with the description we have of our skeleton," Jesse told her. "According to our forensic pathologist, there was a broken leg that had not been properly set, which might fit with his being somewhere with poor medical care."

"There you go," she said. "It is him."

"Maybe," Jesse cautioned. "Do you have any letters or diaries, anything that might give me some indication of his whereabouts the summer he disappeared?"

"I asked my grandmother to send me copies of anything she has from Winston in those years. She kept everything in a box in her study. It was all she had left of him." Molly glanced toward me, then back at Jesse. "I know this was a long time ago, and maybe it's easy to forget that there are victims here, but my grandmother lost her mother and her brother in the same summer. All these years later, it's still painful for her. If we can find out what happened to Winston, I know it will mean a great deal to her."

"We'll do our best," Jesse told her.

"You don't believe that," I said to Jesse as he walked me outside the police station. Ushered me, really—practically escorted me from the building.

"It's as good a theory as any." He put his hand up to my mouth. "And before you yell at me that I'm accusing Eleanor of murder, I want you to understand that I'm not. I am open to the theory that someone was taking advantage of Grace, but that could have been a lot of people, okay?"

I nodded. He lifted his hand from my mouth.

"What was all that 'if we can find out what happened' stuff?" I asked. "Who does she mean?"

"She's just offering to help. He was family, after all."

"She's a kid. She's what, eighteen years old with two whole criminology courses. Don't you find it a little insulting that she's offering to help you?"

He laughed.

"What is so funny?"

"You don't notice a resemblance between her and another person with no law-enforcement experience butting into a police investigation—all enthusiasm and theories but no evidence?"

"No." As I said it, I could feel my neck burning a little and I'm sure my face was turning bright red. But I ignored my embarrassment. "No, I don't," I said again.

Jesse's jaw tensed. "Look, Nell, she's not going to hurt the investigation, and who knows, she may help. I've had some luck with amateur assistance."

"Did you check her DNA against the blood we found on the skeleton?" I asked.

"She didn't come to town until after the mayor posted the blog. The body was at the morgue by then."

"She *says* she didn't come to town until after the blog."

"I'll check her story, and if you want to help . . ."

"I will help, because I'm going to protect Eleanor," I said. "And if

Molly's going where I think she's going with this ridiculous theory of hers, then I'm going to do whatever I have to do to make sure the truth comes out."

"Good. I'll keep talking to Miss O'Brien, and I promise I'll share with you anything interesting she has to say, okay?"

I nodded. I took a deep breath and forced myself to change the subject. "There's something else. Will you look to see if Ed Bryant was ever arrested or involved in any crime? It might be years ago."

"Ed from the movie theater? He taught me science in sophomore year. What do you think he did?"

"Nothing, really. He was just acting weird at the theater today. And Glad said something a few days ago about my grandmother not wanting to be in the same room with him. It's just a hunch, but I want to know for sure there's no reason to suspect him of anything."

"You got it. But I have to tell you he was the world's dullest teacher, so I doubt he had some secret life."

"You might be surprised. I'm beginning to think this town is full of secrets."

"Okay." He kissed me. "I'm making spaghetti. Be at my place at eight." He grabbed my arm at the elbow and hesitated. "Nell, until we get the results of the DNA, we don't even know for sure if that skeleton was once Winston Roemer. But I think we can assume it's him. Which means it might be a good idea to find out where Eleanor was in July of 1975."

"And you trust me to tell you what Eleanor says?"

"The only reason you wouldn't is if Eleanor had done something wrong."

"Then I'll tell you everything."

CHAPTER 27

By the time I got back to the shop, Eleanor's office door was open. But one peek inside made it clear that it was also empty. Natalie was busy with a customer and Jeremy was asleep in his crib. No one could tell me what had happened or where Oliver and Eleanor had gone.

I spent the rest of the afternoon waiting on customers and trying to ignore a growing feeling that I might sound as ridiculous as Molly had sounded to me. Coming to Archers Rest to play detective! Didn't she realize she wasn't needed here? And for Jesse to draw a comparison between us. And be amused by it. I hated to think that deep down he might see me as a silly pest with stupid theories who just got in the way, like Molly O'Brien.

But she had said something that I couldn't pass off as silly—that Winston believed someone had been taking advantage of Grace. I just couldn't imagine who would do it or why anyone would want to harm such a wonderful woman.

Natalie and I closed up the shop at five and, instead of walking directly home, I stopped in at several businesses along the way to ask about displaying quilts in front of their shops on the anniversary weekend. It wasn't a hard sell. The quilts wouldn't block the store windows and probably would even draw interest to them.

After getting a yes from the pharmacy, the ice cream parlor, Jitters, and the post office, I made the last stop on my list—the one I'd been dreading. I went to the movie theater to see if Ed would let me merge the world of quilting with the world of fine cinema. It was only an hour until a movie was supposed to start, so the door to the theater was open, but no one seemed to be manning the ticket counter or the concession stand.

I walked into the lobby with a knot in my stomach. I looked inside the auditorium, but it was empty and the screen was dark. I turned toward the back office when I heard a noise from the projection booth. I thought I caught a glimpse of someone who was slim and probably female. Definitely not Ed. But just to be sure, I walked up the stairs to the booth slowly.

"Ed?" I knocked on the door, but I didn't get an answer. If there was someone inside, he—or more likely she—was not interested in being seen. I turned the knob and went in.

Empty.

The booth was small. An old projector, two chairs, a file cabinet, a large open trunk that had piles of rolled-up movie posters, and a hat rack with a Charlie Chaplin–like hat and cane. I checked for a second door but could find none. I even peeked into the trunk, but no one was hiding in it. I was sure someone had been in here. On the file cabinet was a pink candle with wisps of smoke still coming from it. It had just been blown out. Next to the candle there were a few rose petals, a heart-shaped locket with no photos inside, a small bottle of perfumed oil, and a book of love poems. The whole thing was set on a piece of red velvet cloth. It looked like an altar for a witch's spell, a place where someone might have been setting up to attract love with potions and candles.

Was Ed a witch?

"Whether he is or not is none of my business," I said to myself.

A more important question was whether someone had been able to get out of here in the minute or so it had taken me to get up from the theater to the booth. There was only one door and only one staircase. If someone had been in the booth and left, we would have run into each other. And yet the candle proved that I hadn't been wrong about seeing someone in the booth.

I turned back to the door and pulled the handle. It wouldn't budge. I pulled again. I tried pushing. I pushed again. I stopped, frustrated and a little scared. I was locked in. Someone had locked me in. I took a few steps back from the door and looked around. The candles, the book of poems—nothing was useful for opening a lock. I turned back to the file cabinet and opened the first drawer, hoping to find a stash of tools or even just a lone credit card like they used in the movies. As I searched the drawer, I felt a gust of wind on my back.

I turned. The door was wide open. I didn't stick around to figure out how it had happened. I just ran down the stairs hoping I'd find Ed and maybe get an explanation once I was safe. I told myself it was a stuck door and that the emptiness of such a big, old place was beginning to spook me. There weren't any witches, or ghosts, or anything. Ed, I told myself, would have a perfectly logical explanation for why a locked door suddenly opened, just the way he'd had an explanation for why a heavy metal door could do the same thing.

When I reached the hallway outside his office, I was relieved to hear his voice—but only until I realized how angry he sounded.

"I don't think you understand the situation."

Ed was in his office with the door nearly closed, but I could hear every word clearly.

"Look," he said, "I went along with this because you helped me out, but I don't feel right about it." He paused. "Don't you threaten me. I'm not as big a patsy as you think."

I moved a little to see who Ed was talking to and realized he was on the phone. His office was a jumbled mess of papers, carpet samples, and paint cans. Just as I stepped back, our eyes met.

"I'll have to call you back," he said into the receiver, and hung up. "Nell." His face had gone from angry to smiling. "I didn't see you there."

I pushed the door open wider. Something about the suddenness of his mood change made me nervous. I decided even if he wasn't the person who had locked me in the booth, he wasn't likely to be glad I'd been snooping around in there.

"I just got here," I said.

"Well, then come in, Nell. Sit down. Can I get you something? The soda machine is fixed."

"I'm sorry to barge in, but there was no one outside . . ."

"Slow day. Didn't see the point in paying people to stand around."

"So you're still here all alone?"

"Not anymore." He smiled. "I feel like you keep being drawn to the place today, so what can I do for you?"

"I came to ask you a favor. As you know, I'm in charge of the quilt show for the anniversary celebration, and I'm visiting local businesses to ask for their help."

I could see him relax. "That whole thing is going to be nuts, isn't it? I don't know why I got myself involved in it."

"Maybe it will bring in business."

"Not for me. People won't want to go to a movie with all that other stuff going on. And I don't think tourists come to Archers Rest to sit in the theater."

"I hadn't thought of that."

"Neither had the good leaders of this town." He scowled. "They really don't care what happens to you if you're not part of their clique." He took a breath. "But that's not why you came to talk to me."

"I was just wondering if you would mind if I hung some quilts outside the theater that weekend? The quilt show will be outdoors and all over the main streets of town. At least, that's the plan."

"You can hang them outdoors. You can even hang some indoors, if you need to. That might actually bring people in."

"I appreciate that, Ed."

"Anything to help Eleanor's granddaughter. She's always been so good to my family."

"Really? Eleanor's not much of a moviegoer."

"When you and Jesse came by the other day, I pulled out my dad's files. So interesting to go through the old stuff. It'll take me months to get through everything, but I did find something you might like to hear. Remember that summer in '75 I told you my dad was doing well?"

"You said he took a salary home that year."

"Turns out we nearly closed down. Eleanor loaned my dad the money to keep going." He paused. "I shouldn't say loaned, since my dad never paid her back. It's on my list if this place ever turns enough of a profit, though."

"Why didn't your dad get a loan at the bank?"

"Are you kidding? Those people wouldn't help my dad. Too big a risk."

"Do you know where she got the money?"

"No. And I don't know how I feel about it, either. I just can't imagine what she was thinking."

"That your father needed the money, I imagine."

He nodded. "I'm sure she had the best of intentions."

I started to leave his office, now with more questions than when I arrived. As I got to the door, I turned, hoping to get at least one more answer. "How well did you know Grace's son, Winston?"

He shrugged. "Not well."

"Did he come to the theater often?"

"A few times. There wasn't much to do in Archers Rest in those days. Even men like Winston had to do something with their evenings."

"You didn't like him?"

He furrowed his brow. "Is this about that skeleton? Was Glad right about it being Winston?"

I hesitated before deciding on a small lie. "No, Ed. At least, we're not completely sure yet who it is. It's just that all this talk about the town's past made me curious about Grace and her family. Maybe I could do something to honor them at the celebration."

"That would be wonderful. Grace Roemer was a good woman. And we have to honor the good people in this town and not let a few of them so-called leading citizens dictate who is important and who isn't." He sighed. "I didn't like the man. He came to the theater one day, shouting at my father."

"Why?"

"No idea. And my father wasn't the kind of man you would shout at. He didn't mind getting into a fight. Not like me. I wouldn't hurt a fly." He laughed. "Even if the fly deserved it."

CHAPTER 28

When I got to the house, I ran upstairs to change. Eleanor wasn't home. She was, I assumed, still with Oliver talking about whatever had made Oliver so nervous. At the top of the stairs I peeked into Eleanor's bedroom. Somewhere in that room was a box of photos, old letters, and other mementos. I remembered Eleanor showing it to me when I was a kid. At the time, the pictures that interested me were of my mother as a little girl and of Eleanor on her wedding day. But I hadn't seen everything that box held. As I stood at the entrance to her room, I wondered if maybe there was something inside that box that would answer the growing number of questions I had about my grandmother's life.

I stepped across the threshold.

Eleanor had a blue and white star quilt on her bed and a scrappy nine patch folded up on a chair. I particularly loved the nine patch, as it was made with leftovers from the shop. There was no logic to the fabric selection. There were pastels, stripes, polka dots, bright and jewel-tone fabrics, even a Halloween fabric thrown in. Each piece had been cut into two-inch squares, then sewn together randomly. She made something similar every year from whatever extra bits of fabric she had left from the shop. She brought them home and lovingly pieced and quilted them as though she were creating a family heirloom. In a way she was, because these were the quilts that reminded me most of her. And aside from reminding me of Eleanor, the hodgepodge scrap quilts spoke to another tradition of quilting that I loved. By making use of every inch of fabric you have, you find that things that shouldn't go together often work perfectly—a

Halloween pumpkin next to red polka dots, a blue plaid and an orange stripe, a famous artist like Oliver and salt-of-the-earth Eleanor.

I couldn't help myself. Though I had come into the room to search for the box, I sat on the chair, wrapped myself in the quilt, and enjoyed the comfort of my grandmother's room.

I had been coming to this house since I was a little girl, running through the rooms, jumping on the beds, and enjoying the freedom and security that comes from an afternoon at Grandma's. As close as we had always been, it seemed there was so much about her that I didn't know.

I stood up, refolded the quilt, and put it back exactly where it had been. I knew I couldn't snoop through my grandmother's things. Whatever secrets she had were her secrets. While I might be willing to ask a few questions and butt in where I arguably didn't belong, searching her room was a line even I couldn't cross.

Before I left, I walked over to the window and looked down. I had a perfect view of the backyard and the spot where Winston had been buried all these years. How many times over the years had Eleanor looked out at this window, and what, I wondered, had she been thinking about when she did?

✂

I walked into my own room and got ready for dinner with Jesse. I let the hot water in my shower melt away the tightness in my shoulders and chest. When I stepped out, I grabbed my favorite pair of jeans and a light blue cotton sweater I knew Jesse liked to see me in and went looking for my black flat shoes. They weren't anywhere in my room, so I headed downstairs to the kitchen where I often left them, much to Eleanor's annoyance.

It was only when I stepped out into the hallway that I realized how dark the house was. There was a noise. It was faint and it sounded odd—deep and steady, almost mechanical. Suddenly the tightness in my chest was back.

"It's coming from outside," I told myself. It was getting far too easy to scare me these days, I thought as I crept halfway down the stairs.

Then I realized how foolish I was being. Not because I was scared. I was foolish because I was trying to be quiet, trying to hide my presence and possibly catch someone in the house. I didn't want to catch anybody in the house. I cleared my throat as loudly as I could and stomped my foot on each step as I walked downstairs.

When I reached the kitchen, I turned on all the lights. No one was there. Nothing was disturbed. I peeked out at the backyard and there, too, things were quiet.

"Idiot," I said. I grabbed my shoes and headed for the door, but I was stopped by a blinking light on the phone. A message, maybe from Eleanor. Maybe good news. For a second I was almost optimistic.

But it was Glad. "Eleanor, I need to chat with you. It's rather urgent, and I hope you will make the time to call me back tonight. I tried your shop and you weren't there. Apparently no one knew where you were. Obviously you've been running your business for many years, but it seems to me your employees should be able to reach you at all times." She coughed. "Anyway, please do call me promptly."

I remembered what she had said to the mayor in what was supposed to have been a secret meeting: "We can't let that ridiculous woman ruin everything."

Was I that ridiculous woman, potentially ruining a quilt show? Was that why Glad was so desperate to get in touch with my grandmother? Or was Eleanor the woman in question? Or someone else? And if it wasn't the quilt show, what was Glad so worried about being ruined?

CHAPTER 29

Jesse had the pasta boiling and the sauce bubbling when I arrived, though he looked like a man who was not in control of the situation.

"I burned a batch of garlic bread, so I'm trying again," he told me as I walked in the door. "Cooking really isn't my strong suit, so I apologize in advance."

"What are you worried about? You've cooked for me before."

He blushed. "I haven't, actually."

"Last month you made me fried chicken."

"Actually, my mother made it." He grabbed an oven mitt and pulled nearly burned garlic bread out of the oven. "I just said I'd made it in an effort to impress you."

"That clinches it. Everybody has secrets."

"Who besides me?"

"Eleanor."

As I started to tell him about Eleanor's loan to Ed's father, Allie came running in the kitchen, excitedly explaining about the nice lady who had bought her an ice cream cone that afternoon and promised another one for tomorrow.

"Molly," Jesse explained.

"She's bribing your daughter now?"

"My mother dropped Allie off at the station while she was there. They both like ice cream." He shrugged.

"Should I be jealous?" I asked, teasing. Even in my most insecure moments I couldn't picture Jesse being interested in someone as annoying as Molly.

"Yeah. You probably should be really nice to me and do whatever I ask so I don't end up leaving you for a college freshman."

I laughed. "She can have you if you're going to be that high maintenance."

Jesse heaped spaghetti on my plate and passed me the garlic bread. "She's just enthusiastic about uncovering some old family secrets." He smiled. "I would think you would understand that."

"I do," I admitted. "I just don't want her getting in the way."

Jesse nodded, looked on the verge of saying something sarcastic, then seemed to change his mind.

"While you're checking into Ed's past, you probably should check into Glad's past as well."

"You think Glad Warren has a police record?"

"No, it's just she's having secret meetings with the mayor and leaving urgent messages for Eleanor. And there's something else. That day at the library, I gave her a brief description of the body, and Winston's name just popped out of her mouth. I thought that was odd. I tried to ask her about it today, but she kind of caught me off guard."

"Eleanor saw the body, saw the clothes, and she didn't think of Winston," Jesse said.

"Exactly. And she probably knew Winston far better than Glad Warren. She was living in his mother's house. In his house."

"So why didn't she think of him when she saw the skeleton?" Jesse looked a little suspicious for my taste.

"She didn't think of Winston because she wasn't expecting to find him there."

"But Glad was."

"That seems possible," I said. "Did you find out anything about Ed?"

"No arrests. None for Winston Roemer, either. But there was an interesting incident. Apparently Ed and Winston got into some kind of confrontation on July 3rd of that year. Nothing physical as far as I can tell, but the shouting was bad enough for someone to call the police."

"Over what?"

"No idea. According to the report, the police were called to the bank to break up a fight, and when they got there, Ed and Winston were yelling at each other, accusing each other of something."

"But they weren't arrested?"

"No. They both were prominent men in town. And it sounds like they were just overheated. The chief at the time separated the men and sent them on their way. Apparently he only made a report to satisfy the president of the bank, who seemed pretty upset by the idea of the two men fighting in his bank."

"Glad's father."

"Exactly."

"Who was the chief? Can we talk to him?"

"He died five years ago." He poured me a glass of wine. "But we can talk to Ed tomorrow."

"I talked to Ed about Winston today," I said. "And he never mentioned any fight. But I don't think that's the only thing he's hiding." I told Jesse about the conversation outside the theater and about the candle and other items I'd found in his projection booth.

"Doesn't sound like Ed," Jesse said. "It seems more like something Mary Shipman would do."

"Dru called her a witch. She seemed to think she had something to do with the break-in at the library. I think that's terrible of her to say."

"Have you met Mary?"

"No. I've never even seen her."

"You don't want to. Believe me, she's strange."

"Something else that's strange," I said as I pulled out the note warning me to mind my own business. "I found it on my windshield this morning. I meant to tell you at the station, but the whole Molly thing got in the way."

Jesse studied the note. "This is a threat, Nell." He looked worried.

"So what do I do?"

"I think you do exactly what it says. You stay away from the investigation."

"I've been trying to."

"Well, obviously, someone doesn't believe you've been trying hard enough," he said. "And who knows what they might be capable of."

> ✂

At about two in the morning I slipped out of Jesse's house and made my way home. I left Jesse's quiet street and drove toward the center of town, relishing the silence and anxious to get to my own bed. But just as I was turning from the edge of the cemetery, past the church, and onto Main Street, a woman darted in front of my car.

I slammed on the brakes and watched as the woman ran into the cemetery, not paying attention to where she was going. I watched to see if anyone was following her, but the streets were empty. Just in case she was in trouble, I pulled the car over, got out, and started to walk toward the graves.

As I opened the gate, I heard a noise. I could hear myself breathing but tried to ignore it. This was just headstones and bones, I told myself. I walked a few steps farther. There was no sign of the woman who had run into the cemetery, and I began to question whether it was even a woman. All I really knew was that it was a person, probably no taller than five-five or five-six, wearing a woman's trench coat, running. I wasn't sure of the hair color or the age, or whether the person was drunk, in trouble, or just stupid enough to run in front of a moving car.

I found myself muttering the warning on the note: "Mind your own business, Nell Fitzgerald. Or you'll regret it." I knew that half of me was inclined to do exactly what the note's writer, and Jesse, wanted me to do. And the other half—the stubborn half—was standing in a cemetery in the middle of the night because I'd seen something I couldn't explain. I stood, silently debating which half should win, before finally giving in to fear and common sense.

"Not everything that happens is my concern," I told myself for the third or fourth time today. "And I need to get my sleep."

I'm not a cowardly person. I've confronted people I thought had killed someone. I've broken into houses in search of clues. But walking among headstones on a dark, moonless night, chasing the closest thing to a ghost I'd ever seen, required more bravery than I had in me. I took three more steps before I decided to turn around.

But as I did, something got my attention.

I walked over to the headstones that were placed closest to the church, the oldest part of the cemetery. Most of the headstones in that area date from the sixteen and seventeen hundreds and are worn and faded. Centuries of weather have eaten away at what were once long messages lamenting the loss of husbands, wives, and children. Now many have lost their lettering completely and have even sunk into the ground, leaving stumps where large, proud headstones once stood.

But among this sad collection, one stone is well cared for. John Archer's small grave marker had been replaced recently, with an elegantly carved marble stone engraved with the words: *"John Archer, 1630–1661, From his Sacrifice, in his Honor, a Town was Born."*

Though tonight the words were not so clear. Red paint—at least what I hoped was red paint—had been splattered across his head-stone. I reached a finger hesitantly toward the stone and wiped it across the red mess. I moved toward the street lamp by the church and confirmed my suspicions. It was paint, and it was wet.

I walked out of the cemetery and back toward my car. There was no sense in waking up Jesse in the middle of the night to investigate another vandalism. I called the police station and let the officer on duty know what I'd seen, then I settled into the driver's seat and put the car in gear. Just as I was ready to pull onto Main Street, a car sped past me. It was going far above the twenty-five miles per hour speed limit. Too fast to read the license plate. But I didn't need to see the plate. It was a lemon yellow BMW, and there was only one person in town with a car like that. Glad Warren.

CHAPTER 30

The next morning I headed to Jitters for coffee and to start my search for Glad. It didn't make sense that she would vandalize John Archer's grave, but there was no denying that it had been her car that nearly crashed into mine in the middle of the night.

Glad wasn't at Jitters, but two cups of coffee and a chocolate doughnut were there waiting for me. Along with Molly.

"This seems like a great place to hang out," she said when she saw me.

"It is." I waved to Carrie. "I think everyone in town comes here at one point or another."

"That's why I'm here. So I can talk to people."

"About Winston? Molly, most of the people in town didn't even know him. And those who did don't want to be interrogated over their morning coffee."

"What are my options? It's not like Jesse is giving me addresses of any of his suspects. I have to start somewhere."

Carrie saw me finishing my second cup of coffee and came over with a full pot. "I'll give you a refill if you tell me what happened at the cemetery last night."

"Someone threw red paint on John Archer's grave," I told her. "I think Jesse is there now, trying to figure out which high school kid was in the mood to pull a prank."

"One of my customers said it probably was Mary Shipman's doing, but it won't be investigated because she's Glad's sister," Carrie said. "Personally, I think it's tied into the murder."

"Of my uncle?" Molly asked.

Carrie jumped at the statement. "Your who?"

"Her great-uncle was Winston Roemer," I explained. "She's here to solve his murder."

"Oh, well," Carrie stammered. She looked toward me with a puzzled expression. "Does Jesse know about this?"

"He knows, and so far he's all for it," I said.

"Who is Mary Shipman?" Molly asked. "Can we talk to her?"

"Who's talking, and what about?" Natalie had snuck up behind me and nearly got a cupful of coffee on her T-shirt for startling me.

I didn't want to admit it, but Molly had a point. Everyone kept talking about Mary Shipman, but so far no one had talked *to* her. Maybe she knew something, and there was only one way to find out.

"I'll tell you about it on the way to Mary Shipman's house," I said to Natalie.

"Really? Cool. But you have to drive. I can't fit behind the wheel anymore." She patted her alarmingly large belly.

"When are you due again?"

"July 26th."

"Are you having twins?"

"Actually, I'm having one regular-size baby and about thirty pounds of fat." She eyed what was left of my doughnut. "What's one more pound?" she asked as she grabbed it and stuffed it in her mouth.

✂

"What do you know about Mrs. Shipman?" I asked Natalie as we drove toward her house at the edge of town. We'd left Carrie at Jitters with a shop full of customers, but Molly wasn't willing to stay behind. She sat in the backseat, determined to question Mary about the death of Winston. "Eleanor told me she's Glad's sister, a year older," I said. "They were very close growing up, and now she's the town recluse."

"Her husband died in the mid-eighties. He was really young, maybe thirty-five. My mom said he fell off a ladder," Natalie said. "And she, apparently, had an affair with Ed Bryant."

"Ed Bryant was the man who got into a fight with my uncle," Molly said. "Jesse told me."

"He did? Jesse sure is being generous with information," I said. Far more generous than he often was with me. I turned back to Natalie. "Does Mary have money?"

"She must. She's never worked as far as I know. I don't know what her husband did. Or maybe Glad supports her."

"Any kids?"

"None. She does have cats, though. Lots of them. At least that's what I've heard. And she's supposed to be a witch."

I rolled my eyes. "A Wiccan witch, or a broom-and-pointy-hat witch?"

"Broom and pointy hat, I guess. Kids are afraid of her."

"Jesse says she's strange," I said, as I pulled into the driveway of a drab and uncared-for brown house. Weeds had taken over the front of the house, and what had once been a colorful garden gnome was broken in pieces and trapped by a bush. "And so far, I'm pretty sure I agree with him."

✂

"How charming to have young visitors." Mary Shipman opened the door to her small house with a cat in one arm and what looked like a beer in the other. Her long, graying hair was loosely tied in a ponytail, and she was wearing a lime green T-shirt paired with a long, flowing skirt of the same green but with bright pink and orange flowers on it. She had flat sandals on, showing off red toenails. But what caught my eye was a large, ornately carved silver bracelet dangling from her left arm.

"That's beautiful," I said.

"Thank you. It was a gift."

She waved us inside and what I saw was in stark contrast to the outside of her home. The place was funky, but it was beautifully decorated and alive with color. All around her living room were items from faraway places—Asian art next to pieces clearly from Africa, hanging above sculptures from India.

"Did you get these yourself?" I asked.

"Yes. Years ago. My late husband and I were quite the world travelers. And for a time I went solo. But that's all behind me now."

"Why is that?"

"You don't know? I thought everyone knew," she said. "I'm the crazy woman in the ugly house. I never go out."

"Never?" Molly asked.

She smiled. "Only in the dead of night, and then only to lure strangers to my home so I can use their bones in my spells." She looked at Natalie. "Are you fat or pregnant?"

"Pregnant."

"Well, then I won't offer you a beer. How about you?" she pointed at me.

"Water," I said. "We'll all have water."

She shrugged and left us alone except for a cat here and there that wandered into the room.

"A beer? It's nine in the morning," Natalie whispered.

"I'm not sure she cares about the time."

When she came back, she had three large glasses of water as well as a platter of grapes, strawberries, and cut-up pineapple. Natalie and I sat on a large cream sofa, Molly sat across from us on its exact match, and Mary sat next to her. And she stared. Out of nervousness, both Natalie and I immediately went for the fruit.

"You'll have to forgive my manners," Mary said. "So few people come to see me. Just my sister, and of course, Ed."

"Ed Bryant?"

"Yes. He's a dear friend." She looked at me, amused. "You're not terribly well-informed about the gossip in this town, are you dear?"

"I guess not," I said. "Why don't you fill me in?"

CHAPTER 31

Mary Shipman sipped her beer and stared at me. "Where would you like me to start?"

I considered it for a moment. I couldn't quite determine why, but I felt that she had the answers to all my questions. Maybe it was the amused way she looked at three women she didn't know who had arrived at her door unannounced. Or it could have been the clear, constant gaze directly into my eyes. If she was a witch, she probably was casting a spell on me as I sat there.

"How do you know Ed?" I asked.

"I've lived in this town my entire life, as has Ed. He taught at the high school when I was a student there. Not my teacher. I didn't care for science. But even so, it would be a strange thing if we didn't know each other."

"Why does he visit you?"

"Do you know Ed?"

"Yes," I said.

"And do you like him?"

"He's very nice."

"I feel the same way." She looked from me to Natalie and Molly. "Is that why you came, or is there something else you would like to know?"

"There was a skeleton found in my grandmother's backyard," I said, hoping to start the conversation slowly and build up to love affairs and the other long-buried secrets of Archers Rest.

"Your grandmother is Eleanor Cassidy?" She laughed. "Should have known. She's always jumping in to help, whether she's asked to or not. How's Oliver? Has she agreed to marry him yet?"

Natalie coughed out a piece of pineapple. "You know?" she stammered.

"I hear things."

"From who?" I asked. "You said your only visitors are Ed and Glad, and neither of them is aware of any possible engagement."

"Maybe I just read it in the stars."

I matched her stare with my own and made a guess. "Maggie?"

The corners of her mouth curled up. "She might have mentioned it."

"When did she come to see you?"

"She brought me a cat. A stray had popped up on her doorstep and she knew that I would care for it. One of Maggie's grandchildren is allergic, so she couldn't keep the little thing herself."

"And how did the conversation turn to Eleanor?"

"How does any conversation turn anywhere? We began to talk about our mutual friends. I could see that Maggie was troubled about something, and she confided."

"What was her concern?"

She smiled. "That would be a question for her, Nell."

I sat up straight. "You know my name?"

"You said you were Eleanor's granddaughter. I assume the one that's living with her and dating the police chief. That makes you Nell." She sipped her beer. "And this is Natalie. She's Susanne's daughter and works at the shop." She looked at Molly. "I don't know who you are, I'm afraid."

"I'm Winston Roemer's grandniece."

"I can see a slight resemblance. More to Grace than to her son. Which is a good thing. Winston was an attractive man, in a stern sort of way, but you'd hardly want to take after a man so unhappy with the world."

"Was he unhappy?" Molly asked. "Why?"

"I don't know, dear. He didn't confide in me," Mary said, then turned back to me.

"How is Jesse, Nell? Is he as scared about marriage as it appears? Or is that just you?"

"We're not talking about getting married."

"Other people are talking about your marriage, pushing you toward it. I would suggest, if you're looking for advice, that you put the idea on the back burner for now. You need to be the individual you are first."

"Thanks for the advice. What's your source?"

"It's gossip, not witchcraft, despite what you may have heard."

"Fair enough," I said. "What gossip do you know about Winston Roemer? Aside from the fact that he was unhappy."

"None, but I do have firsthand information," she said. She rested her hand on Molly's. "I don't mean to bring up sad memories of your uncle. You should know that he was a lovely dancer and he had a wonderful laugh. Deep, throaty. He also spoke several languages: Spanish, French, and Latin, if I remember correctly. He was the one who got me interested in world travel. He told me once I had the potential to be anything I wanted to be and I shouldn't let small-town gossips get in my way. I had quite the crush on him."

"Did that make Ed jealous?" I asked.

She laughed. "Wouldn't that have been something? No, dear. Ed and I became involved with each other many years later, after my husband's death, and only for a short time. I knew Winston when I was a girl of only nineteen."

"Did you have an affair with him?" Natalie leaned forward as far as her belly would allow.

"No. Sadly, no. Winston was not available."

"Meaning," I said, "he was already involved with someone."

"Meaning exactly that."

Natalie and I glanced toward each other. "Who?"

Mary smiled. "One of Archers Rest's finest citizens. Can I get any of you more water?" she asked as she got up.

"Yes, please," I said. I was afraid if I said no, it would be my cue to leave, and there was no way I was leaving yet.

"Who do you think she means?" Molly asked once Mary had left the room.

"I don't even know if she was being sarcastic," I answered. "But if she meant it, then Glad pops to mind."

"But she wasn't prominent then. She was a teenager."

"Assuming she meant 1975, and assuming she wasn't just amusing herself at our expense."

"I'm not sure we're going to get a straight answer out of her," Molly said.

"Well, we're going to try." I got up and went looking for Mary.

I found her in the kitchen. As I walked in, she was hanging up the phone. She blushed when she saw me.

"Do you know who might have killed Winston?" I asked. No reason not to get right to the point.

"No, I don't."

"Lots of people in town didn't like him."

"Lots of people in town don't like me. People don't like different. It's scary when someone insists on being who they are regardless of what people think." She smiled a little. "I imagine you struggle with that."

I took a step back. "Why would I . . ."

"The town's own Sherlock Holmes—isn't that your reputation?"

"I don't know if anyone calls me that."

"They do. But you have an instinct about people, if what I hear is right. You help others. You shouldn't run away from that or be embarrassed about it."

Now I was blushing. "I'm concerned about my grandmother," I said.

"Don't be. That will work out the way it was meant to. Focus yourself elsewhere."

"The quilt show or the murder?"

"I know my sister. If you don't pull off the quilt show to her satisfaction, there will be a murder."

"Was she the one? The person Winston was involved with?"

"No, but he would have been her type. She was dating a local boy. Someone her own age. He was cute. He played high school football and ran track. Drove my father crazy because he was, how should I say it, not a member of the country club."

"What happened to him?"

"He became the mayor."

CHAPTER 32

"I don't think that means anything," Jesse said as we ate lunch two hours later. "They dated in high school, more than thirty years ago."

"It's just interesting. They don't seem to like each other now."

"What's hard to imagine is that they liked each other then. Glad dating a local gardener working his way through college? Hardly seems like the type of guy to get her attention."

"You mean she would go for sophisticated, worldly men," I said.

"No, I mean she would go for rich men."

"Like Winston?"

He tilted his head and stared at me. "He was more than twice her age."

"So what?"

He shrugged. "I guess it's a possibility, but I doubt Glad will tell us if it's true."

"Speaking of Glad, did you ask her about last night?"

"Not yet."

"Why not? Did you look at what she did to Archer's grave?"

"What *someone* did," he said. "It was red paint, nearly a whole gallon of it. You were right about that. It must have been the person you saw running into the cemetery, which may or may not have been Glad."

"Whoever it was, I didn't see a paint can in her hand."

"I checked with the hardware store and the art store. No one sold that color paint recently. So either someone already had it, or went out of town to get it."

"She didn't want it traced back to her."

"I have a hard time believing it was Glad," he said. "No matter who you saw drive off."

"Why do you say that?"

"She was the one who raised the money for a new headstone. She personally suggested the epitaph. Besides, she's practically a John Archer groupie. Why would she want to vandalize his grave? Much more likely it was her sister. She is strange, isn't she?"

I thought about it for a minute. "No, she's not," I said. "I actually liked her. She's very . . . she's comfortable with herself."

"She's odd."

"What's wrong with being odd? I'm a little odd."

He smiled. "You're good odd."

"What, exactly, makes Mary the suspect in everything that goes on in town?"

Jesse looked around as if he were embarrassed to be overheard. "When I was about ten, she was arrested for threatening to blow up city hall, while the entire city council was inside."

"I heard something about that. Do you know why she made the threat?"

"What do you mean, 'why?' Is there a good reason for trying to do something like that?"

"No," I conceded. "It just doesn't seem like something she'd do."

"Old friends now, are you?"

"No. But how could she blow up city hall if she doesn't leave her house?"

"She did then. The hermit thing started after that. I'm not sure when. For years she would wander through town, mostly at night. I know some of the older women sought her out for advice and stuff," he said. "The rumor is she would cast spells for them and read their future. But not like one of those storefront psychics. What she predicted was real."

"She pretty much told me she's just sharing gossip she's heard."

He shook his head, unconvinced. "I don't know, Nell. She knows things."

"She said you're afraid of getting married."

"She did?"

"And she thought that you and I should put the idea on the back burner for a while."

He took a breath before speaking. "At this point, any remark I make will somehow get me in trouble."

"Look at that." I laughed. "You know things, too. Maybe you're a witch."

"Me, Mary Shipman, John Archer. The whole town is full of them."

Glad might not have been on Jesse's suspect list, but she was on mine. And if anyone in town was a strange, broom-and-pointy-hat witch, my vote was for her. Something had to explain why the whole town, including Jesse, would be afraid of crossing her, and a spell was as good an explanation as any. I headed down Main Street, figuring I'd grab her at one of her usual hangouts, but Glad, as it turned out, was not an easy person to track down. I called her house, but there was no answer. I called her cell phone, and it went straight to voice mail.

After stopping in at the library, the local hair salon, and Chic, the only shop in town that sold designer goods, I gave up and started for home. But I didn't get any farther than the park.

"I didn't expect to see you here," I said to Oliver, who had a canvas set up on an easel, with paints around him and a very familiar fur-covered face looking to somehow make it into the painting.

"Hey ya, Barney," I said as I patted the dog. Barney jumped up and licked my face, as though he hadn't seen me for years. "What are you doing, Oliver?"

"Painting the gazebo with the river in the background. Maggie is auctioning it off at the church fair."

I glanced at the canvas, which so far had a primer coat of white and some soft blues mixed into the background, with a light pencil sketch of the gazebo over the paint. "How's it going?"

"Look, Nell, don't think you can get any information from me, okay? I've made a promise and I'm keeping it," Oliver snapped.

"Promise about what?"

"That's exactly what I'm talking about. You go talk to your grandmother."

"I would, but I don't think she came home last night." I grinned. "Should I stop by the shop with a bottle of champagne?"

"No. Listen, just forget the whole engagement. Eleanor and I are fine as we are. That's the end of it."

"Did you ask her? Did she say no?"

"I didn't ask her. I changed my mind, and that's the end of it." Oliver's voice was shaking.

I reached out and took his arm. "It's fine," I started to say, "it's—"

"Hey there, folks." The mayor was walking toward us, with Molly right beside him. Barney walked forward to greet them, but I stayed where I was.

"Hi," I called out. "Oliver's doing the painting for the auction."

Oliver's shoulders stooped and he picked up a brush, halfheartedly painting a streak of blue on the canvas.

"You two have gotten chummy," I said to Molly as she and the mayor reached us.

"The mayor's been telling me all about himself. Did you know he was the gardener over at my house—Grace's house—when Winston was alive?"

"I did," I said, letting it slide that she called Eleanor's house "my house."

The mayor seemed enchanted with her. "I think you've got competition here, Nell. This one has been asking a lot of questions about the old days, about her uncle."

"What have you told her?"

"Well, everything." He laughed. "I was just so pleased to find out that we had a Roemer in town. A member of one of our most prominent families back for the anniversary! It's kismet."

"So you told her . . ." I prompted.

"I told her how Winston knew the Latin names of all the flowers I planted. I also mentioned, though I said it meant nothing, that I once overheard Winston and his mother have harsh words about Eleanor."

I looked at Molly, who stood expressionless but still seemed rather pleased with herself. "What do you mean, 'harsh words'?" I asked Larry.

"I don't remember what they said. It was some years ago. But I do remember the tone. He was very angry, and he said something about how Eleanor was the cause of it."

I glanced toward Oliver, who was uncharacteristically quiet. Oliver had always jumped to Eleanor's defense whether she needed it or not. For him to be silent now made me even more curious about what had happened between my grandmother and him.

"Nell, I want a word with you." Larry grabbed my arm and walked me a few yards from the others. "I have something very important, and very delicate, to discuss with you." He whispered—though the mayor's whisper was still loud enough for anyone to hear. "I need you to talk with Eleanor for me."

"What about?"

"I was thinking that we could have tours of her house during the anniversary weekend."

"It's an old house, Mayor, but it's not really historical. It's been remodeled and the furnishings—"

"It's not the house I was thinking of."

"The hole in the backyard."

He nodded. "Would generate a lot of interest."

"There's no way Eleanor will allow you to do that."

"But if you ask her."

I laughed. "Not a chance."

"Okay. Maybe you're right about that. It would be a little intrusive to have people walking around her backyard," he conceded, "so maybe we just have a few people go up there now and take some pictures."

"The police already took pictures."

"Nell," he said, his frustration with me boiling up. "We could get a lot of press about a possible Revolutionary War soldier found in a leading citizen's garden."

"Mayor, you know that isn't true . . ."

"Look, Nell, this town needs something more than a beautiful spot on the Hudson if we're going to get tourists up here. I'd like to see that happen, as the mayor and as a business owner. I'll bet if you ask any shop owner in town, your grandmother included, if they'd like to see more people coming here to spend their money, the answer would be yes."

"I know that. But making up some story about a soldier and getting my grandmother to play along isn't the way to bring tourism dollars to Archers Rest."

"Don't be so sure about that. I've already gotten some interest from several newspapers. Regional newspapers. They want to come up and take some photos of the place. All I need is for you to get her to say yes."

"I can ask, but I don't think—"

"That's fine. Nell, thank you. I'll call the newspapers and tell them you will expect them in week or so."

"Mayor, you probably should talk to Jesse before you bring a bunch of reporters up here."

"I don't need the permission of my chief of police."

"I'm not saying that. It's just that he's getting a DNA sample from Winston's sister."

"I know a way to talk to these reporters that hints at something without saying anything. And unless Jesse has a one-hundred-percent-positive identification of the skeleton . . ."

"Not yet, but . . ."

"Then all I need is Eleanor's permission. And I'd rather you got it for me. Talking to Molly has brought up a lot of old memories of my time at the Roemer house. I haven't shared them all with Molly. Not yet. But I think if Eleanor and I spoke now, it might naturally come up." As he spoke he looked back toward Molly. "And I think we'd all rather forget any unpleasantness from the past, don't you?"

CHAPTER 33

I walked from the park in a daze. The mayor had threatened me. At least it felt like he had. And Oliver was backing away from a future with Eleanor. Whenever I got involved in an investigation I always searched for the truth. Now what I wanted more than anything was a time machine to go back to the day when Oliver and I came up with the stupid idea of digging up Eleanor's garden.

I went toward Someday Quilts. At the last minute I decided I wasn't ready to face my grandmother, so I ducked into Jitters in the hopes of talking things over with Carrie. Instead I walked straight into the one person I'd been looking for all afternoon.

"Nell, dear. You do spend a lot of time in this place."

Glad's voice dripped with a combination of concern, sarcasm, and condescension. If I spent years trying to imitate it, I wouldn't have managed to pull off such a trifecta of superiority.

"Most of the town hangs out in here." I pointed toward the full tables and long line of people in front of us. "Carrie makes the best coffee."

Carrie, at the mention of her name, widened her eyes and stared. She had a message for me; that much I could figure out. But since Carrie had a half-dozen caffeine-hungry patrons waiting for her, it would have to wait.

I settled into the line next to Glad and smiled as friendly a smile as I could. "I've been looking for you," I said.

"There's a problem with the show?"

"No. Everything's going well. I'm working on my quilt. I have promises now for more than twenty others, and most of the local businesses have agreed to let me display quilts outside their windows."

"It's going to be outside?"

"Yes. Won't that be nice?" I asked, more rhetorically than as an attempt at approval. Not that it mattered; I could see Glad wasn't approving.

I tried again. "We'll have quilts up and down Main Street and on several of the side streets in the downtown area. I'm looking for a couple more slots, and of course I have to secure the permits, but I think it will dress up the whole town, making it very bright and colorful for the anniversary celebration."

"Assuming it doesn't rain."

I counted to three before speaking. "Well, if it rains, that spoils more than the quilt show," I reminded her. "The parade, the carnival, and the fireworks are all taking place outside."

"Which is why it would have been nice to have the quilt show indoors. So people would have somewhere to go if it rained." She sighed and looked at me with pity and sadness. "Still, I know you're only doing your best, Nell. And you're not very experienced with an event of this importance."

"Is that why you called my grandmother?"

She looked puzzled, then her gaze hardened. "I didn't call your grandmother."

It wouldn't be worth challenging her directly. I knew that much about Glad. I simply smiled. "I'll do my best with the show," I said.

"That's all I ask."

"Thanks for understanding," I said, trying to keep my voice light and friendly. "That's not actually why I wanted to talk to you. I just wanted to see if you were okay after what happened last night."

"Of course I'm okay. Nothing happened last night."

"I nearly ran into your car."

She glared at me. "When?"

"When I was pulling out of the cemetery at about two this morning," I said. "You drove right past me, and you were driving pretty fast. I only missed your car by inches."

"I was in bed at two in the morning, Nell. And my car was in my garage. You must be mistaken."

"You drive a yellow BMW, don't you? It's the only one I've ever seen in town. That was the car that drove past me last night," I said. "It's kind of hard to miss."

"It wasn't mine."

"Could it have been your husband driving?"

I rarely saw Glad's husband, an executive with an electronics company who traveled for business. Or, if I believed the rumor, just to get away from his wife.

"It wasn't my husband," Glad said. "He's in London. He wanted me to join him, of course, but I'm here working on the celebration and absolutely couldn't get away."

"You didn't loan your car to anyone?"

"No. And anyone I would trust my car to wouldn't be out at that hour. Only people looking for trouble are out at that hour."

"That may be," I said, ignoring the implication. "Especially considering what happened to John Archer's headstone."

"What happened?"

"Someone threw a can of red paint on it. I'm surprised you hadn't heard."

"When?"

"Right about the time your car drove past me."

"You mean, right before you exited the cemetery?"

I smiled. "I *found* the red paint, Glad. I didn't put it there. In fact, I reported it to the police."

"You and Jesse must have the most interesting pillow talk."

Just as she and I were about to get to the front of the line, Glad tapped her foot impatiently as if she couldn't wait a second longer, then turned and walked out of Jitters.

"What was that about?" Carrie asked me.

"Nothing. What do you want to tell me?"

"Natalie called over here looking for you. I think it's about Eleanor. Have you seen her lately?"

"Not since yesterday. Her bedroom door was closed when I got home last night and still was closed when I got up this morning. And I just had the oddest conversation with Oliver. I really have to talk to her."

"She's at the shop now. I saw her go in." Carrie poured me a cup of strong black coffee in a to-go cup. "You need to go across the street and talk to her. And then come back and tell me everything she says."

CHAPTER 34

I rushed into Someday Quilts to find Natalie, her mother Susanne, and Maggie in a huddle.

"Where's Eleanor?" I asked.

"Her office," Natalie told me. "But don't go in there. She said she'll be out in a minute."

"What's going on?"

"No idea. But she asked where you were."

"I'm here. I'll go tell her," I said.

Maggie grabbed my arm. "She said to wait."

"Is something wrong?"

Susanne walked over and patted my shoulder. "I'm sure everything's fine, Nell. Just give Eleanor a minute to compose herself and she'll come out and tell us what this is all about."

"Maggie," I said as I looked toward her. "Do you know what's going on?"

"No. Eleanor called me this morning and asked if I would come to the shop."

"Why?"

"I don't know."

"Do you think Oliver asked her to marry him?" Natalie asked. "That's the only thing that would make sense."

As she spoke, Bernie walked in. Aside from Carrie, this was the entire quilt group.

"If Oliver asked her," Bernie said, "she must have said yes. Otherwise she wouldn't have gathered us all together."

"That's true," Susanne agreed. "You don't get your friends together to say you've turned down a man's proposal."

"Unless she found out we all knew and didn't tell her," Natalie said. "Do you think she'd be mad?"

I didn't want to tell them that an engagement was very unlikely. Instead, we all stood watching Eleanor's office door for what seemed like an eternity. There was no sign of movement from inside. I almost knocked on the door, but Maggie stopped me. "She'll come out when she's ready."

"Do we still have our quilt meeting tomorrow?" Bernie asked.

"I can't believe tomorrow is Friday," I said. "So much has happened."

"Like those teenagers in the cemetery," Susanne said.

I turned to her. "Are you talking about Archer's headstone? Why do you say it was teenagers?"

"That's what the mayor said. I ran into him coming out of the police station."

That didn't make sense to me. The paint was still wet. If it had been a group of teenagers, I would have heard them or seen them. All I saw was a figure running into the cemetery. And whoever was driving Glad's car.

After five more minutes had passed, I lost my patience. No matter what anyone said, I was going to open Eleanor's office door and demand to know what had happened. Just as I moved toward it, though, Eleanor emerged. Smiling.

"Nell, I was about to give up on ever seeing you again. What time did you get home last night?" she asked.

"Just after two. What's going on?"

"Nothing. Nothing bad, anyway."

"Does this have to do with Oliver?"

"A little," she said. "Natalie, will you do me a favor? Lock the door and put out the CLOSED sign. I want us to have a minute to ourselves."

We all waited as Natalie did as she was asked, then turned back to Eleanor.

"Oliver and I had a nice long talk last night," Eleanor said. "He wanted to ask me something and he was actually quite nervous. He thought I would be against the idea. Sweet, really."

While I stood with my heart in my throat, the others smiled, ready to spring into a group hug and act surprised if she told us that she and Oliver were engaged.

"Oliver must go to Paris for an art exhibit. Some of his work will be shown there. And he's asked me to come with."

"Is that it?" Bernie asked. "That's the news?"

Eleanor's face fell. "What's wrong?" she snapped. "I haven't taken a vacation in years."

"That's not what she means," I said.

Eleanor blushed. "Do you think I'm foolish to go? You and Natalie can mind the store, can't you?"

"Of course," I said. "It's wonderful news."

"We're just jealous," Maggie said. "A trip to Paris. All that wonderful food and the beautiful sights. I haven't been to Paris since the early sixties, but I remember it fondly. It was my favorite city."

"I've never been there," Natalie laughed, "and it's my favorite city. How romantic!"

Bernie came forward and hugged Eleanor. "When are you leaving?"

"July 5th. I'll be around for Nell's birthday cake and the quilt show. Can't miss that."

I laughed. "No, of course not. You wouldn't want to miss me tearing my hair out and possibly killing Glad Warren."

She relaxed. "You don't think I'm crazy to go?"

"I think you'd be crazy not to," I told her.

✂

For about an hour we celebrated the way only quilters can, with everyone giving Eleanor a list of fabric shops in Paris along with requests for beautiful Provençal fabrics in saturated yellows, blues, and reds. Eventually, though, everyone left, and Eleanor and I found ourselves alone in the shop.

"This is coming along nicely," she said, pointing toward my devil's puzzle quilt blocks still displayed on the design board.

I studied it for a moment. "It's not bad. I didn't know if I liked the colors at first, but it's coming together."

"These fabrics are a tie to our quilting past," she said. "There might have been a woman more than a hundred years ago who made this pattern in these colors."

"I think that's the one thing that's tolerable about doing this show, and putting up with Glad. It will be nice to see all the centuries of quilts represented. To see how it's evolved and yet, somehow, kept its traditions," I said. "I think it will surprise people to see how many beautiful quilts there are from so many generations of women. Assuming everyone turns in the quilts they've promised."

"Speaking of which, I've chosen a couple of my quilts to show. One is from the seventies. It has appliquéd brown owls on orange backgrounds. It's hideous, but it's authentic. And I have one I've been working on. It's blocks of solid colors, in greens and blues. All the quilt magazines keep talking about the new modern movement in quilting—lots of geometrics, simple lines, bold colors. I thought I'd give it a try."

"Sounds perfect."

"And if it's okay with the chairwoman of the quilt show," she said as she smiled at me, "I'd like to add in a couple of Grace's quilts. They're from the thirties, both appliquéd quilts. One is butterflies and the other has flowers."

"Are you talking about the ones you keep in the living room at the house?"

"Those are the ones."

"I'd be thrilled to display them. And I promise to take very good care of them."

I took a deep breath. Maybe this wasn't the time to tell her, but it was an opening. I wanted her to hear it from me before she heard it elsewhere. And I had a feeling that Molly was going to track her down with a load of questions about some long-ago conversation the mayor had overheard.

"Can I ask you a strange question?"

"You frequently do, Nell."

"Where were you in July of 1975?"

"Is this about the skeleton?"

"I'm not sure. Not yet," I said. "But it might be."

"Nova Scotia, with Grace and the children," she said. "We went every summer, and that summer was the last time we went."

"What do you remember about it?"

"It was very hot, I remember that," she said. "Grace's health was fragile. She couldn't take the heat in Archers Rest, so it was decided to bring her up north, where it was a bit cooler. We stayed in the home of some friends of hers. She was able to sit on the beach and look out at the ocean. We had long talks while the kids played in the water. It was a lovely time."

"How long were you gone?"

"The whole month of July. We left the first of July and came back August 2nd."

"You remember those exact dates?"

"Grace died exactly a week later. It may have been too much for her, poor thing. I've always wondered about that, but she wanted to go. And when someone is nearing the end of their life, how can you deny them what they want?" Eleanor looked at me. "What have you found out?"

"I think I have some news."

"About Grace?"

"About her son, Winston."

Eleanor's eyes flickered, but she stood calmly looking at me. "What about him?"

I knew I was breaking my promise to Jesse, but it was better this news came from me than from Molly. "He may be the one."

"The one what?"

"The . . . the person we found in your rose garden."

Eleanor swallowed hard. "Oh." And with that she left the room.

$\mathcal{C}$HAPTER 35

J ust as I was about to go after her, I heard shouting coming from the street. I ran outside just in time to see an unmanned squad car roll into a fire hydrant, causing the hydrant to gush water all over the street.

Jesse and several officers were on the scene in moments. A few members of the volunteer fire department, Ed and the mayor among them, soon joined in and brought the fire hydrant under control.

Jesse's eyes met mine. "This is crazy," he said. "Someone purposefully put that car in neutral and headed it in the direction of the fire hydrant."

"Is anyone hurt?" I called back.

"No, but it's going to take all day to clear this up." He could have been frazzled. After everything that had been happening in town he certainly had a right to be, but Jesse seemed calm and in charge. Off to the side a dozen or so people watched the action with a combination of amusement and concern. Carrie and many of her customers came out of Jitters. I walked over to Carrie, but Molly intercepted me.

"You wouldn't think a town like this would be so dangerous, but my great-uncle gets murdered, and now all these acts of vandalism . . ."

"There was a thirty-five-year gap between those events."

"I guess. But it makes you wonder if any of us are safe."

I wanted to say something snarky, something about going back to crime-free Boston and leaving Jesse, and me, to figure out what had happened to Winston, but she was just a college freshman looking for answers to a family mystery, and I knew I was overreacting.

"It's really a nice town," I said instead, softening my voice to a friendly tone. "You've just caught us at a bad time." It was the best explanation I could come up with for why peaceful Archers Rest had suddenly turned into a vandal's paradise.

"I don't know about that," Molly said. "I got an overnight package from my grandmother with some of Winston's papers. I was supposed to deliver it to Jesse, but I started looking at it, and there's some interesting stuff in there."

"Like?"

Molly looked around at the people on the street and leaned in close. "Can we go inside Jitters?" Molly asked.

We moved past the crowd and into the coffee shop. I pointed toward a small table in the back and we sat there. I could see Carrie staring at us, so I asked for coffee.

"I'll bring it to the table," she called back. I knew she was more interested in joining the conversation than bringing coffee, which is why I agreed.

"So what did his papers tell you?"

Molly reached into her computer bag and pulled out a large envelope, from which she began to pull smaller envelopes. The small ones were old with beautiful handwriting on them, and they were addressed to Elizabeth.

"These are letters Winston wrote to his sister," Molly said. "He seemed pretty upset about something."

"About what?"

"I don't know." She pushed the letters toward me. "Read them yourself, and maybe you can tell me."

Dear Elizabeth,

It's hot here. Miserable. And I'm miserable. What have I agreed to? I would do anything to protect Mother and to see that she's happy. I know that she had a right to be concerned about me. But, this place? With these people? I know that you have a fondness for Archers Rest from our childhood summers, but you have no idea how corrupt and underhanded these people can be. And I'm stuck with them. I have made terrible mistakes and now I'm black-mailed into an awful choice. The worst choice possible.

I know you disagree with that. Like Mother, you think it's time for me to be a good heir to the throne and do what is expected of me. I know I will be rewarded for it, but I'm not doing this for me. I am doing this to protect Mother from what I'm sure will be great harm.

Winston

The letter was dated July 3rd, 1975.

"What do you think it means?" I asked Molly. "What choice was he blackmailed into?"

"I don't know."

"And what awful harm was he protecting Grace from?"

"I think someone was trying to kill her."

"Any thoughts on who that might have been?"

She took a long, deep breath, and I watched her study me as she did it. "What about Eleanor?"

"That's crazy."

"I'm sure it is. It's just, well, he did have that argument with his mother about Eleanor."

Carrie walked over with two cups of coffee—a fresh iced one for Molly and a hot cup for me. "Anything else I can get you?"

I looked up, the anger evident in my eyes. "No thanks. Molly and I are going over to Someday Quilts."

✄

"Grandma?" I called out as we entered the shop.

"Back here, knee-deep in hand-dyed woolens," she called back, and as she did I could see her leg from behind the last row of shelves. "I tell you, Nell, there are so many beautiful hand-dyes coming out. Just when I say I've made all the quilts I want to make in my lifetime, a new pattern or a new line of fabric comes out and I'm hooked all over again." She peeked out at me and saw Molly. "Who is this? A new recruit? I warn you, young lady, quilting is addictive."

"This is Molly O'Brien, Grandma. She's just come to town."

Eleanor dropped her fabrics and came toward us. "I know that name," she said. "Do I know you?"

"You know my grandmother, Elizabeth Sullivan."

Eleanor's eyes widened, and she took a step back. "My heavens. I can see Elizabeth in you. And your great-grandmother, too. Grace Roemer. Did you know I worked for her?"

"She did," I said.

Eleanor looked at me, taking a second before it was clear she had made the connection. "You're here about Winston."

"I came down from school in Boston to represent the family," Molly answered her. "I understand you knew him."

"I knew him, yes."

We could have spent a lot of time on small talk leading up to the reason I'd brought Molly to meet Eleanor, but I didn't have the patience.

"Molly thinks that someone was trying to kill Grace," I said. "Apparently someone was trying to cheat her, or at least that's what Winston believed, and Molly is wondering if that person was you."

Molly turned bright red, but Eleanor laughed.

"Nell is a bit more direct than she is polite. Why don't we sit in the classroom and talk?" Eleanor turned to the only customer in the shop, a regular who came in at least twice a week. "Shout when you're ready to have your fabrics cut," she said. "We'll be in back talking over old rumors."

Once we settled into the classroom, I couldn't help but notice Molly staring at the quilts. My devil's puzzle blocks were still on the design wall, waiting to be sewn into a quilt top. But there were finished quilts as well, used as samples for kits and classes, that decorated the walls.

"These are beautiful," she said. "When this is all over I want to make one."

"No one better to teach you than Eleanor," I said. "Assuming you haven't gotten her arrested for killing Winston."

Molly blushed again. "I'm sorry," she said to Eleanor. "It's just that you were closer to Grace than anyone, so if she was in danger . . ."

"Either it was from me or I might know about it," Eleanor finished Molly's thought.

"Exactly."

"Well, I'm sorry to disappoint you, dear, but as far as I know, Grace wasn't in danger. Certainly not from me, I can assure you of that. And not from anyone else, either. She was ill. What would have been the point of anyone trying to kill her?"

"What about cheat her?"

Eleanor shrugged. "Not that I know of. This is a good town, with good people. I can't think of anyone who would do something as heinous as cheat a dying woman."

"The mayor said something about Winston and Grace having an argument about you," I said, getting to it before Molly could.

Eleanor blushed. "I'm sorry to hear that."

"No idea what it could have been about?"

"They didn't see eye to eye about a lot of things. But I can't think of why anyone would harm Winston."

"But someone did," Molly pointed out. "And I think it's because he knew something. Maybe someone wanted her money."

"Her children were her only heirs, and they adored her," Eleanor said. "Besides, Elizabeth was in California, as you know, and Winston . . ."

"He was the one raising the alarm," I pointed out.

Eleanor nodded. "Her money was in trusts, as far as I know. Winston was in charge of them. If he wanted her money, all he had to do was take it. And he was very careful with it. Grace used to call him Scrooge." She laughed, then looked embarrassed when she glanced toward Molly.

"Well, he was worried about something," Molly said.

She pulled out the letters her grandmother had sent her, and Eleanor read them one by one. As she did, I noticed that a batch of photos was also included, and I went through them. Most of them were of Winston with Grace.

"When were these taken?" I asked.

Eleanor looked at them. "That summer," she said. "Right before we left for Canada. Winston had come back in May for a visit and stayed."

"Was he planning on staying long?" Molly asked.

"He wasn't at first, then he changed his plans. And then he changed them again," Eleanor said. "Or at least I thought he had." She put the photos on the table in front of her. "All those years in that garden. That poor man. And to think I spoke ill of him at his mother's funeral. I thought he had left without saying good-bye to his dying mother. I thought it was the most selfish thing in the world."

I picked up the pile of photos and began going through them carefully. One immediately caught my eye. Winston and Grace posed in front of the rose garden, the very spot that would become his grave. But far from being the thick brush of weeds it had been since my childhood, the ground was covered in orange, pink, and yellow roses.

"It was lovely," I said.

"Wasn't it?" Eleanor glanced sadly at the photo. "I'm ashamed of myself for not keeping it up. I've just never been a gardener, and for so long I couldn't afford to pay anyone. It just got away from me and became the neglected mess that you and Oliver tried to clean up."

"Maybe if someone had been tending to it, they would have found Winston sooner," Molly said.

"Maybe," Eleanor answered her. Her face was neutral, even friendly, but there was a defiance to her voice that I was quite proud to hear.

CHAPTER 36

"I'm happy to report that we now have forty quilts promised to us for the show," I told the group at our Friday night meeting. "Many of them are reproductions, but we also have some genuine antiques that have been generously loaned to us. Ed offered us the movie theater as a space to hang quilts, so I intend to hang the antiques there to protect them. What we need to work on now is what we'll hang the quilts on, and also who will help me organize things that day."

I looked around, hoping for volunteers. No one was listening. The door had opened behind me and the newcomer was drawing everyone's attention.

"Sorry to be so late."

I turned to see Molly. Eleanor jumped up. "This is Grace's great-granddaughter. She's in town about poor Winston being found in the rose garden."

Though we hadn't discussed it, as I looked around the room, I could see that no one was surprised to hear Winston being identified as the skeleton, or of Molly being in town. Now that Eleanor knew, there was no sense in the rest of us pretending we didn't.

"Grab a chair and join us," I said. "There's coffee and cookies on the cutting table."

"I was looking at your quilts yesterday," Molly explained to the group, "and I thought they were just lovely."

Bernie leaned forward and studied her. "Are you a quilter?"

"No. Grace was the last quilter in the family."

"Maybe not," Maggie said. "We'll get you started, if you like."

And they did. Susanne and Carrie showed her patterns that

would be easy for a beginner and Eleanor helped Molly pick out fabrics. But I wasn't buying it, and when I looked over to Natalie, I could see she wasn't convinced either. I sat next to Natalie and we watched as the others ran around the shop finding all the tools that would turn Molly into a quilter.

"I've seen lots of non-quilters making their first pieces," Natalie said in a low whisper, "and they all have this excited, overwhelmed look in their eyes."

"And she doesn't," I agreed. "She's studying Eleanor. She thinks Eleanor killed Winston."

"But she has an alibi, I thought. She was in Canada."

"She was," I said. "Molly must assume Eleanor hired someone to kill him."

"That girl is nuts. The good news is Jesse is the best there is. He would never believe such a stupid theory."

Natalie and I crossed our arms and watched Molly wander the shop, making our suspicion of her as plain as we could. Not that anyone noticed. They were too busy indoctrinating the new recruit.

"So you knew Winston, too?" Molly was asking Maggie as they walked back toward us.

"Yes. When he was growing up, he came up from New York every summer with your grandmother and Grace. Very smart man. Very articulate." I could see Maggie straining to compliment a man she had disliked.

"And did you spend much time with him that last summer?"

"Not really. I saw him a few times when I visited Eleanor at the house. We had nothing in common, of course, so we rarely said anything more than hello to each other."

"What about Eleanor?" Molly asked.

"Eleanor and I have a lot in common, dear. That's why we've been friends for so many years." Maggie was being deliberately obtuse, and enjoying herself in the process.

"I mean Winston and Eleanor." Molly looked up at me and I smiled back. I knew she was looking for help, but as my expression made clear, she was looking for it from the wrong person.

Maggie seemed to be having fun, though. "You know, I've said many times there was no one fonder of Grace than Eleanor. And no one fonder of Eleanor than Grace," Maggie said. "When I see Eleanor now with Nell, and the relationship they have, I am often reminded of Grace and Eleanor. Eleanor was Nell's age then, and Grace's was Eleanor's age now." Maggie sighed. "Funny how time flies. It feels like just the other day I had small children running around the house, and now my grandchildren are having children. Did I show you a photo of my great-granddaughter?"

I could only sit back in admiration. Maggie had thrown Molly, who had been reduced to polite nodding and a strained smile. Of course, she'd used the photo of her family on me just a week ago, and I'd gotten just as confused.

Finally Molly got a word in. "I was thinking that I might try to retrace Winston's steps that last month he was here."

"How can you?" I asked. "Did you find a diary in the papers your grandmother sent?"

"No," she admitted, "but I have his letters and the photographs. I know he went to the bank several times and to the movie theater. I know he spent time at the house, obviously. And I know he got into an argument with Ed." Molly stood up. "The movie theater is still open, right? I know everything else in town is closed, but people go to movies on a Friday night, don't they?"

"The last movie on a Friday starts at 8:45," I told her, "so it's still playing. Ed should be there."

"Well, then I'll go talk to him."

"I've already asked him about Winston," I said, not adding that his answers apparently had been lies.

"I'm sure you did, Nell," she said, "but I'd like to talk to him myself."

Molly smiled a half smile, and for a second I could sense the same smugness that people disliked in Winston in his grandniece. She waved good-byes to the rest of the group, still gathering tools and fabrics for her, and headed out the door.

CHAPTER 37

After the meeting, I went to Jesse's house to talk with him about the night's events and let him tell me about his day. He was exhausted. Half the town had stopped by the police station, he told me, insisting he do something about all the vandalism. He'd spent much of the day explaining that he was trying, but no one seemed pleased with that answer. Least of all him.

"We've got a broken window at the school, books thrown about at the library, paint on Archer's headstone, a pentagram in front of the church, and a police car running into a fire hydrant," Jesse said as we curled up together in his bed. "What do they have in common?"

"Aside from being pretty small acts of vandalism?" I asked. "Nothing."

"Right. No one's house was broken into. Nothing has been stolen aside from a few pages from that book on Archers Rest history."

I sat up. "They're all aimed at institutions in town. The school, the library, the church, and our founder's grave. These are all places that matter to a lot of people in town, not just to one particular person. Whoever is doing this is trying to make a point about the town."

"What? That it's a bad place? Who feels that way?"

"Molly," I said.

"The school break-in happened before she got to town."

I leaned against his shoulder. "As far as we know, she may have come to town before the school break-in. She lied about why she was here, so maybe she lied about when she arrived."

"You don't like her," he said.

"I don't like that she seems to think Eleanor might have killed

Winston. And I don't like that you're giving her information about an ongoing police investigation."

"I give you information."

"That's hardly the same thing."

"Are you still jealous?" He was smiling.

"For heaven's sake, Jesse, I don't think for a second you're interested in a barely legal busybody, or that she's interested in an old man like you . . ."

"Hey . . ."

"But you have been feeding her details of the investigation. And when I think of all the times I've had to drag it out of you, it just seems unfair."

"One of the many things I've learned since we met, Nell, is that interested parties have a right to information. And Molly is an interested party. I'm not telling her anything I wouldn't tell you." He saw me about to protest. "In fact, I'm telling her a lot less than I tell you." He wrapped his arms around me.

"What are you telling me that you're not telling her?"

"I love you."

"About the investigation. What else about that?"

He sighed. "I think you're on to something about the institutions. Maybe I need to put men out patrolling the other churches in town, the post office, and city hall."

"City hall is next to the police station. I doubt anyone would vandalize the building next to the cops. They'd be caught in a second."

"It would make my job simpler."

"Or if you didn't catch the guy, it would make Glad and the mayor even more upset with you than they already are."

We made a halfhearted attempt at making love, but both of us were tired and our minds were elsewhere, so we just held each other and fell asleep watching television. Three hours later I was woken up by a particularly loud commercial. I wanted desperately to stay curled up in Jesse's arms, but I knew that if I did, I would stay until morning, so I got up.

"Come back to bed." Jesse reached an arm out toward me.

"Be quiet. Allie will hear you."

"I don't think it's safe for you to be going out there at night by yourself. Remember the note," he said. "And Allie has to find out sooner or later. Just stay. I'll explain it to her."

"Explain it to her first. Then I'll spend the night," I said. "I'll be fine." I kissed him on the forehead.

"I'll walk you to the car."

"It's parked outside your window. Just stay in bed. I'll be fine."

"Call me when you get home," he said.

"I'll wake you up."

He grabbed my hand. "Nell, I'll stay awake until you call me."

"Okay. As soon as I walk in my door."

>8

I drove down Jesse's street, turned the corner, and drove past darkened houses, past the cemetery, and into town, looking constantly for someone who might be up to no good. But there was no one.

I reached the town center, where all the shops were dark. As I passed the small square park that bordered Main Street, I saw that the base for Glad's statue had been poured. She was, apparently, going ahead with it despite the general lack of enthusiasm for the idea. Past the park, the movie theater was quiet, as were the bank and the travel agency. On Main Street, Jitters was closed, and as I turned to the other side of the street, I was expecting to see the same quiet darkness at Someday Quilts. But I didn't.

Something—someone—was lying on the ground.

I threw my car into park, leaving it in the middle of the street, and ran toward the figure.

"You okay?" I called out.

There was no answer.

I went closer. It was a woman. Young. Not moving.

"Molly?" I yelled. "Molly. Are you okay?"

The streetlight was just close enough that I could make out something odd about her dark brown hair. It was wet, but what had caused that I had no idea. Three steps closer and I had my answer. Blood. I leaned down and confirmed that Molly had been hit on the head with something.

"Molly?" I felt her pulse. It was there. Faint. But it was there. "Molly, I'm going to call an ambulance. Can you hear me? Can you understand?"

There was no response.

I grabbed my cell phone from my purse and dialed 9-1-1. Once they were on their way, I pressed the first number on my speed dial.

"You're home already? That was fast." Jesse's sleepy voice was cheerful and reassuring.

"I'm not home. I'm outside Someday Quilts. Molly O'Brien is hurt. I think it's bad."

"On my way."

"She's alive," Jesse said to me as I waited by the front door to Jitters. The ambulance with Molly inside had sped to the hospital moments before, and all of Jesse's officers were out combing the crime scene.

"Did she say anything to you?" I asked.

"No. How about you?"

"Nothing. I don't think she was conscious."

He grabbed me and held me tight. "I knew you shouldn't be out by yourself this late. I don't know what I would do if anything happened to you."

"I'm okay, Jesse." Though I wasn't sure if I felt okay.

"I'll tell you one thing. This isn't kids having fun." There was anger in his voice, and I was glad of it, because I felt just as angry.

"I can't imagine why anyone would do this. No one in town even knew her," I said.

"Maybe she was just in the wrong place at the wrong time."

"What was she doing back at the shop?"

"Maybe she was going to break in and look for clues," Jesse offered.

"Or maybe she caught someone else breaking in."

As I spoke, Jesse's phone rang. "The station," he told me as he answered it. "Yeah . . . where?" he said into the phone. "Are you kidding me? I'll be right there."

He hung up and turned to me. "There's been a break-in. And you won't believe where."

Remembering our earlier conversation, I said the first thing that popped into my mind. "City hall?"

Jesse slowly moved his head back and forth. "Worse. The police station."

CHAPTER 38

Only two of the Archers Rest police force had stayed behind at the station when the call about Molly came in. Six were off duty, and the other four were outside Someday Quilts, still working the scene for whatever evidence might have been left there.

"What happened?" Jesse's voice boomed with anger as we walked into the station.

The two officers practically tripped over each other offering excuses. They were both good guys—Tony, just out of the state police academy, and Mike, a part-time police officer, part-time auto mechanic with five years to go until retirement—but neither had Jesse's background as a New York police detective or his instincts about the job.

"We were up front," Tony said, "and we heard something in back, so we went back to investigate. The back door was open. Just wide open."

"Isn't it supposed to be locked?" Jesse asked.

The men looked at each other sheepishly.

"It's a shortcut to Jitters, if one of us needs to make a coffee run," Tony said. "I really thought we had locked it. I would have sworn it. But, I guess, we forgot to lock it when we came back after the last run."

"Which was when?"

"Hours ago, Chief. We haven't left the building since maybe eight," Mike said.

"Okay." Jesse glared, but he sounded calm. "So while you were both back there looking at an open door . . ."

"Yeah," Mike took over, "while we were back there, someone did that."

He pointed toward a brick that was lying near the broken front window of the station.

"So you didn't see anyone?" Jesse asked. "You didn't see the brick get thrown or anyone driving off? Anything?"

"We heard it," Tony offered.

"Anything unusual about what you heard?"

"No. It just sounded like a brick through a window."

I felt sorry for the guys, and even sorrier for Jesse, who looked ready to burst a blood vessel. But I was most interested in the brick.

"I think it has a note attached," I said as I walked over and bent down.

"Great. The criminals think we're such idiots that they have to help us out with notes," Jesse yelled. He turned to me. "Don't touch it, Nell. I'll do it."

After he made me, Mike, and Tony stand back, Jesse put on gloves and examined the brick. He pulled out a piece of paper that had been rolled up and stuck in a hole in the brick. "It's an old newspaper clipping."

I moved forward. "Of what?"

"It's an announcement of Glad Warren being named president of the Garden Club."

"What's on the back?"

Jesse turned it over. "An ad for a special showing of *The Exorcist* at Bryant's Cinema. Both stories have letters circled." He slowly read each letter out loud: "W—I—N—S—T—O—N."

"What do either of those things have to do with Winston's murder or what's going on now?" I asked.

"I don't know right now, but I'm going to find out."

After he'd made photocopies of both sides, Jesse put the clipping and the brick in evidence bags to be sent for fingerprints. Then he and I sat and studied the articles. The article on Glad was the standard one for a small-town newspaper. She was described as a leading citizen, an asset to the community, and a proud native of Archers Rest. Someone was quoted as saying that Glad knew all the Latin names for the flowers, making her the ideal choice for Garden Club president.

"Nothing here," I said. "What about the movie ad?"

"Nothing. It was shown as part of a week of classic horror movies.

Just a listing of times for the showing as well as a special offer for a T-shirt for anyone who went to all five movies that week: I SURVIVED HORROR WEEK AT BRYANT'S CINEMA." He pointed toward the corner of the ad, which featured an orange T-shirt with black lettering that dripped the way blood would. "I guess it was another one of Ed's promotions."

"Would you wear a T-shirt like that?" I asked.

"I'll wear anything if it's clean."

"So what was the person trying to say?"

I leaned back in my chair and closed my eyes for a moment. I was pretending to think, but really I was just tired. My eyes stung from lack of sleep and I couldn't focus anymore.

Jesse, on the other hand, was wide awake. "Someone is trying to point to Ed or Glad as suspects in Winston's murder."

"Then why not just say it, instead of sending cryptic messages tied to bricks?"

"Or maybe it's the killer's way of telling us that one of them is the next victim."

"Or if the killer is Glad or Ed, it could be a way to throw us off," I suggested.

Jesse grunted. "I think the real message is that the police of Archers Rest are such idiots that we can't catch a vandal even when he comes right to us."

✂

It was almost dawn when it suddenly occurred to me that Jesse had left Allie at the house by herself. Even though he was on the phone with the hospital, I walked over and mouthed the word *Allie*. He nodded, finished the call, and took my hand.

"I'm a terrible father," he said. "I pulled her out of bed, rang my mother's doorbell at three in the morning, and dumped my poor sleeping child into my mother's arms."

"At least she's okay," I said.

"This was not how it was supposed to be. Coming back here from New York. When I was a kid, this was such a quiet town. I thought it would be a nice place for Allie to grow up."

"It is a nice place," I said. "And you are a good father."

He leaned his forehead against mine. "And you're exhausted. I should get you home so you can get some sleep."

"I'm fine," I lied. "Everything will be okay."

I didn't know if I sounded as unconvinced as I felt.

CHAPTER 39

After a quick—and not terribly restful—two hours of sleep, I poured coffee into myself and headed toward Main Street. Someday Quilts wasn't open yet, and its exterior looked quiet and clean. One of the officers who had been at the scene the night before had washed the sidewalk down, removing the blood, though I could still see traces of it. It was hard to believe it had been just a few hours since I'd come across Molly lying at the spot, and harder still to believe that in just a few weeks a break-in at the school had escalated to violence. What was next I didn't want to think about.

Rather than go into the empty shop, I headed across the street to Jitters. Going there every morning had become a ritual for me, and I knew I wasn't alone in that.

"Rough night, Nell?" Ed peered at me over his newspaper. As always, his coffee and apple spice muffin were in front of him.

"Long night would be a better description," I said. "Have you talked to Jesse?"

"No. Does he need something?"

"I think he's just checking some things," I said.

I decided it would be better for me not to give Ed any information about the note or the brick. Whatever he was going to say to Jesse, I didn't want to give him a chance to rehearse it.

"Did you know that Molly O'Brien was attacked last night?" I asked.

"I did hear about an attack. A visitor in town. The mayor mentioned it when he came in this morning for his usual fix of caffeine and glad-handing."

"She's Winston's grandniece. Last night when she left Someday Quilts she was on her way to the movie theater to talk to you."

Ed frowned. "Why would she want to talk to me?"

"It was about the fight you had with Winston in the bank just before he disappeared."

Ed turned white. "I remember that. It wasn't anything."

"The police were called."

"Yes, they were."

"What was it about?"

"It was about the town. He was putting us down. Calling us uneducated hicks. I was a science teacher, Nell. I went to college. I've traveled. I didn't take to some rich kid calling me a hick."

"Was that the last time you saw him?"

"Yes, as far as I remember."

"And what about Molly?"

"She didn't come to the theater, Nell. Or if she did, I didn't see her. I was in the projection booth last night. It wasn't working correctly. Again."

"And you didn't hear anything or see anyone unusual last night?"

Ed paused. I wasn't sure if he was trying to remember or struggling to come up with an alibi. "I had a couple of people working the front, at the ticket counter and at concessions. They're both high school students, so they don't come in until late afternoon, but you can come by and ask them if she stopped in. But now I have to go to the bank. And this," he held up his muffin, "is sort of my last meal."

"Bad news at the bank?"

"Bad news everywhere, Nell." He smiled a half smile and headed out of Jitters and down Main Street in the opposite direction of the bank.

"How's Molly?" Carrie asked me when I reached the counter.

I gulped down the last of my drink and handed her the cup for a refill. "Jesse got word this morning that she's awake. She's stable, and the doctor thinks that she'll be able to answer questions this afternoon."

"Has she said what happened?"

"Not as far as I know," I said. "But considering how much blood there was last night, I'm just relieved she can say anything."

"Maybe she'll say who hit her, and that person will confess to being Winston's killer. Then we can put this whole mess behind us."

"Wouldn't that be nice," I said, even as I knew that it couldn't be that easy.

✂

We had to get the doctor's approval to talk with Molly. Although he told us the injury wasn't as serious as it looked the night before, the doctor made it clear she was being monitored carefully and needed to be treated with kid gloves—no stress, no long conversations. When we got into the room I was half expecting to see her wired to monitors, but she was sitting up, eating an individual serving of strawberry Jell-O, and watching TV.

"How are you feeling?" I asked.

"Not bad, considering. The doctor said I had a concussion and a gash at the back of my head." She turned her head to show us the bandage. "I need bed rest for a few days, but I'll be fine."

She was bruised and scratched, with several of her long, black fingernails broken off. She looked young and a little scared. And who could blame her?

"What happened?" Jesse asked.

"I don't know," she said. "I guess someone hit me."

"You didn't see anything?"

"No. I was walking down the street near the quilt shop. I heard someone behind me. The next thing I knew, Nell was standing over me, yelling my name."

"What were you doing at the shop?" I asked.

"I thought you guys might still be there."

"It was the middle of the night," Jesse said.

She shrugged. "I don't know. I just walked back there." She winced, either from pain or to avoid us pushing her further on the subject.

"Where did you go when you left the shop?" I asked her. "You said you were going to the movie theater."

"I did go. I asked someone at the ticket counter if I could talk to Ed, and she said he was in the projection booth. I wrote a note and she took it up to him. I thought maybe he would come down and talk to me, but he didn't. I waited about twenty minutes and then I left."

"What did the note say?"

"That I was Winston's grandniece and I believed he knew something that might help me solve Winston's murder. Stuff like that."

"But he didn't respond to the note?" Jesse asked.

"No. The girl came back down, but she was busy and I just left."

"Then where did you go?"

She seemed tired. Or maybe she just didn't want to answer. "I walked around. I've been so busy since I came to town that I haven't really seen anything. There wasn't much open, though, so I went to a place called Moran's Bar."

"You're not twenty-one," Jesse said.

"I had a Coke."

"Did you talk to anyone?" I asked. I noticed Jesse was tapping his leg, a sure sign he was getting impatient, so I stepped closer to Molly. "Or leave Moran's with anyone?"

"I talked to the bartender. And not about anything in particular. He told me that Jesse was overwhelmed with everything that had been happening all over town. He said we needed to get county police in here if the vandalism was going to stop."

"And that was it?" Jesse's voice had an edge to it.

She sat up a little straighter. "I saw the mayor, but I don't think he saw me. He was talking to that woman from the committee meeting, and they seemed very serious."

"Glad?" I asked. "The woman who turned you down for a job at the historical society."

Molly lowered her eyes a little and nodded.

"Did you talk to them?" Jesse asked.

"No. Like I said, I don't think they even saw me."

"But you talked to the mayor earlier," I said. "What did you say to him then?"

"Nothing. I just asked about my uncle. And I told him I was

expecting some letters from my grandmother that might shed light on the whole situation."

"Did you tell anyone else about the letters?"

"In the note I left for Ed," she said. "And Nell and Eleanor know about them."

"Where are those letters?" Jesse asked.

"In my tote bag." She looked around at the edges of her bed. "It must be in the room somewhere, or maybe the nurse could tell you what they did with my stuff."

I shook my head, remembering the scene from last night. "You didn't have your bag with you when I found you," I said.

"Someone took my bag?" Molly sat up and the pressure seemed to pain her. "Winston's letters. They were all my grandmother had left of him. And they're gone?"

CHAPTER 40

"It could have been a simple mugging," I said to Jesse on the way back to the police station.

"It could have been."

"She said she had twenty dollars in her purse plus her ATM card. Someone could have stolen her purse looking for that."

"Makes sense."

"But you don't believe that."

"No."

"Why?" I asked.

"A dark-haired young woman standing outside of Someday Quilts. In the middle of the night . . ."

"You think someone could have mistaken Molly for me?"

"You did get that threatening note."

"Yeah, but . . ." I didn't have an answer for that. It was possible that in the dark someone might have made that mistake. "She was hit from behind, so I guess the attacker might not have realized it was Molly."

"Winston also was hit over the head," he said, "and from behind."

"You think it's the same person?"

"I don't know," he said. "But when we were talking about Molly's tote bag, it made me wonder about something else. What happened to Winston's stuff? If he didn't leave for South America, wouldn't his passport and clothes have been at the house? Wouldn't Eleanor have found them when she and Grace returned from Nova Scotia?"

"I don't know," I admitted.

"It has to be asked." He sounded stern and ready for a fight.

"I know. But you might want to ask in a different tone of voice, because if I know my grandmother, she's not going to be as patient and understanding as I am."

He smiled. "I'll keep that in mind."

✂

Ten minutes later we were at Someday Quilts, asking Eleanor the question that Jesse had asked in the car.

"All of his things were gone," she said. "He'd told me that he was planning to make a trip to Lima, Peru. He had some work at a university there and he wanted to retrieve it. Something for a new book he was writing. Then he was going to come back. When Grace and I returned from Nova Scotia in August, he wasn't there, but we weren't expecting him to be there. I thought he had gone to Peru. And when he didn't return, I assumed he'd decided to stay."

"It didn't strike you as odd," Jesse asked, "that he never came back?"

"As I told Nell, I thought it was cruel for his mother not to have a chance to say good-bye. But aside from that, his staying in South America seemed perfectly logical."

"Why?"

Eleanor nearly smiled but didn't. She could not be pushed around or intimidated. "Because it did, Jesse. Winston loved South America, and he did not love Archers Rest."

"And you had no correspondence with him while you were away. No letters or telegrams or anything."

"It was 1975, for heaven's sake. We may not have been able to text each other or . . . what is that thing with the birds?"

"Twitter," I said.

"Right, but we had the telephone. We didn't need smoke signals or the pony express to communicate."

"So did you speak to him by phone?"

Jesse was annoyed at Eleanor, and I was annoyed at Jesse for being annoyed at Eleanor. Eleanor was the only one of us who seemed relaxed.

"What are you asking her?" I stepped in.

"I'm asking her if she spoke to him by phone."

"Once," Eleanor said. "When we arrived at the house where we were staying in Canada, I called to let him know we were there. Winston and I spoke for a few minutes before I handed the phone over to Grace. He didn't say anything of consequence. He didn't seem worried about anything. He just asked how the flight was and how my children were. He told me he was making arrangements for his trip. As far as I can recall, that was the extent of it. It was an ordinary call in every way except it turned out to be the last time he spoke to his mother."

"Did he leave you a number to reach him in Peru?"

"No. He was supposed to, but he didn't. That was why I wasn't able to contact him when Grace died." She paused. "Well, it wasn't why, clearly, but it was why it didn't raise any alarm bells. I had no way of knowing he didn't arrive in Lima, and neither did his sister. She was more used to his running off than I was, so she thought nothing of it. And because she wasn't worried, neither was I."

"And there's nothing else, Eleanor?" Jesse asked. "Nothing that you can add."

"If I knew something that would shed light on Winston's death, I would tell you," she said. "But I don't."

Jesse nodded. He stepped back from my grandmother and glanced at me. His eyes were sheepish. He'd overstepped some invisible line, somehow accused my grandmother of something, and he knew it. He was looking for me to tell him that it was okay. I hesitated, just for a moment thinking that maybe I should tell him off, but then I took his hand.

"You're just doing your job, Jesse," I said as I kissed him on the cheek. "You're completely wrong and you're wasting your time, but no hard feelings."

He kissed me back. "Something doesn't make sense," he whispered in my ear.

And then he left the shop, leaving Eleanor and me to stand in awkward silence.

I turned from Eleanor and instead watched Jesse walk down the street toward the police station. As I did, I saw Ed walking toward Jitters.

"Did something happen between you and Ed Bryant?" I asked Eleanor.

"Is this another interrogation? Because I'm quite finished answering questions for the day."

Her tone was calm but unmistakable in its certainty. Too bad for her I could be just as stubborn.

"So something did happen," I said.

"Like what?"

"A love affair?"

"You have one theory after another, Nell. Your imagination might be put to better use designing quilts than delving into my uninteresting past."

"But you did, at some point, date someone, maybe love someone?"

"At some point I did something with someone, yes. That very statement could apply to you."

"It could, but I'm not defensive about it."

"Neither am I. And I don't want to fight with you, Nell. I have a lot of work to do if I'm going to leave this place to you in just under a month. I have to put in fabric orders. I have to do inventory. And there's a pile of unpaid bills that must be paid or I won't get any sleep tonight."

I wasn't going to be moved off the subject. I blocked her path to her office. "Was it Winston?"

"Now I had an affair with Winston?" she asked. "First Ed, now Winston. Didn't I get around?"

"Well, did you have an affair with Winston?"

"What kind of a question is that for you to ask your grandmother?"

"A completely supportive and nonjudgmental question."

"No, Nell. On my children's lives, I did not have an affair with Winston Roemer," she said. "And I didn't kill him, either, just in case that's your next question."

"Do you know if he was having an affair with anyone in town?"

She looked at me. "What do you think of me, Nell?"

"I don't understand the question."

"Do you think I'm a good person?"

"You're the best. You're the kindest, strongest, most decent human being I know."

She smiled. "I would say the same thing about you." She took a breath. "Would I intrude on your life like this? Demand to know answers to things that are none of my business?"

"You do it every day."

"Well, then that's a bad example."

CHAPTER 41

Eleanor was deliberately avoiding my questions, and by extension, me. Just as I was about to push her harder, she suddenly remembered the shop needed pens and sent me out to buy more. We didn't need pens, and we both knew that. She just wanted to get rid of me.

I stood outside the shop, wondering if I should go back in and confront her again, or just recognize that I was outmatched.

"Are you okay?"

I looked up to see Maggie.

"I told her," I said, "about it being Winston."

"And what did she say?"

"Nothing. Nothing useful."

"Maybe you should just let this whole thing drop."

"It was a murder."

"Years before you were even born. Weren't you going to stay out of it, Nell? Isn't that what you said when the skeleton was discovered?"

"That was before Molly O'Brien was insinuating that my grandmother was involved. There's no statute of limitations on murder, Maggie. Eleanor could be in serious trouble if she knows something . . ."

"That's an excuse to get in the middle of it. You hate not having answers. But you have to learn at some point or another that in life you don't get all the answers. You don't get—whatever that word is," she paused, "closure. Things are messy and difficult and sometimes you live with not knowing."

"So I should just cross my fingers and hope that Eleanor isn't arrested?"

Maggie scowled. "Seriously, Nell, is there any real possibility that Jesse will arrest Eleanor?"

"No," I admitted.

"Then let it go. Eleanor and Oliver are happy and looking forward to a wonderful trip together. Maybe it's not the wedding we'd hoped for, but it's what they want. Let's just be happy for them and not let our egos get in the way of their future."

She was right. Even someone who didn't know Eleanor could see that she had no reason to kill Winston, and a solid alibi for the time he disappeared. She wasn't in danger of being arrested. It was just me and my get-in-the-middle-of-everything ways. I sighed, determined to put my focus on the quilt show and nothing else.

But just as I vowed to stay out of things, I noticed something that was reflecting the sunlight. On the ground, next to the shop's door, was a campaign button. I leaned down and picked it up. ARCHERS REST: 350 YEARS OF AMERICAN LIFE.

I opened my purse and dug through it. Stuck in a corner was another button with exactly the same words on it, the one I'd gotten at the committee meeting.

"Maggie, do you still have that button the mayor gave us?"

"I suppose." Maggie went through her purse and took out a button. "Are you collecting them?"

"No. Just wondering."

I looked again at the button I'd found. My fingers felt something on the back of it, and when I turned it over I saw a small piece of black plastic.

"What is that?" Maggie asked.

"Part of a fake fingernail."

I had a choice to make. I could take the button I'd found to Jesse, or I could go looking for answers myself. I could have pretended to struggle with it, but I knew from the moment I recognized the button what I was going to do. Despite all my best efforts, I couldn't help myself.

✄

Maggie headed into Someday Quilts and I took a short walk to the hardware store, owned by the mayor's sons. One of them was making keys and the other was unpacking boxes. Neither had seen their father. I went around the corner to the Williams Travel Agency, the first business Larry Williams had created. Aside from the travel agency, it also housed his insurance and tax businesses. But its real function was as the unofficial mayor's office.

As I was walking in, Larry walked out, looking tired and annoyed. As soon as he saw me, though, he put on a politician's smile. "Nell Fitzgerald. Are you here about the anniversary celebration or thinking of taking a trip?"

"Neither, actually. I'm here about this." I held up the button. "Do you have a minute?"

"I need to get to city hall."

"It will only take a minute."

He frowned. "Walk with me and tell me some good news."

The day was getting warmer and the mayor, despite his extra weight, could walk faster than me. I found myself sweating just to keep up with him.

"Have you spoken with Eleanor about having some photographers at her place?" he asked.

"Not yet. But I did talk to Molly. She told me she saw you and Glad in Moran's last night."

"How is she? I heard she'd been injured when she encountered one of those hooligans that have been vandalizing town property."

"There's no proof that it was one of the vandals. She doesn't know who hit her."

"But she'll be okay?"

"Yes. It seems that she'll be fine."

"Poor thing, after coming up here to see about her uncle." He looked over at me. "Is it for sure then, that it's Winston Roemer?"

"Jesse's still waiting on the final DNA results, but from everything we've found it seems likely it's Winston Roemer. What do you remember about him?"

"I was the gardener over at the Roemer house when I was a kid. My father had a local business, tending to the summer homes of folks like the Roemers."

"What was he like?"

"He was a lot older than me. I was just out of high school the last time I saw him, and he was a grown man. An accomplished man.

I don't think he and I exchanged ten words in the whole time he came to the house."

"I've heard he wasn't a nice man. I guess he wasn't nice to you."

"Why would he be? I hardly appeared to him as the kind of person who would end up, well, where I ended up."

"As mayor, you mean?"

"And a successful businessman. I was just the help."

"Glad didn't see you that way, either, did she? Is that why she broke up with you?"

Larry smiled. "You do have the most curious way of asking a question, Nell. I think you find a reason to be suspicious of everyone."

"Why would I be suspicious of you?" I asked.

"I have a feeling that's what you came to talk to me about."

CHAPTER 42

"She was a good woman, that Mrs. Roemer. And so is your grandmother. Eleanor knew I wanted to go to college and couldn't afford it, so she tutored me. It was she who got me interested in history. Helped me get a scholarship and gave me a new direction for my life."

"But the other day, you hinted at something . . . Eleanor wanted to keep hidden," I said.

"I was just bluffing. Eleanor was—and is—a true friend to everyone in town. You should know that better than anyone."

I loved hearing of how Eleanor had helped the people in town. But it also made me feel a little inferior. Eleanor was known for her strength and selflessness. I was mostly known for being curious and headstrong.

But I also noticed like any good politician, Larry had changed the subject to one he wanted to talk about.

"But there were people in town who didn't like Winston," I said.

He ignored my statement. "You said you weren't a hundred percent sure it was his body."

"No. Not one hundred percent."

"Then maybe this should be kept under wraps."

"I don't think that's possible. It's pretty much all over town by now."

"That's just the town, not anywhere else." He seemed to be formulating a plan, and I was pretty sure I wanted no part of it. "You have influence with Jesse."

"Not that much influence. He wouldn't delay an investigation to please me, and I wouldn't ask him to."

"But you could steer him in a different direction. You always have a lot of wild theories about things."

"I don't think I *always* do . . ." I started, but we were getting off track. "But even if I do, Jesse doesn't. He's very serious about doing his job. And he's very good at it."

"No argument there. I'm just thinking that Jesse could stretch this out a little, give it a little play, as they say in the news business. I'd rather he find out whoever is behind this crime spree we're having. Vandalism and theft, that's bad publicity. No way to spin that."

"I agree."

"Which is why he focuses on the crimes and I hint to the world that we have uncovered something quite interesting in the backyard of one of our leading citizens. If the identity can't be hidden at this point, that's okay. We can use it to our advantage. We can plant stories about the old days when a lot of prominent families used to summer up here. A bit of nostalgia, a few ghost stories . . ." He was getting excited.

"I don't know if that's in good taste, Mayor. Considering what happened to Molly. A visitor to town gets attacked and left for dead. That's the kind of bad publicity you want stopped, isn't it?"

"Of course."

"This was found near where Molly had been hit." I showed him the button again. "The other day you handed out one each to the members of the committee."

"So what?"

"Is that all the buttons there are?

"For the moment. The rest are ordered. They'll be here a week before the celebration."

"So someone who was in that committee room dropped this button at the spot where Molly was hurt. And Molly's fingernail got stuck in it, maybe when she pulled it off her attacker."

"Exactly what I'm talking about, Nell. You and your wild theories. It could be the button I handed you."

"It wasn't. I still have mine. Maggie still has hers. That leaves you, Glad, and Ed."

"And Molly."

"She gave hers to Dru Love over at the library."

"Well, then any one of us could have walked past your grand-mother's shop and dropped it. Or given the button away. Or thrown it away. That's the sort of thing Ed would do."

"Where's yours?"

He stopped. "Not on me, if that makes me a suspect. It's probably in my office."

"You still haven't explained about last night. Molly saw you in a serious conversation with Glad at Moran's, and it's not the first time the two of you have met in secret."

"It was perfectly innocent, but coming out of your mouth it sounds like something clandestine. Not that I mind. Might be great for my reputation. People think my only interests are my businesses and the future of Archers Rest. I was thinking of taking up golf if I could find the time for it, but I don't know where I can . . ."

I wasn't letting him take me to a safer subject twice. "What were you doing with Glad?"

"Dog with a bone, Nell Fitzgerald," he said. "Glad and I are both very committed to making this anniversary celebration a success. It's more work than either of us imagined and she's a little—no, make that a lot—concerned about it coming off without a hitch. She's wor-ried some of our team chairs don't have the right experience."

"I'm aware." I winced a little at the insult but kept up my line of questioning. "Is that what you were talking about at the library? Am I the 'ridiculous woman' she was afraid would ruin everything?"

"Yes, but not just you. Everyone. Glad's a control freak. She's decided to install window boxes around town, painted in a bright red, with white and blue flowers. She's very insistent about the color scheme, at least that's what I heard."

"What you heard? She didn't talk about it with you?"

"I only heard about it because she bought the paint from my son's hardware store. She told him. But why should she tell me? I'm only the mayor."

"Your son told Jesse that no one had bought red paint recently."

He took a breath. "I know what you're thinking, Nell, but Glad wouldn't deface Archer's grave. You have no idea how many times we've discussed that very event. Given how Glad's purchase could be misinterpreted, my son and I thought it would be better if she didn't have to explain herself."

"Why? If she has nothing to hide . . ."

"She has a reputation to uphold, and enough trouble doing so considering the sort of things that are said about her sister. She asked that we not mention it, and we didn't. That's all."

"That's what you're talking about? Her reputation?" I asked. "Not old times?"

He laughed. "Not that it's any of your business."

"You're right. I'm sorry," I said. "It's none of my business. It's just Mary Shipman . . ."

"That's an interesting lady."

"Yes, she is. She mentioned that you and Glad had dated."

"A lifetime ago. We were kids. Glad was . . ." He searched for a word. "Less formal, less offended by the world. She was even fun, if you can believe it."

"I'm not sure I can," I admitted. "Mary said her father didn't see you together either."

"Hated the idea of it. Thought I wasn't good enough for her. He did everything he could think of to break us up."

"It obviously worked."

"No, it didn't, actually." He stopped walking and looked down for a moment at the pavement, smiling sadly. "We were madly in love. We were seventeen, eighteen, so you have to put that in context, of course. Her father couldn't keep us apart." He sighed. "We put an end to it ourselves after about nine months of serious puppy love. Our differences started to matter, and we found ourselves fighting. The last one over a Yankees game. I wanted to go to New York on the day her mother was having a tea or some such nonsense. She said if I went to the game, it was over, and I went to the game anyway. That was it." He shrugged and started walking briskly again. "Eight months later, I walked into an ice cream shop and met a girl named Bunny Giordano. You know her better as Mrs. Williams. We've had thirty years of wedded bliss, so I'd appreciate your not suggesting otherwise."

I'd only met the mayor's wife twice, but I had to admit that both times the couple seemed devoted to each other. Which didn't mean he was telling the truth about his meetings with Glad—only that there might be something more dangerous than an affair going on between them.

We were at the steps to city hall, a one-story brick building that housed the mayor's official office, as well as the city council meeting room and the Archers Rest Historical Society.

"I heard Mary Shipman threatened to blow this place up once," I said.

"At least once." He chuckled and headed up the steps and into the building.

CHAPTER 43

I was next door to the police station, so I stopped in and told Greg, the detective in charge, about the button I'd found with Molly's fake nail still stuck under the pin. He put it in an evidence bag and promised to tell Jesse once he returned from a meeting with Glad about security during the anniversary celebration.

As I walked out of the station, I had a weird feeling. For the third time in weeks, I felt as if I were being watched. I looked around. It was a bright, warm day and there were people on the streets, but no one was paying any particular attention to me.

I took a deep breath and made a few careful steps toward Main Street. As I did, I kept an eye on everyone around me—even on the buildings that I passed. I couldn't see anyone that should concern me. But I could *feel* it.

I walked slowly down Main Street, toward the river. If someone was following me, it would be harder to do once there were open spaces and fewer people. I headed toward the park, keeping myself near the edge of the river, looking around as discreetly as possible. No one was there, yet I felt as if I weren't alone.

Finally, I couldn't stand it anymore. I turned around, hoping to catch whoever was behind me. But there was no one. There was a patch of trees behind me. I could have searched them, but suddenly the idea scared me.

Keeping myself from breaking out into a run and reminding myself that this was broad daylight, I turned back toward the town center and kept walking until I reached Jitters.

"Anyone behind me?" I asked Carrie when I walked inside.

"Behind you how?"

"Watching me?"

She looked behind me. "No. What's going on?"

"Nothing, I guess. I'm just chasing my tail. I was talking—"

"Oh my God." Carrie was standing behind the counter pouring a cup of coffee, but she was focused on whatever was going on outside her window.

I turned. Ed was standing outside Someday Quilts talking, and laughing, with Eleanor.

"I guess Glad was lying," Carrie said.

"I guess so."

We watched as Ed and Eleanor hugged, and then he walked down the street.

"I'll pay for this later," I said as I grabbed my coffee and ran off after him.

I wasn't sure if I was following him or trying to catch up, so I kept a normal pace. Ed walked briskly, like a man with an appointment to keep. I've seen dozens of movies where people trail a suspect. They follow closely, and duck into doorways or between buildings when they're about to be caught. Unfortunately for me, all the doorways along Main Street are flat to the sidewalk, and there are no spaces between the buildings, so I tried to look casual, and kept walking. I was feeling pretty good about my ability to follow someone unde-tected, when Ed turned around to face me, just as he reached the theater.

"Hi there, Nell," he said. "Lovely day."

"It is. Nice day for a movie, I suppose."

"Today? No. Too much sunshine and summer breezes for sitting in air-conditioning. No one will come for a movie today. Might as well keep the place closed."

"I wanted to ask if I could take you up on your offer to display some quilts in your theater. It has so much space in the lobby, and it would be great to keep the antique quilts indoors."

"Absolutely. I'm happy to help." He paused. "Is that it?"

"Yeah. Were you out taking a walk?"

"Yes. Just over at the park. I love to watch the kids on the swings, don't you? But I have to admit, I'm always very tempted to jump on one myself. I used to love that as a kid. The freedom I had when I would swing high, as if I were soaring into outer space. You know what I mean?"

"Sure," I said.

His whole attitude was light and playful, like a kid on Christmas morning. As he spoke, he rocked a little, and when he opened the door to the theater, he hummed. If I hadn't known Ed had just been talking to my grandmother, I'd say he was a man in love.

After he told me about the playground, he smiled, turned his back on me, and headed into the theater. I stood there long enough to hear him bolt the door.

✁

"So Ed lied to you," Natalie said when I told her about the conversation.

"And for the second time. Eleanor and Ed were laughing and hugging not five minutes before."

We were at the back of Someday Quilts, whispering and hoping that the sound of the longarm machine would keep Eleanor, who was at the front of the shop, from overhearing.

"They weren't just hugging outside," Natalie told me. "They were talking for about twenty minutes."

"About what?"

"I don't know. Ed came in looking for her, so I sent him back to her office. She closed the door. I couldn't hear a thing."

That deflated me. That, and the feeling that I had to rely on eavesdropping to find out about my own grandmother. Eleanor was hiding something from me. It wasn't that she couldn't have parts of her life that were none of my business. Of course she could. But she had never been anything other than direct and open—until now.

"I did hear one thing," Natalie said. "I don't know what it meant."

"What?"

"When they were walking out of her office, I heard Ed say that *she* had done exactly as Eleanor had instructed."

"She who?"

"He didn't say. Eleanor told him to be sure that she kept it up. She said to do a little bit every day, nothing too big, just enough to keep the momentum going."

"A little bit of what, I wonder?"

"I don't know, but as they were walking out the door, Eleanor said that Glad was next."

"Glad was next for what?"

Natalie threw her hands up. "Nell, stop asking me questions I don't know the answers to. I told you everything I overheard. After Eleanor said that about Glad, she and Ed went outside the shop."

"That's when I saw them hugging and laughing," I said.

"What could they be doing?"

"Whatever they're doing, they certainly don't hate each other."

"Then why would Glad say they did?" Natalie asked. "And why is she next?"

"It's not so much why that concerns me," I said. "It's what. What will happen to Glad?"

"I don't know, but whatever happens, it will be because Eleanor told Ed to make it happen."

CHAPTER 44

The answer to what would happen to Glad came just a few days later. I was in the middle of a great dream, getting my first good night's sleep in days, when my cell phone rang at 6:25 AM.

"Is somebody dead?" I asked as I answered the phone. "Because it's too early to call for any other reason."

"Nice way to say good morning," Jesse answered back.

"Good morning."

"Can you meet me at the park?"

"Now?"

"Now."

✄

I hung up and got dressed as quickly as possible. Since Barney was whimpering by the door, I grabbed his leash and took him with me. It was a beautiful morning, and I was enjoying the walk enough to let Barney sniff at his leisure, a delay I hoped Jesse would understand. June was midway through and the flowers were in bloom. It would have been the perfect day for a romantic picnic breakfast, but I knew by the tone in Jesse's voice that romance was not on his mind.

When Barney and I arrived at the park, Jesse and several of his officers were huddled around the area where the John Archer statue was supposed to be erected in a few weeks.

"What happened?" I asked as I arrived.

"Look for yourself," Jesse said, and pointed toward the base for the statue.

A poster-size photo of Glad with a knife stuck through it was secured to the base. The word *killer* was spray-painted in red across the photo.

"That's bizarre," I said. "Who would do that?"

"The town vandal," Jesse offered.

"It seems fairly elaborate, doesn't it? I mean, the person would have to get a photo, get it blown up . . ."

"A service unfortunately not available in our little town," Jesse said, "so it's going to be fun to try to track down where it was done."

"And this is different from the other things. This is personal."

"So was hitting Molly over the head," Jesse reminded me.

"Assuming it's the same person."

"I hope it is, Nell. Otherwise we have at least two people running around town. One hurting property and one hurting people."

Jesse stepped back as one of his detectives took photos of the scene.

"You haven't heard of any threats against Glad, have you?" he asked.

"Are you kidding?" I said. "I've been close to killing her a few times myself."

He rested his hand on my waist, a simple action that felt so reassuring. "Molly gets out of the hospital this afternoon, so that's something. Except I'm not comfortable letting her stay on the hill."

"On the hill" was the town expression for an old colonial-era home that was the one bed-and-breakfast we had. It was a small place on the edge of town, only a block from Mary Shipman's home.

"I can ask Eleanor," I said, reluctantly. We often had people staying at my grandmother's large house, but they generally didn't suspect her of killing their relatives.

"If you could," he said. "And if you have any theories about this . . ."

"I don't."

I debated briefly about whether to tell him of the conversation between Ed and Eleanor that Natalie had overheard. I felt that by telling him I would be betraying Eleanor, though not telling Jesse also felt like a betrayal of sorts. I decided that I would delay sharing the information until I'd had a chance to speak with Eleanor.

I left Jesse and the other officers and walked to Someday to drop Barney off at the shop when Eleanor came out into the street, her face red and angry.

"There are people at the house," she said. "I got a call from the neighbors. There are people walking all over the backyard and jumping into the hole."

"I'll go there and stop it."

"Take him with you, as protection," she said, pointing to our nearly deaf, slightly addled dog.

"I'll take him, but I don't think I'll need the help. It's just the mayor," I said. "I forgot that he asked me to ask you for permission to take photos of the backyard."

"I would have said no if you had asked me."

"That's what I told him."

"Well, now go tell those people trampling on my property," she said. "Imagine, exploiting poor Winston for tourism. What is happening to people?"

"I don't know. It's getting crazy. Jesse just showed me something in the park. Someone had put a knife through a photo of Glad and spray-painted the word *killer* on it," I said.

I knew my grandmother well enough to know the shocked look on her face was genuine—at least, I hoped I knew her well enough. After reassuring her that I would put a stop to whatever was going on at the house, I left her at the shop and ran home.

✂

As I passed the movie theater, I saw a woman walk inside. Though I couldn't see her face, I could make out a distinctive silver bracelet dangling from her arm—it was the same one Mary Shipman had worn the day I went to her house.

When I arrived at the house, I saw two cars parked in the driveway. I recognized the mayor's, but the other car was new to me. I ran to the back, and just as had been reported by the neighbors, there were three men milling about: the mayor, a man who was talking to him, and a photographer taking photos of everything from the rose garden to the back of the house.

"This is private property," I shouted. "And none of you have permission to be here."

"I told you to ask Eleanor if it was okay," Larry said.

"And she said no," I told him. "And I say no. This was a man's grave, Mayor, and the site of an open murder investigation. This isn't a tourist attraction."

As I spoke, the photographer snapped a photo of me.

"I'll call Jesse and have all of you arrested for trespassing if you take one more photo or stay on this property one more minute."

"Now, Nell, don't upset yourself," the mayor said. "This is news. Big news. A leading citizen of Archers Rest spent more than thirty years buried in the backyard of one of our most beautiful and historical homes. Don't you think people will want to read about that in the city papers?"

"Don't care."

He turned to the two men with him. "Nell Fitzgerald is our town's favorite amateur sleuth. She and the police chief often collaborate on investigations, among other things." He chuckled. "Perhaps you would like to be interviewed. Give your take on the story. Everyone likes a little publicity."

"You want publicity, Mayor? Then maybe I should talk with these men about the library, the school, the pentagram at the church, Molly O'Brien, and what's happening at the park right now. You want that kind of publicity?"

The mayor pursed his lips. "I think we have enough for now, gentlemen. Why don't we take some photos of our beautiful Main Street?"

The men walked ahead, but the mayor stayed behind and whispered to me, "What's happening in the park?"

"Someone stabbed a photo of Glad," I said.

"I don't understand why someone would do that."

"Neither do I," I admitted. "But I have a feeling it's not the last thing that's going to happen before your big celebration gets under way."

CHAPTER 45

It took a few more minutes with the photographer frantically taking pictures before I could get them off the property. It was just a garden, and just a hole in the ground, but it was such an invasion of Eleanor's privacy, and of Winston's.

I sat on the grass near the torn-up rose garden and looked at the overgrown weeds, the black dirt, and the empty space that for so many years had held Winston's body. Three hundred and fifty years ago, John Archer had felt driven to leave New York because of rumors about him, and now Mary Shipman seemed to hide herself away because people thought her odd. Winston hadn't been a likeable man, at least to the people of Archers Rest, but had he been so unlikable that he deserved to die? They were all people, it seemed to me, who were honest about who they were—and paid a price for it. So far the only price I paid for my reputation was a little teasing from the folks in town, but maybe it was better to hide who I was and just fit in. It certainly would be safer.

✂

I decided to head back to the quilt shop and an afternoon of sewing to clear my head, but five minutes after I'd left the house, I got a call from Jesse that meant I had to turn around. Molly had been released from the hospital, and he was bringing her over. I called Eleanor at the shop and got her approval for the scheme, quickly changed the sheets on my bed, and threw some of my clothes on the sofa bed in the sewing room. Much as I didn't care for Molly's suspicions, I couldn't let someone just out of the hospital sleep on the lumpy mattress in that couch. Then I went downstairs and put the kettle on.

When she arrived, with a bandage on her head, Molly, Jesse, and I sat down for tea and some Oreos, the only cookies I could find in the house.

"My grandmother will be appalled I didn't serve you anything homemade," I said.

"I don't want anyone to go to any trouble. But I do feel a bit safer here than I would at the hotel."

"If someone is trying to hurt you," Jesse said, "then that's where they'll look for you. But we'll keep your being here under wraps. Eleanor and Nell won't tell anyone."

He looked toward me, and I nodded.

Molly got up and walked to the back window. "Is that where?" She pointed toward the dug-up rose garden.

"Yes," I said. "It was really beautiful when Grace lived here. There were bushes of huge roses, yellow and pink and a really pretty orange. It's small comfort, but it was a quiet place for him to rest."

"I suppose. But seeing it just makes me want to know more. I feel like I owe him that much."

Jesse stood up. "Molly, what you can do for him is rest and recover. You got a bad blow to the head. You're just lucky that all it did was cut your skin and give you a mild concussion. It could have been much, much worse."

"It could have been fatal," she said, not taking her eyes off the rose garden.

"And to make sure that there isn't a follow-up, I need you to stay here. Out of sight and out of trouble," he said.

She nodded. "I have no intention of getting myself killed."

Jesse looked to me. "Do you want to walk me out, Nell?"

"Okay. There's more tea, Molly," I said, but she was lost in thought.

Jesse and I were at the front door before he stopped me. "If you were her, would you stay here and rest or would you be more determined to find out what happened?"

I bit the inside of my cheek. "I don't think you want to know my answer."

"I was afraid of that. I'm going to send one of my guys over to watch the house. Not so much to keep anyone from getting in, but to keep her from going out."

"I assume I can still go out," I said.

He brushed a stray hair from my cheek. "I know better than to try to stop you."

✂

After Molly's police protection arrived, I went back to the shop and collected the reproduction and antique quilts that some of our regulars were already dropping off. The quilt show was more than two weeks off and I already had sixteen quilts ready to hang.

It was as comforting as ever to spend my time looking at quilts. As much as I wanted to worry and stress about a growing collection of questions, I soon got lost in the fabric choices and the beautiful stitching.

They were an amazing group of quilts. The antique ones dated back to the Depression, and I had promises for quilts from just after the Civil War. But I also had quilts made in the 1970s, 80s, and even ones made less than ten years before. Even though most of the older quilts didn't have labels to identify who had made them, each quilt provided insight into its maker—a collection of choices in color and pattern that revealed the true passions of the woman behind it.

Some, like the log cabin quilt in bright blues and purples, were exciting and lively, even as a close examination revealed wobbly rows, large stitches, and mismatched seams.

"A beginner who wasn't afraid of color," I said to myself. "That's someone who plunges in headfirst, without a worry about right or wrong."

Another quilt was a small star pattern, with a carefully planned-out color scheme of reds and taupes. Intricate appliquéd flowers bordered the quilt.

"An expert," I decided. "Someone who likes order. Someone with discipline and patience."

"Who are you talking to?" Natalie asked.

"I'm determining the personality of each of these quilt makers. It's amazing what you can tell about a person by their quilts."

"I suppose it's always been a place for people to let their guard down, just be themselves," she said. "I think we all get so caught up in what other people need us to be that it's easy to forget what we need. I know when I quilt it's one of the rare times when I'm truly seeking only to please myself."

"Mary Shipman was suggesting I try to do that," I said. "When I talked to her in her kitchen she said I needed to be comfortable with who I am, as the town busybody . . ."

"You only are a busybody if it's for a good cause . . ."

"Maybe, but her point was that it made me uncomfortable to be seen that way. She said that my worrying about what other people thought was getting in my way. It was weird how she picked up on that, because I've been thinking about it a lot lately."

"Did she give you a potion to cure it?"

"She's not a witch, Natalie."

"That's too bad. I was hoping she'd cast a spell over the baby when it's born, so it will sleep through the night from day one."

"I think she was trying to tell me something," I said.

"Something other than what she actually said."

"Yeah. Something about Winston's murder. Maybe someone is not showing who they really are."

"Like?"

"Who are our suspects? Ed had a fight with Winston at the bank . . ."

"And then there's Glad, who might have had a crush on him that he didn't return," Natalie said.

"Which puts the mayor in play. He was Glad's boyfriend; maybe he was jealous."

"Or maybe Mary was jealous that her sister was involved with the man she wanted."

I sighed. "My head is spinning. There are too many suspects, and those are the ones we know about. What about the maybe dozens of people that Winston encountered in the time he was in Archers

Rest? Maybe he insulted someone we don't even know about and got hit over the head for it."

"Maybe," Natalie said, a hesitancy in her voice. "But why would that person take all of Winston's things?"

"I don't know. Winston was being blackmailed. He said so to his sister. If we find out what that was about, then we find his blackmailer."

"And probably his killer," Natalie finished my thought.

"I hope so," I said, caught up once again in the thrill of solving a case. "And then we have to figure out who is turning Archers Rest into a hotbed of petty crimes."

"You don't think it's . . ."

She didn't have to finish. I knew she was talking about the conversation between Ed and Eleanor. "No, I don't," I answered quickly.

"Well, Eleanor did say that Glad was next," Natalie said. "And less than seventy-two hours later, Glad's picture has a knife sticking out of it."

"Does that sound like Eleanor?" I asked.

"No. But it doesn't sound like anyone in town."

"If there's someone in Archers Rest who seems to know more about people than they know about themselves, it's Mary Shipman," I said.

Natalie frowned. "I think all you'll get are more of her riddles. But at least you know where to find her."

"Maybe," I said. "Unless she's hiding something, too."

CHAPTER 46

Twenty minutes later, I was ringing Mary Shipman's doorbell for the third time and getting no answer. Standing there felt a lot like this murder investigation, the vandalism around town, and Eleanor's newfound secrecy—I was putting in a lot of effort and getting no answers anywhere.

I walked around to the back of the house, looking for signs that someone was inside. The windows were all covered with heavy drapes, and I couldn't see a thing. I did find an empty gallon of red paint in the backyard, but it seemed odd and really careless for Mary to spill the paint on the headstone and then bring the empty paint can back to her own house. Still, I couldn't just assume she wouldn't.

I headed back to the front of the house and rang the bell one last time. Just as I was about to leave, convinced that Mary Shipman was the person I saw earlier disappearing into Ed's theater, the door opened. Only instead of Mary, it was Glad.

"What are you doing here?" I asked.

"It's my sister's house. What are *you* doing here?"

"I've come to talk to your sister."

"She's sleeping. She had a headache, so I suggested a nap."

"But she's home?"

"She's always home. My sister has a crippling fear of leaving her house. She's struggled with it for years."

I had no choice but to take Glad at her word, so I turned around and headed for my car.

"Nell," Glad called out to me.

I turned back.

"Come inside for a minute."

I walked back to the house and followed Glad inside. As soon as I crossed the threshold, she slammed the door behind me and locked it tight.

"What's wrong?" I asked.

"Didn't you see what someone did to my picture this morning?"

"Yes. Strange."

"And terrifying. I've had to hide out here because I think someone's trying to kill me."

"I don't know if that's the case."

"They wrote *kill* across the picture," she said, her voice trembling, her hands shaking.

"They wrote *killer*," I corrected her. "It was more of an accusation than a threat."

"Why would someone accuse me of being a killer?" she asked. "Who could I have killed?"

"I don't know. Winston, I guess."

She sniffed, displeased at me. She walked ahead to the living room and sat on the cream-colored couch, pushing a sleeping cat from its comfortable spot. I sat opposite her with my back to the door, a position I felt gave her an unseen advantage.

"I was only a teenager at the time," she said, her fear now gone, replaced with Glads trademark sense of superiority. "I barely knew the man."

"And yet you knew exactly who was in that grave based on a description of his height and clothes."

"No one in Archers Rest wore anything made on Savile Row except for Winston Roemer," she said. "He was the very embodiment of sophistication to me."

"But you were dating Larry Williams. Maybe you wished it was Winston?"

She shook her head. "I only had eyes for Larry. It was one of the loveliest times in my life, when he and I were together."

Based on the mayor's recollection of the experience, I wasn't expecting her to feel that way. "He said it was puppy love."

"It wasn't. It was real, true love. I wanted to marry him," she said.

"For years after, I would have dropped everything to be with him."
She sighed. "I don't know why I'm telling you this."

"Maybe the fright of seeing your picture stabbed . . ."

"Maybe."

Or maybe, I thought, you want me to believe you didn't have a
motive to kill Winston. But I kept that to myself. Instead I told her,
"The mayor said you broke up over a baseball game."

"We did."

"If it was real, true love, why break up with him just because he
wouldn't go to your mother's tea?"

"We were supposed to announce our engagement at my mother's
tea. Then at the last minute he said he preferred to go to a baseball
game, and we'd do it another time. I wanted to know if he was getting cold feet, and he said that he was. 'Ice-cold,' I think he said. And
that was the end of it."

"Was that before or after Winston died?"

"Given that at the time I didn't know Winston was dead, I would
hardly be able to use that as my point of reference."

I had to concede she had a point.

"What's all the chatter?" I heard from behind me.

I turned to see Mary walking into the room. She wasn't alone.
Oliver was with her.

"Hi, Oliver," I said. "What are you doing here?"

He didn't answer. He seemed to be blushing, but it was hard to
tell, because he turned his back to me as if he hadn't noticed I was
there. Then he left without saying a word.

"Nell, how nice of you to come for a return visit," Mary said.
"And spend time with my sister, the fugitive."

"You're not a fugitive if you're a potential victim." Glad was scolding her, but there was something good-natured and warm about it.

"Glad said you were sleeping."

"I was visiting with Oliver."

"I didn't know you two knew each other."

"Don't feel bad about that. I'm sure I have a lot of friends you
don't know about."

"Why was he here?"

"Advice, I suppose." Mary plopped down next to her sister and grabbed Glad's hand. "More and more sinister happenings. Have you figured any of it out yet?"

"Not a thing," I admitted. "But I am discovering that everyone in this town has a secret."

"At least one," Mary said. "What's mine?"

"Glad says you're afraid to go out of the house, but you were at the movie theater this afternoon."

"Was I? What makes you think that?"

"I saw someone go into the movie theater. I only saw her arm . . ."

"Not much of an ID," Mary said lightly. "A lot of people have arms."

"The arm I saw was wearing that bracelet," I said as I pointed to the jewelry.

"This one?" She held up her hand for closer examination. "Oliver just gave it to me. It was a gift for Eleanor, but she didn't care for it, so he regifted it to me."

"He couldn't have given it to you just now. You had it on when I was here before."

"You're right. It was another visit."

"You said you only got visits from Ed and your sister. Then you added Maggie to the list, and now Oliver."

I could see Glad stiffen and get ready for a fight, but Mary patted her hand and leaned toward me. "It's true I didn't give you an exhaustive list of my visitors, but I had no idea you required one. Now that I know it's important to you, I'll begin keeping a guest book."

She could have sounded angry, but she didn't. She was playing, having fun. As I looked at the sisters, it was obvious she was Glad's opposite. Not just in the way they dressed, though Glad was in a dark blue designer suit with an A-line skirt, nylons, and three-inch pumps, while Mary wore a pink T-shirt and patched jeans. But what made them opposites was in their attitudes. Glad was closed off, unwilling to show herself to anyone. If her sister was telling the truth, Mary's phobias might make her a prisoner in her own home, but in so many ways, she was far more free than Glad.

"Mary, my grandmother said that if I wanted to know what was going on, I should talk to you," I said.

"What did she mean by that?"

"I'm guessing you know."

Glad and Mary exchanged glances and seemed to agree on something.

"People come to me for advice," she said. "I help them. Or at least, I try."

"So you are a witch."

Mary leaned back and smiled.

CHAPTER 47

"That's slander," Glad said. "I don't know why people glamorize such ridiculous rumors."

"Hush," Mary told her sister. "I'm not a witch, though honestly if I could make people's lives better with a mix of herbs and incantations, I would do that. Sadly, I cannot. All I offer is a sympathetic ear."

"People depend on her advice," Glad said.

"Did my grandmother come to you for advice?"

Mary looked puzzled. "Did she tell you that?"

"No," I admitted. "I just had a feeling."

"And your instincts usually are right."

"What would she need advice for?"

"We all need advice from time to time. And I needed help with something."

"With what?"

"You live up to your reputation, Nell. As curious as any one of my cats."

I looked at the sisters, side by side on the couch, so different but approaching me as one. I wished I could question them separately, but I knew that I couldn't make that happen. Not now.

"The book from the library," I said. "The one your father wrote."

"*The History of Archers Rest?*" Mary asked.

"You have a copy, I assume."

"No," Glad said, but it was too late. As she spoke, Mary was saying, "Of course."

"I'd like to see it."

Mary and Glad exchanged glances. Glad seemed worried, but Mary was relaxed.

"I have several copies on that bookcase behind you."

I walked over and searched for the book, finding a half-dozen slender red-leather copies with gold embossed lettering. "Why did he write this?"

"He wanted to make sure that the history of our town was recorded for all future generations," Glad said.

"And when he retired, he was bored," added Mary. "It's mostly hearsay and the like. John Archer hadn't lived the kind of life that made it into the history books. Much of what my father says is his interpretation of rumor."

"Except for the fact that Archer founded the town." Glad sounded proud. "We know he did that."

"What pages went missing?"

"I believe the pages about his worshipping the devil," Mary said, amused.

"We seem unable to escape that nonsense," Glad said.

"Or capitalize on it." I grabbed a copy of the book and put it next to me as I sat back down on the couch. "I'm surprised the mayor hasn't used this information to turn us into the new Salem."

"I wouldn't stand for it," Glad said.

"And you make the rules?"

I could see Mary put her hand across her sister, as if to stop her from striking me. Not that Glad looked ready to. She seemed more shocked than angry at my challenge.

"My sister," Mary said, "like your grandmother, is someone who has earned influence and respect. And like your grandmother, Glad may have occasional cause for regret, but I don't judge an entire life on a few unfortunate choices."

"Meaning?"

"Whatever you would like it to mean."

I stood up. "Please stop talking in riddles. Everyone I talk to hints at something but won't directly come out and say what they mean.

Someone killed Winston Roemer. I don't know if either of you did it or know who did it."

"We didn't, and we don't know who did," Glad answered.

"And someone has been running around town breaking into buildings, tearing up books, mugging people, and stabbing photos . . ."

"I'm the victim of that," Glad said.

"Or you want people to think you're the victim of it," I said. "Or your sister does."

"You're working yourself up, dear," Mary told me.

"I'm fed up. What do you know, Mary? Just tell me."

My voice was at a near shout, and I was, as she had pointed out, working myself up, but I was at the end of my patience with Mary, Glad, and even Eleanor.

Mary sighed and watched me for a moment before directing me to sit down again. "What I know," Mary said calmly, "is that Eleanor feels responsible for Winston's death."

"Why?"

"He had been scheduled to leave town in June but stayed at her request."

"Why did she ask him to stay?"

"I believe it had to do with Grace."

"If she asked him to stay because his mother was sick, was dying, why should she feel guilty about that? Anyone would make the same request."

"I don't think that's it," Glad said. "Ed and Winston had a fight about your mother in the bank, just before he was killed."

"How do you know that?"

"I was there," Glad said. "Mary and I were both there, visiting Daddy."

"What did you hear?" I asked.

"Winston was there, going over Grace's account with Daddy. Ed came in, already angry, looking for Winston," Glad said. "They exchanged some words. I didn't hear everything, but I did hear Ed say that people like Winston thought they could buy and sell anyone they liked, but that Eleanor wasn't for sale. Winston said that he was the one that had been bought and paid for."

"'He,' meaning Ed?"

"No. Winston was talking about himself. He said, 'I'm the one who's been bought,'" Mary told me. "I guess someone had bribed him."

"Blackmailed him," I said, more to myself than to the women.

"Blackmailed him about what?" Glad was sitting up straight, caught up in the conversation.

"I don't know. But I know Ed lied. He said the fight was about comments Winston had made about the town," I told her.

"He was just trying to protect your grandmother's reputation. I think Winston paid her off, got her to take Grace away so he could steal Grace's money," Glad said. "Daddy told me once that nearly thirty thousand dollars was missing from Grace's account, but Grace was too sick to do anything about it."

"And you think Winston took the money?" I asked.

"Who else would?" Glad asked. "The only other person who was authorized to draw funds from the account was your grandmother."

CHAPTER 48

I walked to my car, put the key in the ignition, switched it into gear, and began driving. At least I assume I did, because by the time I was fully aware again, I was driving away from town, going toward the road to New York and away from everything that was familiar to me. My conversation with Glad and Mary kept playing in my head, over and over.

Someone was stealing money from Grace. Eleanor had access to the account. Winston found out. His body ended up in Eleanor's rose garden and his belongings disappeared. If the participants were anyone else, the killer's identity would be obvious. But this wasn't anyone else. This was Eleanor. And Eleanor as a killer was unthinkable.

Suddenly a beeping sound came from the passenger seat, and I almost jumped out of the car before I calmed down enough to realize it was only my phone.

"Have you seen Molly?" Jesse sounded annoyed.

"She's at the house," I said.

"I had one of my guys go over to the house. He rang the bell several times and no answer."

"She's probably sleeping."

"That's what I thought, but Eleanor came home while he was there and they searched the place together. She's nowhere."

"Then I don't know what to tell you."

I had enough trouble keeping track of the quilts, the murder, the vandalism, and Oliver's plans—I didn't really need to add an eighteen-year-old supersleuth to the mix. And judging by the tone in his voice, I could tell Jesse felt the same way.

"She's not under house arrest," I said. "You warned her to stay put, but if she doesn't listen to you, that's not your problem."

"It is if she gets into trouble."

I turned the car around and started back toward the center of town. "I'll check the shop, Jitters, and the library," I said.

"Thanks." He hung up without another word.

✂

Natalie hadn't seen Molly, nor had Carrie. Though Carrie did have some interesting news.

"Ed was in here about an hour ago, and just as he was leaving, Glad pulled up in her car, got out, and practically hit him," Carrie said. "Ed's got to be a foot taller than Glad, and I swear, he looked like a child being yelled at by his mother."

"For what?"

"I couldn't really hear. The coffee machines are extremely loud." She looked back at her espresso maker with disdain. "So as soon as I could, I snuck over to the door and caught the end of their conversation."

Just as she was about to tell me what it was, a customer ordered a half-decaf cappuccino, no whip. I've always thought Carrie made those drinks quickly, but standing there waiting for her to finish up with the customer, it felt as though a year had gone by.

"So what did you hear?" I asked as soon as the customer left.

"Glad said that Ed was responsible, and he'd have to pay for the damage he caused," she said. "What I don't understand is if Glad knows that Ed is the one doing the vandalism, then why go to him and not Jesse?"

"Maybe she's not talking about the vandalism."

"Maybe. As soon as she was done yelling, she got in her car and drove away. I've no idea where she went, but she was pretty angry."

"She went to her sister's house to pretend that she was afraid someone was trying to kill her."

Carrie had stopped listening. Something had drawn her attention to the front door of her shop. I turned around and saw Molly walking Barney. It wouldn't have drawn any attention except Molly, a bandage still on the back of her head, was dragging a large, dirty suitcase.

I ran out of the shop and grabbed her.

"What are you doing? You're supposed to stay at the house," I yelled.

"I'm going to talk to Jesse."

"You could have called him. He's been looking for you all over town."

"I found this. And I wanted to bring it to him. I wasn't going to stay in that house knowing a killer was there." She pointed toward the case. "It's Winston's suitcase."

"Are you sure?"

She pointed toward the initials WLR embossed in faded gold lettering on the top of the case. "I can't open it, but those were his initials: Winston Lawrence Roemer."

I grabbed the case from her and brought her into Jitters. "Sit down," I said, "and I'll call Jesse."

Within minutes he was there. Molly looked as if she were about to collapse from the effort, and I was worn out from trying to open the rusted lock.

"Where did you find this?" Jesse's voice was gentle. He knelt in front of Molly, who was shaking, trying not to cry. "What happened?"

"I went out for a walk in the woods. Barney wanted to go out, so I took him, and we walked down by the river. We found the case half-buried by a tree. Barney's the one that dug it up."

"By what tree?" Jesse asked.

"I don't know. A big one by the river."

"I've walked those woods a thousand times," I said. "I've never seen a suitcase."

"Maybe you missed it," she said.

"Maybe it wasn't there."

Jesse stood up and nodded at me. "Maybe it was put there."

"Obviously." Molly stood up to go toe-to-toe with him. Since she was barely five-three and Jesse was over six feet, it was more comical than threatening.

"I think he means maybe it was put there recently," I told her.

"Who would do that?"

"Someone looking to implicate my grandmother."

"Oh." She sat down again. "But how would they know someone would find it?"

"Because Barney walks those woods every day."

"And the townspeople know your dog's habits?"

"Oddly, they do," Jesse answered for me. "Barney's quite loved in this town."

Jesse patted the old dog, who seemed pleased to be in the center of the action but completely confused as to why.

"If Eleanor had that suitcase all these years, she'd find a better place for it than in the mud by the river."

"I think we should ask her," Molly said. "Or at least we should open it. I couldn't find any tools in your grandmother's house."

"That's because she keeps them in the garage," I said.

"Well, let's open it now." She reached for the case, but Jesse stopped her.

"I think you should go back to Eleanor's house and get some rest," Jesse told her. "And this time I'm positioning my guy inside the house."

✄

One of Jesse's deputies came to Jitters and drove Barney and Molly back to the house, but only after Jesse got a promise from Molly that she wouldn't snoop in any of the rooms or stray past the front door. I wasn't entirely satisfied with her assurances, but there was nothing I could do.

Once she was gone, Jesse bought me a cup of herbal tea and we sat on the purple couch, quietly staring at Someday Quilts across the street. Finally, our eyes both went to the suitcase, still sitting where Molly had left it.

"I'll bet Carrie has a screwdriver," I said.

"Get it."

It took twenty minutes and more than a few curse words from

Jesse, but he finally got it open. I don't know what I was expecting, but all there was inside were some men's clothes that looked as though they had gotten wet over the years, a fading passport with Winston's name on it, and a gold ring.

"Was he planning to get engaged?" I asked when I saw the ring.

Jesse held it up. "This is a man's ring."

"I thought he wasn't married."

"Maybe he was about to get married."

"And someone stopped him," I said. "And then took the case so it would look like Winston went ahead with his plans to leave for South America. So why bring it back today after hiding it for so long?"

"Because they wanted to point a finger at Eleanor," Jesse said.

"So, somehow, we're getting close."

"Maybe. Was anyone at your house today?"

"The mayor and some photographers," I said. "But anyone could have planted it. You can walk over from next door, or if you stay by the river, you could come from the center of town if you wanted to without anyone seeing."

"You could also drive up if no one was home. And it would be easy to see if Eleanor was at the shop. Or you were."

"Or it could have been put there last night."

"It does tell us one thing," he said.

I nodded. "Winston's killer is still alive."

CHAPTER 49

"'John Archer was a man with many secrets and few friends,'" I read to Jesse as we sat in his bed at three in the morning, both unable to sleep. "'He took what talents he had and turned them into greatness, despite the obstacles that often stood in his way.'"

"This book is giving us one important piece of information," Jesse said. "Glad's father is no writer."

I looked at the red leather history of our town and shrugged. "He meant well. He was trying to preserve the image of a man who mattered to him and to the town."

"He's saying he's a devil worshipper."

"He is not, actually. He's saying," I turned the page and began reading again, "'Archer was rumored to have pagan beliefs that could, in his time, have meant jail or worse. This may have been the reason he came north to what is present-day Archers Rest. There was also some speculation that he was responsible for the death of his neighbor, or even that he had taken money that did not belong to him and was fleeing for his life. Whatever the reason, Archer's life cannot be judged by a single action, however wrong it was. It is only in looking at the totality of his accomplishments that we come to know the man.'"

"Jeez, he makes it sound like Archer invented the wheel," Jesse said. "He just did what probably hundreds, maybe thousands of other people did at that time. He went north of New York, claiming land for settlements. Half the towns on the Hudson River were founded around the same time as Archers Rest."

"He obviously admired the man," I said, "almost as much as his daughter does."

"She's transposing her father onto Archer." Jesse chuckled. "I cannot wait to see what that statue looks like. Odds are John Archer will be wearing a three-piece suit and have a bank ledger in his hand."

"I wonder why she didn't have copies of the book," I said. "Considering how much she admires her father, and Archer."

"Because he was a devil worshipper."

"Stop saying that."

"Now you're a member of the John Archer fan club?"

"No," I said. "I'm just tired of innocent people getting painted with silly rumors. So what if he cast spells, or danced around trees, or did whatever it was he did. Who cares?"

"He could have murdered his neighbor. That's what the book says."

"Do you think that's why the pages were torn out? Do you think it was a clue?"

"I think it's three in the morning and I need to get some sleep." He took the book out of my hands and put it on the nightstand. "And tonight you're staying until the morning." He turned off the light and pulled me toward him. I curled myself into his arms and listened to the rhythm of his breathing, growing steadier and calmer as he drifted off to sleep.

But I wasn't sleeping. Somewhere just outside my grasp was an answer, and my mind wouldn't shut off until I pulled it closer.

✂

Five hours later, I stumbled from bed and into the kitchen, running straight into Allie as I was buttoning the last button on my blouse.

"You and Daddy had a sleepover," she said.

"We did. Is that okay?"

"Sometimes I have sleepovers at Grandma's," she told me. "We read stories until I fall asleep."

"You know something, Allie, that's exactly what your dad and I did last night. I read to him about the history of Archers Rest."

"It sounds boring."

Jesse entered the kitchen. "It was. Get ready for Grandma's, Allie." As she ran out of the room, Jesse turned to me. "And where are you off to?"

"I'm picking up the poles to hang the quilts. Ed's letting me store some of the stuff at the theater, since there isn't enough space at the shop, so I have to go there, too. And somehow today I have to find the time to finish my own quilt. What about you?"

"I'm praying for a nice, quiet day."

Allie came running back in with a twelve-inch-square piece of fabric. On closer inspection I could see it was a small quilt made from strips of brightly colored cottons, some of which I'd helped her pick out, and held together with small tied threads rather than stitched. An easier, and just as traditional, way to attach the three layers of a quilt.

"Can I enter this in the show, Nell?" She held up her work.

"I'm thrilled," I said. "I'll hang it next to my quilt."

"Okay, but afterward you have to give it back so I can give it as a present when you and Daddy get married."

"That's really sweet," Jesse said, "but you know Nell and I aren't getting married anytime soon."

"But Eleanor said . . ."

Jesse looked at me.

"I'll say something to her. So you can stop panicking."

"I'm not panicking. I'm just surprised Eleanor would say that."

"Oliver's ring," I reminded him. "She thinks you bought it."

I kissed him on the cheek, then did the same to his daughter. "Thanks for the quilt, Allie. It's the perfect way to show everyone that quilting has a long future."

✂

I spent the day doing what I had told Jesse I would. I finished sewing the blocks of my devil's puzzle quilt into one large quilt top, then readied it for longarm quilting. I went to the hardware store and picked up the poles that would hold the quilts up. It looked like a metal jumble to me, but when I brought them to the theater, Ed promised to help assemble them the night before the show.

I noticed right away that his mood seemed changed. I also noticed that, for once, everything in the theater, from the soda machine to the ticket counter, was operating perfectly.

"Something's going your way," I said.

"Things have improved, Nell. Sometimes even a guy like me catches a break."

"You deserve it, Ed," I said. "Were you able to get a loan?"

"No. Bankers don't have vision. They look at this old place and see worn carpet and broken equipment. They don't see what I see."

"Which is?"

"Rainy Saturdays made fun, first dates made easy, difficult afternoons made bearable. That's what a movie theater is, Nell. It's a place anyone can go to—alone, on a date, with a crowd, and, just for a little while, escape," he said. "You know what I mean?"

"I do," I admitted. "And it sounds like you've convinced someone else, too. A buyer?"

"An investor," he said. "An opportunity that needed just the right nudge to make it happen."

"It wasn't Glad, was it? I heard you two had a few words outside Jitters."

He looked down at his feet for a moment. "I'm sorry that's getting around. It was a bit of a misunderstanding, that's all. Glad thinks that she knows what's best for everyone, but sometimes she doesn't."

"She's certainly gotten everyone under her thumb for the anniversary celebration," I said.

"You know, I was thinking about that. I know she's got some fancy reception planned at the library for before the fireworks, but I was hoping maybe we could do something here. Something simple, in the afternoon, to celebrate the quilts."

"I'd love that." I was a little uncomfortable broaching the subject, but I knew I had to. "I talked with Glad and Mary. They remember the fight you had with Winston a little differently than you do."

He seemed to blush. "It was a long time ago. I'm surprised they remember it at all."

"You said something about Winston buying someone off."

"That's what the rich do, Nell. They buy loyalty, silence, love . . ."

"Is that what Winston did?"

"That was what I thought at the time. But maybe I was hard on him. I didn't know everything. I couldn't know everything about what he had to do, what sacrifices he made. But I've been learning a lot lately."

"Like what?"

He smiled. "I know, for example, what my father and Winston were fighting about when Winston came into the theater."

"Which was?"

"It wasn't actually a secret. I just didn't know about it. But you've inspired me to investigate this old place. I looked through all the old papers, making sure there weren't any debts I didn't know about— like the money owed to your grandmother."

"I'm sure she doesn't care about that, Ed."

"She probably doesn't, but I will pay her back. And I can now, with things looking up. I mentioned it to Eleanor the other day, and she said she was just happy to see the theater in the hands of someone who loved movies. It was 'an investment in Archers Rest,' she called it. And in good people like my father." He seemed about ready to cry.

"She's right," I said. "But you were talking about the fight."

"I was, sorry. I get off track sometimes. My father had some papers with Grace's name on them. She'd hired the theater for the whole day on July 1st of '75. Then Winston came in and canceled it. It must have been what the fight was about, because my father had written *jerk* across the contract," he said.

"No idea why she hired the theater?"

"Can't help you there. But whatever the reason, I think she had a lot of nerve trying to hire the whole place, knowing how I felt about her son."

"Wouldn't that have brought in a lot of money?"

"I don't need Roemer money, and neither did my dad."

"So you can't be bought like Winston apparently was?"

He looked at me, sort of angry and sort of puzzled, but then he grinned. "Not by the Roemers, anyway."

CHAPTER 50

"It's a beautiful evening," Oliver said as we sipped wine on the back porch of Eleanor's house.

"It is," Eleanor agreed.

She smiled at him, and he smiled back. There was such love between them that I wanted to propose for him right then and there. It was only the dug-up rose garden a few feet away that stopped me. That, and the fact that granddaughters shouldn't propose marriage to their grandmothers.

I hadn't asked Oliver what he had been doing at Mary's, and he hadn't offered an explanation. I was trying, in my own small way, to learn the difference between being concerned and being intrusive. Even though it was killing me.

And I was enjoying a rare quiet evening at home.

It wouldn't last. Molly came down the stairs, with Jesse's favorite detective, Greg, right behind her. Barney followed, and then Jesse rang the doorbell. None of us had spoken of Winston's suitcase since Molly had found it almost a week earlier. Everyone agreed it had been hastily planted in Eleanor's yard for the purpose of being discovered, so it seemed pointless to do anything but wait for fingerprint results and hope for the best.

"There were none," Jesse reported when he joined us on the back porch. "The case was wiped clean inside and out."

"But it was Winston's?" Molly asked.

"Yes. And the DNA results came back. The lab was able to determine that the skeleton was a close relation to Winston's sister."

Eleanor sighed. "So it's certain now. He's dead."

"It's certain."

We all, without meaning to, turned our attention toward the makeshift grave and stared into the night. I'd never met him, and based on all that I'd learned, I wouldn't have liked him, but the confirmation of his death still saddened me. He had mattered—to Grace, to his sister, and to Molly. And because of that, he mattered to me.

"I've only seen one photo of him," I said, "and a grainy one in the newspaper. I'd love to see what he looked like again."

"I have some photos," Eleanor said. "In the box upstairs in my closet. Why don't you and Jesse bring it down?"

✂

Just a few weeks ago I had hesitated to go looking for the box, and now Jesse and I were sent to retrieve it. Though I had her permission, I still felt I was prying.

"Where do we go from here?" I asked Jesse once we were alone in Eleanor's bedroom.

"Nowhere, at the moment. We're at a dead end. I've told Molly it might be best for her to go home for the rest of the summer. We're releasing Winston's body so his family can finally bury him. I talked to his sister, and she would like to have him cremated and sent to California."

"I guess she wouldn't want him buried here, given how much he hated the place," I said.

"It's a fair point," he said. "Especially since I can't find out what happened to him. I've spent the last few days tracking down the places he bought his clothes, his shoes, even the ring."

"And no luck?"

"None."

"Maybe there was something we missed in the suitcase. A secret compartment . . ."

"The instincts of a seasoned detective." He winked at me. "I checked. And there was. Not a secret compartment, but a small zippered pocket that had been protected from the elements. It had a plane ticket in it. New York to Lima, Peru. He was supposed to take off July 5th."

"And when was he scheduled to come back?"

"He wasn't. It was a one-way ticket."

"But he had a teaching job . . ."

"I don't know what to tell you, Nell. It's one more unanswered question." Jesse sighed. "I feel like I've let his family down."

"It's such an old case, Jesse. Something that's been unsolved for so long. It would be nearly impossible to find all the answers."

"But the killer is alive and taunting us with evidence."

I heard my grandmother call out to us from the bottom of the stairs. "Everything okay up there?"

"Yes, sorry," I said. "We've found the box."

✄

The five of us sat around the kitchen table and went through the items one by one. Most were old Christmas cards, yellowing letters, and a few odd recipes, as well as a box of photos that seemed to mix pictures of my grandfather Joe with shots taken only a few years ago.

"I really need to organize these," Eleanor kept saying. "One of these days . . ."

"What's this?" Molly held up a postcard sent from Santiago.

"I remember that," Eleanor said. "Grace was terribly worried about him. Things weren't very stable there at the time, and Winston didn't seem to be taking it seriously."

Molly turned the card around and read, *"Wonderful people, but can't stay here. Will go north to Mexico and write from there. Miss you mother, Love W."*

"He actually came here," Eleanor said. "It was '73, I think. He stayed a while. Grace tried to talk him into taking some kind of teaching position, but he wouldn't go for it."

"But he did eventually," I said. "In '75 he took a job as the head of the anthropology department at Avalon. He had to give a huge donation to get it, too."

"Why not just apply instead of buying his way in?" Jesse asked.

"That was his personality," Eleanor said. "If he applied for the job, he would have had to work his way up to chairman of the department. Winston didn't like to wait."

"Besides, he had plenty of money to throw around," Molly said. "And he stood to inherit from Grace."

"And that was a substantial amount of money?" Jesse asked.

"It was," Eleanor said. "Several million, and that's in 1975 money."

"What happened to it?"

"Elizabeth took control of the estate when Winston couldn't be located," Eleanor said. "At the time she set up some kind of trust for his half of the money, just in case he returned."

"It's still there," Molly said. "She wouldn't have him declared dead, so the trust is still set up, waiting for him to claim it."

"She loved her brother very much," Eleanor said. "Even though she had a family of her own, she somehow felt alone in the world without her brother. It broke my heart anytime she wrote to me about him."

I opened the photo box and took out a handful of pictures. I began going through them one at a time. Winston was in a few early ones, and he even seemed to smile occasionally, making him look far more youthful and approachable than either his reputation or the earlier photos I'd seen. There were also pictures of Grace. One I particularly liked was a photo of her in the backyard, the red, yellow, and pink roses behind her. She had fabric on her lap, and she was clearly hand-piecing something.

"That's a cathedral window," Eleanor said. "She was only half finished with it when she passed away."

"That's the quilt you have hanging over the couch," I said.

She smiled. "It is. Grace thought, given the name, it was a fitting quilt to make as she came to the end of her life. She said it helped her think about what came next." She took a breath and continued. "But it's time-consuming. Large squares of muslin fabric folded and sewn like origami flowers, with little bright squares inserted into the openings. She poured her heart into it, as we all do with all our quilts. But this was special because she knew it was her last. She wanted to do it all by hand."

"And you finished it for her," I said.

She nodded. "That photo was taken only four or five days before she died, so, yes, I finished it for her. I wanted to give it to Elizabeth, but she said the quilt belonged with the house. Every time I look at it, though, I see Grace's beautiful stitches next to mine. Even now I'm not the quilter she was."

I rested my hand on Eleanor's. "I think she would be very proud of you," I said. "The quilter you've become, the strong, independent person you've always been. And she'd be so happy to know you've found Oliver."

And, in a move that was quite uncharacteristic of my grandmother, she left the table in tears, stepping out to the garden before anyone could stop her.

CHAPTER 51

"Maybe I should go," Oliver said.

"No, I will. I'm the one who said whatever it was that upset her."

I walked out of the room looking for Eleanor, who was standing next to the ruined rose garden. "You okay?"

"Fine, dear. Sorry about that. Just missed Grace for a moment."

"I'm sure you miss her all the time," I said. "And I imagine all of this has brought up a lot of old memories."

"It has," she said, before wiping her eyes. "We should go back inside."

"I just wanted to ask you one more thing while we're alone. Do you know why Grace would have rented out the movie theater if she was going to Canada with you?"

"I remember that," she said. "She could be quite extravagant. She wanted to throw a party, a large one, and she didn't have air-conditioning in this old house. She grew up in an era without it. So did I, for that matter. She didn't see the point in installing it, so we lived our summers with the windows open. Except it was a very hot summer that year and she didn't want people to faint in their lemonades."

"What was the party for?"

She paused. "For Winston. To help him get to know the people in town, since he'd be living here."

"And Winston didn't approve of the idea?"

"Winston saw it as Grace spending his inheritance on people that he didn't care about." She looked back at his grave. "Not to speak ill of the man, but he could be quite self-involved."

"Did you know he was being blackmailed?"

She looked startled. "That's ridiculous. Who would blackmail him, and for what? He didn't do anything other than read and study. I don't even remember him playing sports or watching television."

"No girlfriends? Like maybe Glad or Mary?"

"They were teenagers, Nell. He was too proper for something like that. He would have been more comfortable living in 1875 than 1975. He wouldn't have chased young women, even pretty young women like Glad and Mary."

"It looks like he was about to marry someone," I said. "And maybe that's the reason."

"And you think that's the reason he was killed?"

"Could be. Or he could have been holding the ring for someone else." I threw my hands up. "Or it could be something else entirely. There were people who were angry at him."

"Like who?"

"Like Ed." I'd been waiting to say something since I'd spoken with Glad and Mary. It had never been the right time, and now certainly wasn't, but somehow it had slipped out of my mouth.

"Mary told me," Eleanor said. "She called me when you were at her house with Molly and Natalie. And she called me after your conversation with Glad."

"Was she reporting in on my whereabouts?"

"She wanted to know what, well, I guess what I wanted her to say."

"And what did you say?"

"I know you mean well, Nell, but it was so long ago. Why does it matter?"

"Because of that." I pointed toward the hole in her garden. "Why did Ed think that you had been bought and paid for?"

As she looked at me, the tears were vanishing and her clear, certain stare was back. "He was trying to ruin my life." She grabbed my arm. "But he didn't. It all worked out fine."

"Are you sure he's not trying to ruin it now?" I asked. "Planting suitcases on your property."

"He didn't kill Winston," she said.

"Are you sure?"

The certainty was gone. She looked at the hole in the ground. "I don't know anymore," she said.

✄

The next morning I sat in my car, unsure of what to do next. I wanted to talk to Ed, but the theater was closed. I could have gone back to Mary, but I wasn't sure I could handle another conversation that twisted and turned until I didn't know what to think. There was only one person left who could offer me advice: Maggie. Even though she'd suggested I drop the whole thing, I knew that as a friend, she would at least listen.

As I was driving over to Maggie's house, I saw Jesse talking with the mayor. I waved hello, and Jesse motioned for me to stop the car.

"Everything okay?" I asked as soon as I parked.

"Fine. We're just going over the plans for the anniversary," Larry said. "I think there will be quite a lot of people in town, thanks to this." He held up a New York newspaper with a small article that was headlined: ARCHERS REST CELEBRATES 350 YEARS OF MURDER AND MAGIC. It went on to detail the rumors about John Archer all the way to the skeleton of "a once-prominent citizen who now is said to haunt a local home." Next to the article was a photograph of Eleanor's house.

"She's going to kill you," I said to the mayor.

The mayor wasn't concerned. "It's good for the town. It will bring in people, and that will bring in business. Your grandmother may be a little upset, sure, but wait until her shop is swamped with customers. She'll forgive me." He grabbed the paper from me and walked into city hall.

"He's working on a Sunday?" I asked Jesse.

"He works every day." He turned to me. "His heart is in the right place, you know."

"I'll let you tell Eleanor that."

"You want to get something to eat?" he asked.

"I'm actually headed to Maggie's."

"That should be fun."

"It should be," I told him, "I'm just not sure it will be."

✄

Five minutes later I rang Maggie's doorbell, and waited. I could hear shuffling and voices, but it took several minutes for Maggie to open the door. And when she did, she didn't open it all the way.

"Can I talk to you?"

Maggie stepped outside and closed the door behind her. "Absolutely, Nell. What would you like to talk about?"

"Can we go inside?"

She looked back at her door. "The place is a mess."

"I don't care." I sighed.

Maggie didn't budge.

"Okay," I tried again. "I was talking to Eleanor and she said that Ed had tried to ruin her life."

Maggie nodded. "I guess this is something we have to talk about inside." She opened the door.

CHAPTER 52

Maggie led me inside the house, and I saw immediately what she had been trying to hide. Ed was sitting on the couch, looking worried and upset.

"If one of you is going to confess to something, I'd better call Jesse," I said.

"What we have to confess does not require law enforcement," Maggie said as she directed me to a brown leather chair across from the couch.

She sat down next to Ed and patted his hand.

"Oh my God," I said without thinking. "You and Ed had an affair. He's your son Brian's real father. Is that what you've been hiding?"

Ed and Maggie burst out laughing. While I was glad to see the tension diminish, as the laugh went on I felt increasingly stupid. When they finally were able to compose themselves, Ed and Maggie turned to each other, seemed to wordlessly consult, and then turned back to me.

"While I would have been proud to have been Maggie's better half," Ed said, "if anyone could be better than Maggie, I was actually in love with a different woman that year."

I hesitated but guessed anyway. "Eleanor."

He smiled. "Eleanor."

"And she was in love with you?"

"She was cautious, of course. She had the children to think about, but I think she could have been persuaded to that way of thinking eventually."

"What stopped her? Was it Winston?"

"No," Maggie said. "It was me."

"You?"

"I didn't think Ed was ready for marriage, for an instant family. He was . . ."

"Struggling with maturity," Ed said. "Eleanor came to talk to me one day in early June about the nature of our relationship."

"I persuaded her to," Maggie said.

"It terrified me." Ed shook his head. "I backed off. We'd only been dating for a few months, and while being with Eleanor was a dream, instant fatherhood was . . . well, it was more than I could imagine for myself."

"So you broke up?" I asked.

"We broke up."

"And never spoke again until the other day? Glad said you disliked each other."

"We did speak, but only politely, and only when we had to," he said. "That was my choice, not Eleanor's."

"But it wasn't because of the breakup, it was because of what happened after." Maggie nodded at Ed, encouraging him to continue his story.

"A few weeks later I went over to the house to talk to Eleanor," he said. "To tell her I'd changed my mind. But Winston wouldn't let me speak to her. He wouldn't even let me in the house. A few days after that, Eleanor, Grace, and the kids were in Canada. Gone for a whole month."

"When did you argue with Winston?"

"July 3rd. I remember distinctly. I was going into New York for the holiday and I went into the bank to get some cash. It was before ATMs, you remember, so I had to get it there. Winston was just leaving the bank manager's office. He saw me and, well, one thing led to another."

"Because he'd kept you from talking to Eleanor? Why would he care about your relationship? Eleanor wasn't in love with him. Was he in love with her?"

Maggie shook her head. "No. Nothing like that."

"Then what?"

"People with money, as F. Scott once said, they're different than you and me," Ed said. "Winston flaunted his money and supposed superiority. He kept his thumb on people like Eleanor."

"I can't image Eleanor being under anyone's thumb."

"She was different in those days. She had children and no money, no education beyond high school, and no husband. And when Grace died, nowhere to go," Maggie said. "The day she opened Someday, her hands were shaking. Hard to believe now, but that goes to show you how strong a person can get."

"Is that where she got the money to open the shop? Did Eleanor know something about Winston stealing money from Grace's account and he paid her off to keep her silent?" I said.

Ed shook his head. "Eleanor never would have stayed silent about something like that. I assumed he paid her to take Grace to Canada, to get Grace out of the way."

"They went every year, didn't they? Eleanor said it was to get Grace out of the humidity of an Archers Rest summer."

"They did," Ed said, "but Eleanor was afraid the trip would be too much for Grace. Her health was very fragile."

"But Winston insisted they go," Maggie added. "So Eleanor took her. And within days of their return to Archers Rest, Grace died. Eleanor felt, as I did, that the trip killed her."

I sat watching Ed. And watching Maggie. There was regret in both their eyes. But there didn't seem to be guilt. I was glad of that. Considering for even a second that my dear friend Maggie had hurt someone was almost as unthinkable as imagining Eleanor capable of murder. But as far as Ed was concerned . . .

"After Eleanor returned," I said, "and Grace had died, why didn't you talk to her then?"

"I did. She told me that it was too late."

"Why?" I asked.

"She didn't tell me."

I looked at Maggie and then at Ed. "Do you know now?" I asked.

"I know what a mistake I made, and what a lucky man Oliver is," he said. "And that's all that matters to me anymore."

CHAPTER 53

Maggie walked me to my car and hugged me a long time, as if I were going away somewhere.

"Ed and Eleanor have spoken. Whatever hard feelings there were between them are gone," she said. "By the way, I have another quilt for you. It's a grandmother's flower garden made using reproduction 1930s fabrics, just like the one you wanted to make. I think it would make a nice addition to the show. I know its name might have an unfortunate connection to what's going on, but I think if we want a beautiful traditional quilt in the show, we should do it."

"Why did Ed come to your house?" I asked.

"My friendship with him ended when Eleanor and he broke up—out of loyalty to her."

"And now . . ."

"We can all be friends again, so some good has come from all of this," she said.

"The summer Winston died . . ."

She squeezed my hand. "I'll bring it by the shop tomorrow."

Then she turned and went back toward the house, where Ed was waiting for her.

Once she reached him, he smiled at me, and they both went inside and closed the door.

✄

There was nothing left for me to do but go back to Someday and think. Surrounding myself with fabric often put me into a peaceful sort of trance. My brain would quietly work on my problems as I focused on color and pattern. Even if I hadn't needed to finish my quilt for the show, I would have gone back to the shop to piece a few blocks of something. People always assume quilters do what we do so we can have a finished product. And, I admit, there is little more satisfying than sewing in the final stitch of the binding and knowing that another quilt is done. But mainly we quilt because we like the process of quilting. It is our meditation, our therapy, and our connection to the soul.

I got in my car and headed back toward Main Street, feeling confused, sad, and tired, but anxious to work on my devil's puzzle quilt. But just as I pulled up in front of the shop, my cell phone rang.

"When's the last time you saw Molly?" Jesse asked before I'd even had a chance to say hello.

"Again? When I left the house this morning, Mike was with her. He said he would stay at the house until Eleanor got home."

"I just got a call that a woman fitting her description, with a bandage on her head, was seen breaking into the bank. Mike said she went up to take a nap, but when I called, he checked on her and she wasn't there."

"I'll meet you at the bank," I said.

><

Jesse was at the scene before me, as were a half dozen of his force. Being a Sunday, the bank was closed, but their cameras were working. Jesse and one of the bank's security guards checked the tape, and sure enough Molly was using a screwdriver to open the back door to the bank. It looked like she was doing pretty well, too, until the alarm went off and she ran, leaving her screwdriver—actually Eleanor's screwdriver—behind.

"Where could she be?" Jesse asked.

"Out trying to solve the case."

"And maybe getting herself killed in the process."

I grabbed his hand. "I never thought I'd say this, but amateur detectives really get in the way of an investigation."

He laughed. "I don't know. Sometimes they come in very handy."

"Chief?" Greg, one of Jesse's detectives, approached cautiously. "I just got a call. There's another problem."

"Of course there is."

"There's a bomb threat at city hall. They're clearing the building now, but someone has to go check it out."

Jesse rested his head in his hands. "All right. Everyone stay away. Greg, call the state police and see if they can get a bomb squad here. I'll talk to the mayor."

"Let me go with you," I said.

He shook his head. "Stay here, Nell."

I waited by the bank for a few minutes, then made my way over to the shop. News of a bomb scare had gotten all over town in just the time it took me to make the walk. Carrie, Natalie, and several customers of both the quilt shop and the coffeehouse were outside on the sidewalk, though we were a block and a half from city hall and couldn't see anything.

"There was a threat against city hall years ago," Natalie said.

"Mary Shipman." I took a few steps closer to the end of the block. As I did I saw Ed walking toward the theater.

"What's the fuss?"

"Someone called in a bomb threat at city hall," I told him.

"Good heavens. Who would do that?"

"Not sure. But it's not the first time it's ever happened."

"No." His voice was shaking.

I was about to tell him that Jesse had it under control, but he disappeared into the theater.

✂

After another twenty minutes passed, I walked to the end of the block and around the corner. I could see Jesse talking with several state police. The mayor was there, as were Glad and several more of the town's leading citizens. If there still was any danger, I decided, Jesse wouldn't allow them to be there. And since there wasn't any danger, I walked the rest of the way to city hall.

"False alarm," Jesse said when he saw me. "The state's bomb squad just came out and gave us the all clear."

"What happened?"

"Someone said they would blow up city hall," the mayor said.

"Did you get the call?" I asked him.

"Not me. Glad."

I turned and saw Glad walk up behind me. "Why would someone call you?" I asked.

Glad clutched at the top button of her light pink suit. "I was in the building, at the historical society office. You know I'm the president."

"I do."

"I was getting together a presentation for the unveiling of the statue and I noticed that some of our artifacts were missing. Nothing valuable, just a few pieces. I came out to speak to the mayor."

"You were working in city hall on a Sunday?"

"Yes, I was. I have a lot to do to keep things running smoothly. After that atrocious article came out in the paper, it will be that much harder," she sniffed. "I couldn't find the mayor, so I was going back into the office, and the phone rang. A voice, a muffled voice, said there was a bomb in the building and everyone should get out or someone would be hurt."

"Man or woman?"

"I was so frightened, I couldn't tell."

"You should get home," I said. "And maybe call your sister to see where she was today."

"It wasn't my sister." Her voice hardened. "She only threatened to blow up city hall once in her life, and that was twenty years ago."

"Still, she did make the threat once."

"It was because the powers that be at the time were trying to pass an ordinance that would have limited the number of pets a person could have in their home. It would have meant Mary would have had to get rid of her cats. She didn't actually intend to blow the place up. She was making a point."

"You could say the same thing about whoever called today."

I left Glad to be offended by my insinuation and went over to Jesse, who was talking to the mayor.

"What were you doing at city hall?" Jesse asked, his voice all business.

"I have to get signatures to get on the ballot for the next primary," he said. "It's never too early to worry about reelection."

"Did you hear the call?" Jesse asked.

"No. I was coming out of the men's room when Glad came running out into the hallway in hysterics. She said something about a bomb and that we had to run. So I went office to office making sure the place was empty. It's a good thing this happened on a weekend, because I think we were the only people in the building."

"And that's all you know?" Jesse asked.

"I want publicity. This isn't publicity. This is a disaster." The mayor looked around. "We have three days, Chief. Three days until the anniversary celebration. I can't have this kind of thing hitting the papers and scaring off tourists."

"I know that."

"Solve it or shut it down," he said. Then he patted Jesse hard on the back and headed back into city hall.

Jesse let out a grunt. "This doesn't even make any sense, Nell. Why would someone pull such a stupid prank? Assuming it was a prank."

"There wasn't a bomb," I said, "so what else could it be?"

"A diversion."

"That doesn't sound good. That means something worse is about to happen." I could see Greg signaling for Jesse, so I waved him over. "I think one of your detectives may be about to tell you what's next."

Greg ran over to Jesse and whispered in his ear. It was police business, I understood that, but I probably would hear about it anyway, so I waited until Greg was done.

"Jitters," Jesse said to me, and then took off into the police station.

CHAPTER 54

I ran down the block and around the corner to Jitters, but somehow Jesse had gotten there before me.

"Back entrance of the police station," he said. "I can cut through the alley."

"What's going on?"

"The state police were able to trace the call that came in on Glad's phone. It looks like it came from here."

"Someone in here called in a threat?"

We looked around. The usual customers—students, moms with strollers, folks looking for a good cup of coffee. Maggie was sitting with Natalie on the purple couch. No one in the place looked the type to make a threat against city hall.

"But if you could make the trip from city hall to here this quickly . . ." I started.

"Then so could anyone else," Jesse finished my thought.

"Or maybe it was a completely innocent call," I said. "A coincidence. And Glad could be lying about the threat."

"Always a possibility." Jesse looked around.

I went behind the counter to talk to Carrie, with Jesse close behind. "Did anyone make a call from your landline just before we got word of the bomb scare?" I asked.

"Not that I know of," she said. "It's been really busy, so I guess someone could have."

"But you didn't use it?" Jesse asked.

She shook her head.

"And you didn't notice anyone hovering near the phone?"

"Half the town comes in here," she said. "I leave my cell phone next to the cash register, but the landline sort of moves around. It's cordless, so it tends to be left on the counter or even on a chair. I don't really pay attention. I'm sorry."

"It's okay." I turned back to Jesse. "What now?"

"Another dead end," he said. "I just start investigating one thing and something else happens. I can barely keep up with the manpower I have."

"Maybe that's the point. Maybe Winston's killer is just giving you busywork to keep you distracted."

"And unable to follow up on the evidence from Winston's death." Jesse nodded. "It makes sense. New crimes are more of a priority than a cold case. And I have limited staff."

"And when you think about it, no real damage was done to anything around town. No personal property, all stuff belonging to the town. And it was nothing that couldn't be cleaned up or easily replaced."

"Except Molly was hurt."

"Maybe it wasn't the same person," I offered. "Or maybe she knows something she doesn't even realize she knows."

"Or there was something in those letters . . ."

"I guess we should find Molly," I said, "before she finds out who the killer is the hard way."

"I'm going to get in the car and patrol the streets," Jesse said.

"I'll check a few places and see what I can find out."

He took my hand. "If someone is trying to keep us from solving Winston's murder, then I want you to remember it's someone who is capable of killing another human being. I need to know you're going to be careful."

"Is this going to be a speech about staying out of police business, because—"

"No." He smiled a little. "This is a speech about how lucky I am to have you in my life, and how I don't want to lose you."

"Aren't you smart to have learned that now, instead of forty years from now, like Ed did with Eleanor?"

"I have no idea what that means, but yes, I am."

"I'll explain later," I told him.

"Hopefully we'll get a lot of things explained soon." He kissed me and headed out toward his car.

✄

I agreed with Jesse about the killer being out there, potentially ready to commit another murder. But I wasn't sure I shared his optimism about finding explanations soon. Answers in this case always seemed just out of my grasp, and I could feel my chest tighten at the thought of what might be next.

CHAPTER 55

I walked across the street to Someday Quilts trying to piece together what I knew. The vandalism in the library, at the church, or in the cemetery didn't require any special knowledge of the town. And as far as stealing an old paper from the newspaper office, anyone in Archers Rest could walk in and get access. In a town like ours, people usually aren't on guard.

There wasn't a single event that pointed to, or eliminated, anyone in town. Even hitting Molly over the head didn't offer any special clues. She was small and young, and she was walking an unfamiliar street. It would be easy to watch her, to sneak up from behind and hit her. And as bad as it had initially looked, it hadn't been a strong hit. Anyone could have struck a blow like that.

"What are you staring at me for?" Eleanor asked as I stood by the door looking at her.

"I'm actually looking for Molly."

"She hasn't been in here. Is she up to something?"

"She's trying to track down Winston's murderer."

"What is it with you young people? You have all the things I had as a girl, plus the Internet and television and computer games. And still you spend your time chasing after killers."

"Natural curiosity, I guess."

"Natural stubbornness is more like it."

"I inherited that."

She smiled. "I suppose you did."

"Which is why I'm never going to stop bugging you about what happened thirty-five years ago."

"I'm finding that out."

"So you should tell me."

She looked around. There were no customers to help, no bolts to be restocked, no fabric to be cut. She sighed. "I want you to be proud of me, Nell."

"I am proud of you, Grandma. I won't stop being proud of you if you tell me what's bothering you."

Her eyes welled with tears. She was silent for a moment, and when she spoke she was almost whispering. "Okay. But I just want to ask you one thing. I want you to call Jesse. I think you should both hear this."

Jesse arrived ten minutes later—with Molly in tow.

"I found her trying to walk back to your house by following the river."

"I just wanted to see if it were possible to walk from town to Eleanor's house without being seen," Molly said.

"It is," I said. "What does that prove?"

"I'm not sure," she admitted. "But I did see a woman from the back. She was running along the riverbank. Long gray hair, like that woman . . ."

"Mary," I jumped in. "It had to be."

"So I found a suspect," Molly said, a triumphant tone in her voice. "I knew if I just kept at it . . ."

"You need to stop, Molly. You tried to break into the bank," I pointed out. "Even I'm not that nutty."

"On Friday I asked to see the records of Grace's accounts. Even though they were closed decades ago, they still wouldn't show them to me."

"The bank has been owned by a new company since the mid-eighties," Jesse said. "They probably don't even have the records."

"Besides, you could get jail time for breaking into a bank," I pointed out.

Jesse grabbed my arm. "No one is going to jail. I just wanted Molly to be somewhere that I can keep an eye on her. So that's here right now."

"Fine. She can stay here," I said, "but Jesse, we have to talk to Eleanor."

He nodded. "Any idea what this is about?"

"She wouldn't tell me." I turned to Molly. "Just stay out here and stay out of trouble."

I closed the store and pointed Jesse toward the classroom, where Eleanor was sitting, drinking a glass of water.

"Hi, Eleanor." Jesse's voice was soft, as if he were addressing someone on their deathbed. I thought it an overreaction until I saw Eleanor's face, white and stricken.

"Hello, Jesse. It's good of you to come over."

Jesse took a chair and moved it directly opposite Eleanor, then sat facing her. "I understand that you have something you want to talk to me about."

Eleanor smiled slightly. "You have a nice interrogation technique. Gentle, kind. It makes a person want to talk."

"I'm not interrogating you, Eleanor. Unless I have a reason to."

Jesse looked back to me. I shrugged, hoping my panic didn't show. It was impossible, of course, but a small part of me worried that my dear grandmother was about to confess to murder.

"What is it, Grandma?" I asked.

She looked at me. "I promised myself I would never speak of this again, but I need to tell you both in case it has something to do with everything that's happened. There's something in my past that I'm deeply ashamed of."

Eleanor swallowed more water, emptying the glass. Jesse and I waited. She seemed as if she were struggling for the words. As we waited, I noticed Molly inching toward us until she was hovering near the entrance to the classroom, standing just behind me.

"Is it something to do with Winston?" I asked my grandmother.

"Yes. Obviously." A hint of annoyance in her voice. Whatever had shaken her, my curmudgeonly Eleanor had not been entirely lost.

"So," Jesse prompted. "What is it?"

"As you know, Winston was Grace's son. He spent his time in South America, and his sister was in California by then. Grace had been widowed in '62, and a few years later she sold the family's home in New York and moved up to their summer home in Archers Rest. Winston hired me to be his mother's caretaker."

"How did he meet you?" I asked.

"He put an ad in the paper. 'Looking for live-in companion.' That kind of thing. He wasn't comfortable with the fact that I had two small children. He thought it would distract me. But Grace was very taken with the idea. She loved the life they brought to the house. And her own grandchildren lived so far away."

"And you and Winston became friends?" Jesse asked. I knew he was trying to move the story along, but it didn't seem as though Eleanor was interested in doing that.

"He was gone most of the time. It was just Grace and me and the children. It was lovely, really. We had many happy years. Then Grace's health, which had never been good, took a turn for the worse. Winston came back to make sure Grace's affairs were in order."

"And he found that they weren't," Molly said. "He found that someone was cheating Grace."

"I don't know about that," she said. Then she looked at me. "I don't, Nell."

"Of course you don't."

Jesse put his hand on Eleanor's. "You went to Nova Scotia and Winston stayed in Archers Rest," Jesse said. He was so calm and patient. I stood back, admiring his quiet authority.

"Yes."

"Is that all you know about Winston's disappearance and death?" Jesse asked.

"That's all I know."

"Why would you be ashamed of that?" I asked.

"There's something else," she said, her eyes darting up toward mine, then back at the floor. "I didn't know him very well. Not really. But he and I, we . . ."

"You slept with him?" It popped out of my mouth.

Eleanor blushed. "No. I married him."

CHAPTER 56

The words hung there. Jesse, Molly, and I glanced at each other, then looked away, uncertain of how to react. Eleanor just sat there, for the first time looking old and tired. We waited.

"I didn't have a lot of money saved up," she said finally. "With the kids and old debts, I was just getting by. And once Grace died, I wouldn't just lose a job, I'd lose a home, too."

"But you had Grandpa's life insurance, right?"

"It was just enough to bury him," she said. "He was only twenty-seven. He wasn't expecting to die, so he bought the smallest policy the company had. I know I misled you about that, Nell. It's just you kept asking questions, and I didn't want to . . ."

I could feel myself turning red. I'd pushed her into a corner, forced her to lie. I don't think I'd ever been so ashamed of myself.

"So what did you do, Eleanor?" Jesse asked.

"Grace was dying and she was concerned about Winston," Eleanor continued, "about what would happen after she was gone. She worried about putting so much of the family fortune in his hands, but it was more than that. She thought he had spent too much of his life feeling superior to others. She wanted him to get a job, live an ordinary life. To understand what the rest of us go through."

"How did you fit into it?"

"She thought I would stabilize him, and he would be an answer to my financial worries. We got along all right, Winston and I. And things were different then for a woman like me, with children to take care of. I wasn't the self-reliant woman you think I was, Nell."

She looked up at me with watery eyes.

"You were very strong," I said. "And you still are."

"I was very foolish," she said. "I'd been going around with Ed. Nothing serious, but when Grace came to me with her idea, I went to talk to him. I didn't tell him the details, I just asked where he thought our relationship was going."

"And he broke up with you."

"Yes. So, very quietly, right before Grace and I went to Nova Scotia, Winston and I were married. We got married in New York by a justice of the peace. There was no honeymoon."

She was firm as she spoke. "Grace wanted to throw a big party at Bryant's Cinema to celebrate our wedding, but Winston was offended by the idea. We had agreed with Grace that we would stay married for a year after her death. And at that time, the trust would pass to him. But only if we stayed married. By then, I guess she figured he would have tasted the kind of life she wanted him to live. And maybe he would have liked it. And maybe he and I would grow into a real marriage, instead of the sham it was."

"So you were the blackmail," I said. "Grace blackmailed her son into marrying you by threatening to keep the family fortune from him?"

"I believe so," she said. "I think that may have been why Winston was so intent on finding out exactly what the fortune was, and if it was possible for his mother to disinherit him."

"But he found out something else—that someone was taking advantage of Grace," I said.

"I suppose."

"Who knew about the agreement?"

"As far as I know, only Grace, Winston's sister, Elizabeth, Maggie, and of course, Glad's father. As president of the bank, he was in charge of the trust. But I don't know if Grace or the others told anyone else."

"Did you tell Ed?" I asked.

"No. I was too embarrassed to tell him then. I only told him recently, after Winston's body was found and these old memories came back in a way they hadn't in years. I'd hurt him back then.

When he wanted to get back together I turned him away, with no explanation. I wanted him to have one now."

"Does Oliver know?" I asked.

"Yes." She smiled for a moment. "After all your talk about engagements, I thought Oliver and I should be clear about a few things. The day he asked me to go to Paris, I told him about Winston. He was very understanding."

"Have you told anyone else?"

"No one other than the few who knew about it at the time. And Mary Shipman."

"Why Mary?" Jesse asked.

"Mary is good at helping everyone but herself."

"And Winston wanted you to leave right away after the wedding?" Jesse asked.

"I've always wondered if he wanted to hasten his mother's death by sending her on a long trip," Eleanor said. "And I was so ashamed of myself that I'd married for financial security. That I'd done it to be put in Grace's will . . ."

"It wasn't for you," I said, "it was for the kids."

"Still. It's not something to be proud of. It's not something I ever wanted you, or even my own children, to know."

"And when you came back from Canada?" Jesse leaned toward Eleanor.

"He was gone. And I was relieved he was gone. Relieved he didn't come back," she said. "After Grace passed away, Elizabeth took control of the trust. She sold me the house for a dollar, and I lived off the small amount that I'd saved up until the shop got going. I felt so guilty about the money Grace left me that I gave it away the first chance I had."

"To Ed's father," I said.

She nodded. "At first I expected Winston to show up again, but as the years passed and he wasn't heard from, I assumed what Elizabeth assumed: that he'd died somewhere in South America. But I didn't think about it too much, I'm embarrassed to say. I wanted to put it behind me and forget about it."

Tears rolled down Eleanor's face. "I'm sorry to be such a disappointment to you, Nell. Here you have Jesse with a ring in his pocket and you would rather be an independent woman than marry too quickly, but I jumped at the first chance for security."

I sat next to her. "You could never be a disappointment to me, Grandma. And I think you were right about Winston. He had a one-way ticket to Lima. If he was coming back, he wasn't planning on doing it before the year was up and he could get the marriage annulled."

We sat quietly for a moment and let Eleanor collect herself. As we waited, I heard a knock on the door.

"Looks like you have customers," I said.

"Let them in." Eleanor seemed relieved at the intrusion.

It wasn't a customer. It was Greg.

"I'm sorry to intrude," he said. "I'm just looking for the police chief."

"He's in the classroom."

I pointed toward the semi-enclosed room at the far end of the shop and watched as Greg walked to it. I lingered near the door. Eleanor married Winston? My mind couldn't put them together—the arrogant man who felt he was better than the residents of Archers Rest, and my grandmother, who would never accept such snobbishness.

Jesse emerged from the classroom while I was still at the door. Greg trailed behind him looking worried.

"There's a disturbance at Jitters," he said. "I'll come back as soon as I can."

"This never stops," I said to myself. I walked back to Eleanor. "Are you okay, Grandma?"

"Fine. I just need to sprinkle some water on my face and get myself together. Go with Jesse. Make sure everything's okay across the street."

CHAPTER 57

I ran out the door and across the street, with Molly only steps behind me. We arrived at Jitters just in time to see Jesse breaking up the most ridiculous skirmish I'd ever seen. Glad had spilled Ed's coffee on his lap and apparently had thrown his apple spice muffin on the ground and stepped on it.

"What's going on?" I asked Carrie as we watched Jesse move Ed to the back of the coffeehouse.

"Ed said it was a fine day for a walk, and then she dumped his coffee on him." She giggled. "I tell you, this place is a front-row seat to every interesting thing that happens in this town."

"This is stupid," Jesse said. "You're too old for this, the both of you."

"He is a cruel man," Glad said. "And he's been doing terrible things around town. You ask him."

"Ask me?" Ed stood up, the coffee still dripping down his pants. "Ask her what she and Winston were doing the summer he died. She's your killer, Chief."

"That's the most insane accusation," Glad said, walking toward the door. "I'm not going to stand here and listen to it."

"Yes, you are." Jesse's voice boomed with authority, and the whole place came to a standstill. "You sit down, Glad Warren, or I will arrest you, handcuffs and all. Ed, you sit at the table on the other side of the shop. And everyone else, buy coffee or get out."

He let go of Ed and looked over at Glad, who sniffed a little but sat where she was told.

Jesse sat first with Glad. "Okay, tell me what happened."

"He insulted me."

"Without editorializing, Glad. What happened?"

"He made a remark that was intended to insult me . . ."

Ed waved his hands. "I said it was a nice day for a walk."

"He knows what that means."

Jesse took off his glasses and rubbed his eyes. "I don't know what it means, Glad, so why don't you tell me."

"It was a remark about my sister. About her issues with being outdoors. Ed and Mary were an item for a few years, but he broke up with her because of her agoraphobia."

"I said it was a nice day for a walk," Ed said again. "And she dumped coffee on me."

"Why do you think, Glad," Jesse continued, ignoring Ed's outburst, "that Ed has been doing terrible things around town?"

"Because he's the type."

"That's your evidence?"

"Considering who I am, that should be enough."

"Who are you? A boring stick-in-the-mud, that's who you are," Ed yelled. "Determined to ruin your sister's life."

"Me ruin Mary's life?" she yelled back. "That's a laugh. I'm protecting her. I've always protected her."

"The only person she ever needed protection from was you."

At that Glad got up. "You can arrest me if you want, Chief, but I'm not going to stay and listen to this."

We all watched her leave, including Jesse, who didn't make a move to arrest her. Instead he turned to Ed. "What about her and Winston?"

"I came to see Eleanor one night in late May or June of that year. I walked out onto the back porch and I saw Glad and Winston talking over by the trees."

"So what?"

"Glad was crying. Winston was calling her a child. He said she would get over it."

"I don't suppose you know what he meant?"

"Him, I assume. Don't you?"

Jesse nodded slightly. "Why did you wait until now to mention this?"

"I didn't want to stir up any trouble."

"You were protecting Glad?"

"No. Heavens, no. Mary. She doesn't need to be tarnished with her sister's actions. She has enough of her own problems."

"Okay." Jesse got up from the chair, shaking his head. "Go change your pants, Ed. And get another muffin, on me." Jesse walked toward me. "We should get back to Eleanor."

We walked over to the shop, but by the time we got there, Eleanor was gone and the CLOSED sign was on the window.

CHAPTER 58

"Happy birthday." Jesse kissed me on the nose as I lay next to him in bed.

"What was that for?"

"Does the fact that I wished you a happy birthday provide any kind of a clue?"

"Not if you kiss me like you're my grandfather."

Jesse smiled, leaned over me, and kissed me again. This time he got it right. "Happy birthday," he said again. "What's the plan for today?"

"The show is tomorrow," I said. "And believe it or not, I haven't quilted my devil's puzzle yet. Plus, I have to get all the quilts ready to be hung and make sure that my volunteers are in place."

"Any word from Eleanor?"

"Phone calls. She's been at Oliver's. I think she's avoiding me. She hasn't even come to the shop in two days."

"That poor woman, still feeling embarrassed after all these years." He leaned on his side, looking at me as I lay on my back in his bed. He ran his hand softly down my chest and rested it on my stomach. "But she'll have to see you today."

"True. And one good thing came out of it. We know what she was hiding, so that takes her off the suspect list for Winston's murder."

"Nell, if I were able to be objective about you, or your grandmother, which I'm not, I would say that her marriage to Winston not only does not take her off the suspect list, it actually moves her right to the top."

"Except you know she didn't kill him."

"I do."

"So, she's off the list."

"She was never really on the list."

"Then why are we fighting?"

"Are we fighting?" he asked. "Because if we are, and the fight is over, then we should make up."

With that he moved his hand lower on my body, leaned over, and kissed me again.

✂

When I arrived at the shop later that morning, Natalie and Eleanor were there ahead of me.

"Happy birthday, dear," Eleanor said.

I hugged her. "I've missed you these past few days."

"I wouldn't miss your birthday. Oliver helped me see that I need to move forward, not backward, so I'm ready to help you get the show together. Whatever you need."

"We'll deal with that later," Natalie said. "Happy twenty-seven, Nell. Look what we did for your birthday."

With Natalie's son clapping, Barney barking, and my grandmother and Natalie looking on, I opened up the large gift bag Natalie had placed in front of me. Inside was my devil's puzzle quilt, and it had been beautifully finished.

"When did you do this?"

"When you were out solving the world's problems," Eleanor said. "Natalie did the quilting and I sewed on the binding."

"You could not have given me anything I would appreciate more. It was going to take up my whole day finishing this."

"What's a quilt group for if not to help you get a quilt finished . . ." Natalie started.

"Or investigate a few murders," I said.

"Assuming you don't spend your afternoon doing that," Eleanor interrupted, "what will you do with your day?"

"Hang quilts."

✂

I headed over to Bryant's Cinema, where I assembled the quilt poles for the quilts that would be shown in his lobby. Ed wasn't there, but he'd left me a note saying he'd arranged for *How to Make an American Quilt* to play all day in a salute to the show and the holiday. After the poles were assembled, I hung the twelve antique quilts that would be displayed.

They represented generations of quilters, some beginner, some expert. Some used scraps, like the star quilt of blue denims and white and yellow shirtings that had been made in the seventies. Others were made from quilt kits that dated as far back as the twenties. And still others were made from velvets and silks with elaborate embroidery.

After I'd hung them on the poles, I placed the racks throughout the lobby. Bright appliquéd baskets in one quilt gave way to soft pastel log cabin blocks in another. A quilt from the Civil War faced a quilt made a hundred years later. In each one the maker was evident, and I stood wondering about each of these women and about the hard choices they faced, the rumors they lived with, and the losses they accepted. I felt a part of them, the way you do when you become a quilter. We are all joined by a love of needle and thread, by the usefulness and the beauty of a quilt, and by the friendships that form because of it. But as I looked at each quilt, I also saw the individual behind each piece. You can hide who you are from much of the world, but when you quilt, I realized, your personality finds its way into the finished product.

After I finished, I went to each shop that had agreed to display a quilt outside and I put together the poles, hung a reproduction quilt, and placed it inside the window. At Jitters, my last stop, Carrie and I hung her reproduction Depression-era broken dishes quilt, an easy pattern of quarter square triangles. Each block looks like an hourglass, but when assembled, the quilt looks like a mosaic of broken dishes spread out over a muslin floor. For the borders, Carrie had cut wide strips of muslin and appliquéd dozens of small Scottie dogs to it. Scottie dogs were a popular appliqué item in the 1940s, as a nod to Franklin D. Roosevelt's dog, Fala. While it must have taken hours back then to trace and cut out each three-inch pup, Carrie had made a more modern choice. She ordered the Scotties, precut and ready for appliqué, on the Internet.

"Just keep it in the window until tomorrow at ten a.m.," I said. "That's when all the merchants are supposed to put the quilts out on the street. The parade starts at eleven, so all the people will be watching just outside your store and hopefully enjoying the quilts while they watch the parade."

"What time is the carnival?" she asked. "I'm taking my kids to that."

"It starts at noon. After the parade and the big unveiling."

"Glad's statue." Carrie shook her head. "Any hints on what it looks like?"

"None yet. I passed the park on my way here. The statue was there, but it was completely covered by a huge blue cloth and tied with a rope."

"That's going to be interesting."

"Let's hope it's the only interesting thing that happens tomorrow."

"What's left to happen?" she asked. "Most of the town buildings have been broken into or vandalized already."

"Whoever murdered Winston has done an excellent job of misdirection," I said. "We're no closer to finding the killer than we were when we found the body."

"You certainly have enough suspects," Carrie said. "Everyone seems to have had the finger pointed at them at one time or another."

"Everyone but me," I said. "I'm off the hook."

"Only because you weren't alive in 1975—if that's a hint for a free birthday cupcake."

"I already had one."

"So have another. And make a wish," she said as she put a small pink birthday candle on my cupcake.

"I want Winston's killer to turn himself or herself in. And after tomorrow I want life in Archers Rest to return to normal." I blew out my candle.

"Birthday wishes don't come true if you say them out loud."

"I knew it couldn't be that easy," I said, and bit into a lemon-filled vanilla cupcake with raspberry icing.

CHAPTER 59

The next morning I arrived at the shop, a little worse for the birthday celebrating—excessive champagne, rich Italian food, and a night spent at Jesse's house. But I was smiling. For the first time in a long time, I was determined to focus only on quilting and having fun.

"Let me see it," Eleanor said as I walked in the door.

"See what?"

"The ring."

I held up both unadorned hands. "No ring."

"When is he going to propose? Last night was the perfect opportunity."

"Maybe he has another plan in mind," I said. "When it comes to romance, he's a bit of a perfectionist."

"Jesse?"

I stopped. "Yeah. Jesse. Of course, Oliver is a romantic, too."

"Back to that again."

"Well, the reason you were so against remarrying is that you thought there was a chance you might still be married," I said. "And now you know you're not."

Eleanor raised an eyebrow. "Every puzzle has an answer."

"Not every puzzle. But this one did. What I don't understand is why you didn't have him declared dead after seven years. Couldn't you have done that?"

"But that would have meant admitting he was dead, and his sister wasn't able to do it. Elizabeth assumed it, as I did, but to have it declared in a court of law, that would have been too painful for her."

"Hey, what can I do to help?"

I turned and saw Molly walk in with Natalie.

"You want to help?"

"Sure. I am supposed to be here helping with the anniversary celebration, and it does sound kind of fun," Molly said. "Besides, I figured Grace would want me to pitch in, as a representative of the family."

"We're getting ready to position the quilts in front of the shops," I said. "If you can just walk down the street reminding the shop owners and assisting anyone who needs help bringing the quilts outside, that would be wonderful. And if you can do it without breaking into any banks or questioning any suspects . . ."

She laughed. "I'll try. I may not have solved my great-uncle's murder, but at least I got to know him a little. So I guess that's something. And I have to say," she paused, "I think he might have been wrong about this town."

Natalie threw an arm around her. "You remind me more and more of Grace."

"That's a high compliment," she said.

"But," Natalie reminded her, "Grace knew how to quilt."

"I may give up investigating and take up quilting," Molly said.

"You can do both," Eleanor told her. "Just ask Nell."

I rolled my eyes. "Let's get the quilts out before Glad finds me and throws another fit."

Twenty minutes later, I hung my devil's puzzle quilt just outside the shop, pinned Allie's striped square next to it, and looked up at the sky—bright, blue, and clear.

"A perfect day," I said to myself.

Molly must have felt the same way, because she was smiling brightly as she walked toward me. "The quilts are out, and Ed's theater has all the antique ones ready for showing. He also told me he has the wine and cheese for the reception this afternoon. What else do you need?"

"Tourists, I guess. And coffee."

I ran into Jesse and Allie at Jitters. Allie had dressed herself in pink, white, and blue. The American flag, she told me, but she liked pink better than red. Jesse had his full force out for the day, and he was on duty himself, except for a half hour he had promised to Ed.

"How did I talk myself into the dunking booth?" he laughed.

"I don't know, but I've been warming up my pitching arm all morning."

"You're in a good mood."

"You put me in a good mood," I said.

"Even with an unsolved case on our hands?"

I frowned. "I think this is the one we don't solve, Jesse. Too many clues but too few real ones. And a decades-old skeleton of a man no one seemed to like. Maggie said to me a while back that we should just let this one go. Maybe she was right."

"Maybe. We'll have to let it go for today anyway. Too much else going on." He took Allie's hand and kissed my cheek. "See you tonight at the fireworks display?"

"Are you kidding me? I'll be at the dunking booth at noon sharp."

✂

The parade went off without a hitch. The high school marching band and bands from several towns over all played beautifully. The fire department, complete with fire truck and Dalmatians, was followed by twirlers and kids waving small American flags. Barney led a pack of dogs that seemed to have joined the parade of their own accord. At one point Barney wandered into the marching band, nearly tripping a trombone player, but it just made the whole event all the more endearing to the crowds that had come for the celebration.

And there was a crowd. News of the skeleton had reached major papers, with side articles about our anniversary celebration. It had brought people from New York, New England, and even a few states just to the west of us. It was exactly the kind of day that all of us had worked so hard to bring about. I got myself a hotdog and a glass of lemonade and joined Ed as he walked toward the park, where the parade was scheduled to end right in time for the unveiling of the statue.

"The quilts look great, Nell," he said. "You must be proud of your hard work."

"And you must be, too. This is one amazing parade."

"Thanks, but I probably should go back and check to make sure the parade route gets cleaned up."

"Don't you want to see the statue?"

"And get accosted by Glad again?"

I grabbed his arm. "I'll protect you."

✂

We got to the park just as Glad, the mayor, and several of the town council members were positioning themselves on a small temporary platform next to the still-covered statue. Ed and I stood next to Eleanor and Oliver. Carrie was there with her husband and kids, Natalie with her husband and son, and Maggie with a pile of children I assumed to be her grandkids. Much of the town, it seemed, had turned out. In the distance I even saw Mary, standing by Glad's lemon yellow Mercedes watching the proceedings, as riveted as we were.

"I thought she never left her house," I whispered to Ed. "And yet I keep seeing her in town."

"Shh. I want to hear this." But even as he ignored me, I saw him watching Mary and smiling.

The mayor made a speech about the beauty of our town and its long and vaguely interesting history, but no one was listening. We were all waiting for the main event. Finally, Glad stepped to the microphone.

"This is for all the citizens of Archers Rest, past, present, and future," she said as we waited to see the installation. "We are a small town, and maybe we haven't been a major part of American historical events. But we care about each other and we love Archers Rest, and this sculpture, I hope, will be a simple acknowledgment of that."

With that, she pulled a rope that released the canvas and revealed . . .

"It looks like a potato chip," Eleanor said quietly.

"I think it's a wave, dear," Oliver told her.

"Or a cloud," I said.

Whatever it was, it wasn't a statue of John Archer or Glad's father. After the initial shock had worn off, I realized it was a cool abstract sculpture that somehow fit our little town. It was what you made of it.

"I like it, Glad," I said once she had come down off the platform. "This was a lovely donation."

"Thank you, Nell. I realized that since none of us really know what John Archer looked like, it might be better to have something that represents the freedom he came here looking for."

"It does."

"It's missing the plaque, of course. That's still being engraved with my name. And the flowers. There must be red flowers all around the base. I absolutely insist on it."

After she finished she walked off toward her sister, who stood waiting for her. The two women talked for a minute and then got into Glad's car and drove off in the direction of Main Street.

"I wonder where she's going," I said to Carrie.

"I don't know. But just in case something else happens, where's Jesse?"

I looked across the park to where the carnival was starting. "Encased in a glass booth filled with water."

CHAPTER 60

"Glad's probably just going to sit out the carnival and come back for the fireworks," Carrie offered. "I can't see her taking a ride on the Tilt-A-Whirl."

"I guess." I looked around. "Good crowd, though."

"Amazing crowd. The press is really bringing people up here."

"I guess the mayor knew what he was doing," I admitted.

"You did, too," Carrie said. "People have been coming into Jitters talking about the quilts. They love that they're all over town. It brings a lot of color to the place."

"Well, I have to get back to work," Eleanor said. "I can't leave the shop closed with this many people in town."

"Do you want me to help?" I asked.

"No, thanks. Enjoy the carnival. Natalie is on the schedule for today."

We both looked toward Natalie, who seemed about to fall over. "I don't think she's coming into work." I rushed over, with Maggie, Eleanor, and Carrie right behind me.

Natalie was bent over, breathing heavily. "Baby," she said. "The baby is early."

"Call us from the hospital," I said to her. "We'll be thinking about you."

She sighed. "With all the work for the quilt show, I didn't finish the baby quilt I was making."

Maggie took her hand. "That one and a dozen more will be waiting for you when you get out of the hospital. Now go."

We stood and watched Natalie, her husband, and their son drive away.

"We're off to the carnival," Carrie said, as her kids pulled at her shorts. "It looks like Ed did a spectacular job putting it together."

"He did," Maggie said. "He's very giving. And speaking of giving," she said as she turned to Oliver, "so far we've sold three thousand raffle tickets at five dollars apiece. I'm getting people calling from as far away as Montreal, wanting to have a chance at your painting."

Eleanor leaned into him. "No surprise there."

Oliver put one arm on Maggie's shoulders and the other around Eleanor's waist. "The town raises a little money, and I get the gratitude of two beautiful women," he said. "Seems like a win-win."

"Nell," Maggie said, "come with us for the drawing. We'll have Oliver take his picture with the winner if the winner is around. It should be the highlight of this whole event."

"Sounds great," I said, "but I think I want to head over to the carnival."

✂

They left, but for some reason I didn't move. I couldn't place my finger on it. I just wanted to stay in that spot and stare at the statue. And I wasn't alone. Some tourists were taking pictures of it, and the mayor and several of the town's other leaders were standing nearby talking.

The statue was beautiful. It glistened in the sunlight, its silver color standing out against the blue sky and the Hudson River in the distance. I could picture it years from now as something people talked about—the Archers Rest ripple statue.

But in my daydream something occurred to me. Something that had been there all along but I'd never seen because I hadn't put the pieces together. And now, suddenly, Glad's statue had made it all clear.

I ran through the park to the other side, where Jesse was sitting in the dunking booth in a Yankees T-shirt and denim shorts. I yelled to him, but he didn't hear me. I tried to run back, but the carnival worker wouldn't let me.

"How much for a dunk?" I asked him.

"Two dollars for four chances," he said.

I grabbed two dollars out of my pocket and laid them on the

table. I grabbed the first ball. I missed. Jesse laughed and stuck out his tongue at me.

I threw another ball. It didn't even come close to the target. The third ball was closer but still a miss. On the fourth I threw so wild I nearly hit the carnie.

"It's going to be two more bucks if you want to try again," he said.

"Oh, to heck with it." I climbed over his table and ran to Jesse. "Get out," I yelled.

"What?"

"Get out."

As I was yelling the carnie came up behind me. Before he could pull me away, I jumped up to the target and hit it with my hand. The bench collapsed beneath Jesse and he plunged into the water.

"That's cheating, Miss," the carnie said.

"That's the chief of police. He can arrest me."

Jesse pulled himself out of the water and got out of the booth. "What's wrong?"

"It's Winston," I said. "I know what happened."

$\mathbf{B}$ack at the police station, I waited in the entryway while Jesse dried off and changed. I paced the floor, listening to the music and laughter coming from the streets. Finally Jesse emerged from his office.

"You're sure," he said. "Because you have to be sure."

"I'm sure."

We walked out of the police station and toward Ed's theater, where the quilt reception was scheduled to begin at one o'clock.

"At least I hope I'm sure," I said.

✄

Everyone was there. Along with dozens of townspeople and tourists, Maggie and Molly were looking at the quilts. Glad was talking to the mayor. Oliver sipped ginger ale and talked with Eleanor. Mary sat in the ticket booth watching, and Ed walked around beaming.

"This is the most crowded I've ever seen this place," he said.

"It may clear out soon," Jesse said.

"Let it wait," I told him. "It's waited more than thirty years. Let everyone have this."

Jesse nodded. "I'm putting two guys outside," he said. "Just in case."

For an hour we milled around, talking and laughing and exchanging theories about the quilts. All the while I could see Jesse staring, and I felt a tension that had started in my jaw creep down my shoulders and into my stomach and legs, until every muscle in my body was tight.

Finally the last of the tourists left to return to the carnival and wait for the fireworks. But we wouldn't have to wait for our fireworks. As the last stranger walked out, Jesse closed the door.

"What's going on?" Maggie asked.

"Nell figured out who killed Winston," Jesse told her. "You guys can all leave, but you can stay if you want to. You're going to hear about it sooner or later."

"I'm staying," Molly said. "I have a right to know who killed my great-uncle."

Ed nodded. "Yes, I agree. I think you might as well just tell us."

I looked around at the faces in the room, all people I knew, all people who loved Archers Rest. And one who hated Winston enough to kill him.

"So who was it?" the mayor asked.

I turned to him, saddened that I was actually saying what I was about to say. "You."

"Me?" The mayor laughed. "That's ridiculous. Why would I kill the man?"

"I'm not sure," I admitted. "I know Glad had a confrontation with Winston. He told her she'd get over it. Ed thought it was a romance, but I don't think it was. Glad was too in love with you to cheat on you. I think it had something to do with her father. I think her father was the one taking advantage of Grace."

"You're wrong," Glad bellowed. "This is not acceptable, saying awful things about my father when he isn't alive to defend himself."

Mary walked out from the booth. "Glad, we don't need to protect him. Dad was embezzling from Grace's trust. He had access to it, and lord knows my sister and I liked to spend his money. Winston found out about it and threatened to have him arrested. We all spent weeks waiting for the police to knock on our door, but it never happened. Winston just disappeared. I thought after that confrontation at the bank that Ed had killed him."

"Well, I didn't," Ed said. "And I cannot imagine why the mayor would. He was only a teenager, and Winston was a grown man."

"I know," I said. "But he was a strong kid, a high school football player, and he worked in the garden. That's what came to me this afternoon when Glad was talking about the red flowers around the base of the statue. In a photo of the rose garden taken before Winston died, the flowers were orange, yellow, and pink. And after he died, they were red, yellow, and pink."

"So what?" Glad asked.

"It's a small change," I admitted. "And considering that Grace was dying and my grandmother is no gardener, it was one no one would have noticed. Except the man who tended those roses every week." I looked at the mayor. "If someone had disturbed the garden, and it wasn't you, you would have said something. But you didn't, and you have said that you bugged Eleanor with details about the garden every time you were there." I looked back at Eleanor. "He never mentioned it to you?"

She shook her head. "Not that I remember."

"We think you dug up the orange roses to bury Winston, and they must have died in the process, so you planted red ones instead," Jesse said. "You had time. Eleanor and Grace were gone a month."

"So I changed the roses," the mayor said. "What does that prove?"

"It just bothered me," I said. "And other things bothered me. There was all the vandalism. Jesse and I figured out the killer was trying to keep the police busy with one crime after another. But there were so many and they seemed so random. Except, I started to realize, maybe there was a connection. Your office is on the same floor as the historical society, so you could have stolen the coins and key chain Jesse found in the garden after Winston's body was discovered. You planted them there to confuse us as to the identity. You were at Jitters picking up doughnuts when I sent Carrie the text about Glad naming Winston. She leaves the phone by the cash register, so you could have seen the message. You dumped garbage in her office to keep her from helping with the search. You didn't know Natalie was also looking into it," I said. "You could get red paint from your son's store; you walk into the newspaper office probably every day, so you could have gone through the old papers and found something to put in the brick; and thanks to your newly rekindled friendship with Glad, you would know that the library doesn't have a security system. Plus, you would have to know the same shortcut the police do that cuts the distance between city hall and Jitters in half. You could easily have called in that bomb threat and been back in time to appear to have been in the men's room."

"It's that imagination of yours, Nell," the mayor said. "It's working overtime again. What you're saying could apply to nearly everyone in this room who knew Winston Roemer."

"That's true," I continued. "In fact, yesterday Carrie said that the killer had pointed a finger at nearly everyone in town. There was an ad for Ed's theater in that newspaper clipping that was thrown through the police window. Glad's photo had the word *killer* written across it. There was a threat to blow up city hall, just as Mary had done years before. And the suitcase was found on Eleanor's property," I said.

The mayor shuffled his feet and looked down at the floor.

"At first I thought the killer was trying to set someone up," I said, "but you weren't setting anyone up—you were setting *everyone* up. You didn't want to do any permanent damage, so you did small things to public buildings, things that could easily be fixed. And you didn't want anyone to get in trouble for the murder or the vandalism, so you pointed a finger at anyone who could have been involved. But that was a mistake. Nothing pointed to you. You were the only one who didn't get accused of a crime."

Jesse walked toward him. "You hit Winston with something, buried him in the roses, and took the suitcase because you wanted it to look like he'd gone to Peru. You had to know he was going. It was hardly a secret. And you probably knew he wouldn't be missed."

"Why?" Glad came forward. "Why would you do that?"

The mayor took a deep breath. "To protect you," he said. He buried his face in his hands and started to cry. "I was a stupid kid who was in love with a girl. When Glad told me what Winston intended to do, I confronted him. I didn't want Glad's life ruined. I didn't want to see her unhappy. I thought I could explain it to him, but he was such an arrogant man. He didn't care about anyone else."

"That money my father stole," Mary said. "It was maybe thirty thousand dollars. A lot of money, but there was more than a million in the trust. Winston acted like he'd taken every penny Grace had. I'm not saying what Dad did was right, but he was going to pay it back."

"He just needed time," Glad said.

"That's why your father wrote those things about John Archer," I said, "about judging a man by his whole life instead of just his mistakes. He was talking about himself."

I could see Glad blush. *The History of Archers Rest* had represented her father's admission of guilt. Any hint of imperfection was difficult for her, so she had no copies of the book, but it was comforting for Mary, which was why she had a shelf full.

"Winston wouldn't listen to Glad's father or to me," the mayor continued. "I got mad. Lost control of my senses. I took a shovel and hit him. And kept hitting him." He threw his hands up in the air. "You know the rest."

"Is that why you broke up with Glad?" I asked.

"I felt too guilty. Every time I looked at her, I saw what I'd done. I couldn't take it anymore." The mayor looked to Jesse. "I've done a lot of good in this town. I've dedicated my life to doing good."

"I know, but it doesn't make up for killing a man, Larry." Jesse took his arm and they left the theater, with two of Jesse's officers walking behind them.

We stood quietly absorbing the news. Everyone, including Glad, seemed unable to speak. Mary walked over to Ed and took his hand.

"I thought you couldn't leave your house," I said.

She smiled. "I've been getting help. From Ed and your grandmother."

"Small things," I said. "Eleanor had said something to Ed about doing something small every day. She was talking about you taking steps outside your house. And when she said Glad was next . . ."

"She meant Glad was the next person to know that Mary was trying to get over her fears," Ed said.

Mary glanced over at her sister, still shaking her head in disbelief. "Glad knew something was going on and she was pretty upset with Eleanor and Ed for trying to encourage me."

"Glad didn't think it was a good idea," Ed said. "That's what the arguments were about. She'd helped me a little with the theater, and she thought it had bought her the right to tell me what to do. She thinks she runs the town."

"My sister wanted to protect me," Mary said, patting Ed's hand. "She thought it would be too much for me if I tried again. After I had my little nervous breakdown years ago and threatened to blow up city hall, I used to stay home all day. I was afraid of crowds, and then just being around people scared me. I started to walk through the town late at night when it was quiet. I think that's why people thought I was a witch."

"You were the one watching me," I said.

She nodded. "I was curious where you were going, what you might find out, but I wasn't ready for you, for anyone, to see me."

"And you had some kind of altar in the projection booth."

She laughed. "An altar! It was supposed to be the beginning of a romantic picnic—candles and a velvet tablecloth. But Ed got a call from Glad and it kind of ruined his mood."

I blushed. I had decided it was an altar without ever considering a simpler explanation. "Where did you hide?" I asked. "I looked everywhere."

"Not everywhere, Nell. I came out into the hallway and stood in the dark by the door. When you went into the room, I locked you in to give myself a moment to think. I saw through the crack you had turned your back on the door, so I opened it and ran down into the theater."

"And the night you ran in front of my car at the cemetery?"

"I'd borrowed Glad's car, without telling her," she admitted. "I parked it by the cemetery and I was trying to get to it. I thought I could just drive around. But I was so scared being out on my own. That's when I realized I needed more than Ed helping me. I needed a group, like you have with your quilt group. So I called Eleanor. She enlisted Oliver to help, and she confided in me about her past. I think she wanted me to realize that we all have our fears. Hers was that you would be disappointed in her."

"Not possible."

"I told her that," she said. "I'm very grateful to your grandmother.

Without her I'd still be trapped in my house, known as the creepy witch who stalked the town at night."

"I go through town late at night, too," I said. "So I guess that will be my reputation."

"No," Mary said, "you have your reputation, as an inquisitive citizen . . ."

"A nosy snoop," I said.

"And you should be proud of it. You help people. You solve problems."

"So do you, I gather." I nodded toward Ed. "You're Ed's new partner in the theater."

"See how good you are at figuring things out?"

I looked at the antique quilts that surrounded us, with each stitch a clue to the maker's true personality. "I guess we can't hide who we are. Not forever, anyway."

CHAPTER 62

I sat on a rock near the water's edge and watched the explosions of color in the sky. I wasn't alone. The whole town was out watching the mayor's fireworks display, and it was, as he had promised, the best we'd ever seen.

"Can I join you?"

I looked up at Molly. "Grab a rock."

She sat next to me. "I thought it would be satisfying, you know, to find Winston's killer. Instead it just made me sad."

"I know. I kind of wish that Oliver and I had never come up with the idea of digging up the garden. But the mayor did kill Winston, and he did hit you on the head."

"Yeah, but it wasn't a hard hit. He could have killed me, but he didn't. He just wanted my grandmother's letters in case Winston said anything about the embezzlement. I guess he figured once you and Jesse had a motive, you would somehow trace it back to him."

"Too bad he didn't realize I'd already seen them."

"What I don't understand is why he kept the suitcase all these years. Do you think he just felt guilty?"

"I don't think he kept it. It probably was buried out in the yard somewhere close to Winston's body. Once we found the remains, he must have come back to check that he'd left nothing that would point toward him, and he cut himself on something, leaving those droplets of blood. And when it was clear Jesse wouldn't drag the investigation out for publicity, the mayor probably figured we'd go back and keep digging. If we did, we'd find the suitcase. I heard someone in the yard one night, but I didn't pay enough attention. I'm sure it was the mayor. Maybe he thought he'd get rid of the suitcase, then decided to use it to implicate Eleanor instead."

She nodded. "Still, you have to feel sorry for the man. He's lived his life trying to make up for it."

I pointed to Jesse, who was standing at the edge of Main Street with several detectives. Next to him, watching the beautiful display, was the mayor.

"Jesse agrees with you. He let him out of jail for an hour. He wanted him to be able to see his hard work pay off."

"And it did pay off. You guys had quite a crowd today."

"I'm glad all those people got a chance to see Archers Rest," I said, "but I'll be glad when they go home and it's all quiet again."

And then I heard a scream. Carrie came running over. "It's a girl. Seven pounds, four ounces. Mother and daughter are doing fine."

"And another quilter is born," I said, and hugged Carrie. "Come by the shop tomorrow and we'll finish Natalie's baby quilt for her."

"Deal. But it's not the only quilt we'll have to do quickly."

"What do you mean?"

Carrie pointed toward Eleanor and Oliver, hugging tightly.

"Do you think?" I asked, but before she could answer I ran over.

Eleanor grabbed me. "I'm getting married," she said.

"You asked her?" I looked to Oliver.

"She asked me."

We hugged and cried and planned quilts for the next half hour, before Oliver and Eleanor headed back to the house to get ready for their pre-honeymoon trip to Paris. As I stood wiping the tears from my eyes, Jesse came up behind me.

"Everything okay?"

"Eleanor figured out who the ring was really for."

"And?"

"I'm going to be a maid of honor soon."

"What about being a bride? I know you think I'm scared, but . . ."

"One wedding at a time, Jesse."

He laughed. "Okay. It would be too many wedding quilts to make all at once."

"My thoughts exactly," I said, settling into the arms of the man I loved, and surrounded by a town I loved almost as much. "But don't get too comfortable. I'm going to start collecting fabric."

COZY UP WITH ALL THE BOOKS IN
CLARE O'DONOHUE'S
BELOVED QUILTING SERIES

ISBN 978-0-452-28979-6

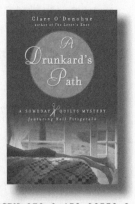

ISBN 978-0-452-29558-2

ISBN 978-0-452-29642-8

ISBN 978-0-452-29737-1

Available wherever books are sold.

VISIT WWW.CLAREODONOHUE.COM

Plume
A member of Penguin Group (USA) Inc.
www.penguin.com

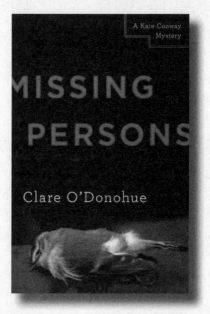